R.D. BRADY

SURRENDER THE FEAR

VINCI
BOOKS

Vinci Books

vinci-books.com

Published by Vinci Books Ltd in 2026

1

Paperback ISBN: 9781036700874
The EU GPSR authorised representative is Logos Europe, 9 rue Nicolas
Poussion, 17000 La Rochelle, France contact@logoseurope.eu

By R.D. Brady

The Nola James Series

Surrender the Fear

Escape the Fear

Tackle the Fear

Return the Fear

The Belial Series

The Belial Stone

The Belial Library

The Belial Ring

The Belial Recruit

The Belial Children

The Belial Origins

The Belial Search

The Belial Guard

The Belial Warrior

The Belial Plan

The Belial Witches

The Belial War

The Belial Fall

The Belial Sacrifice

The A.L.I.V.E. Series

A.L.I.V.E.

D.E.A.D.

R.I.S.E.

S.A.V.E.

Into the Cage

Into the Dark

Chapter One

NOLA

The cries of thirteen-month-old Abigail Miceli carried through the open window of the second floor. The two-story colonial was in a not-so-great neighborhood of Modesto, California. It was a rental sandwiched between two other rental homes on postage-stamp-sized lots. It was a good choice of locations. Rental neighborhoods were notorious for not knowing who belonged and who didn't.

The lack of guardianship was both a blessing and a curse for those who'd taken Abigail. A blessing because the neighbors had taken little notice of the group moving into the home, even though the child with them had had her face plastered across TV stations for the last forty-eight hours.

But Nola James was committed to making sure that same apathy to strangers bit the kidnappers in the ass.

Because the same neighbors who hadn't noticed the group also hadn't noticed Nola James slide up the driveway. No one glanced out a window or walked by when she incapacitated the guard at the back door with a quick kick to the back of his knees and a slam of his head into the railing, followed by a chokehold.

Reaching down, Nola checked the man's pulse. It was beating strongly. She rolled him onto his stomach, which took a little effort because the guy was dead weight, a lot of dead weight. He was easily three hundred pounds, very little of it muscle.

She shook her head as she pulled his arms behind his back. Another man suffering from big man syndrome: he'd figured his size alone would give him the edge in a fight.

Didn't give you much of an edge with me, did it? She thought as she pulled a zip tie from the pocket of her black jacket and quickly wrapped it around his wrists.

She pulled a strip of black duct tape from the sleeve of her jacket. She'd placed it there for just this occasion. She slapped it over the man's mouth, careful not to cover his nose. She didn't need him dead, just out of the way.

Straightening, Nola glanced around. There wasn't a single person in sight. No one peered out at her through the windows of the home along the backyard. Loud music played from two houses down, but that was the only indication of activity anywhere nearby.

Nola climbed the three concrete steps leading to the back door. Gripping the door handle, she paused, listening for any noise from inside.

The music from down the street made that a little hard. She turned the handle, unsurprised to find it unlocked. It wasn't exactly a brain trust running this operation. The guard "securing" the back door had had his back to the driveway, leaning against the house while he watched a show on his phone, completely oblivious to Nola moving in.

Now Nola eased the door open, wrinkling her nose at the smell of old Chinese food. Takeout containers and bags littered the cracked linoleum counters and a scarred wooden table. Four metal folding chairs stood around the table, littered with plates and takeout tumblers.

These guys deserve a beating just for being complete slobs. She closed the kitchen door quietly behind her.

No sound came from the first floor.

That meant everyone was on the second floor. She knew from the plans she'd gotten from city hall that the kitchen emptied into a small living room at the front, with an enclosed porch beyond that. There was a small dining room off the kitchen.

A staircase led from the living room to the second floor, which held two bedrooms and a full bath.

There were four individuals on the second floor, not including the child. Two of them were guards, really more hired muscle than any sort of professional security. If they were anything like the back door guard, they wouldn't be a problem. The third was a nanny, in the loosest sense of the term.

And the fourth, the fourth was definitely someone who should not have come. He should not have let himself be seen anywhere near this mess.

But Nola wasn't overly surprised by his presence. Every step of this case was dogged by ego and entitlement, hallmarks of the Hannigan family.

Nola made her way through the small kitchen to the bare living room. It held only a ripped green futon and two more folding chairs. A large mirror above the futon, rimmed by a peeling gold frame was the room's only decoration. Checking the mirror, Nola scanned the stairs. No movement, but voices indicated at least two people were close to the top of the stairs.

As she passed, Nola caught the shortest of glances of her own reflection. Dark jeans with black Hi-Tec boots, blended into a fitted black jacket that she'd had specially designed to hold dozens of tools from knives to her lockpick kit. It even had a pocket that could hold a small grenade. A ski mask hid her face, and the dark outfit unintentionally complemented her slim athletic build.

A deep gravelly voice rolled down the stairs. Nola flattened herself against the wall and peered up.

No one in sight.

Leaning back, she grimaced at the sticky residue along the wall. She didn't even want to think about what it could possibly be. The building was a far cry from the luxury the owners of it usually enjoyed. The Hannigans were titans in data storage and management fields, but their fortune extended into dozens of enterprises, from hotels to transportation to even clothing lines. Their personal fortune extended well into the billions.

As expected of a family of such wealth, they had residences all over the world, which had made finding this place difficult. Searching through all their holdings had taken time.

But with a little help and a search of shell company after shell company, she finally found the purchase of this 1967 dream. It had been bought for $50,000. That alone made it stand out amongst the Hannigans' homes.

They should have paid cash or at least used an untraceable account. Instead they did what they always did: threw money at a problem to make it go away.

Another shrill cry came from upstairs, followed by a mumble of angry voices. Nola's gut clenched. She knew that cry. Her own daughter had made a similar one a few times. It wasn't the cry of the hungry or the tired. It was the cry of abandonment. The cry of a child feeling desperately alone and needing some comfort.

Abigail wasn't going to get any from the people in this house. From what Nola knew of the people upstairs, none of them had ever experienced comfort from their own parents, never mind being able to provide it to another child.

The child in question was the biological daughter of Rachel and Frederick Hannigan's youngest son, Max. No one disputed that fact.

The dispute was over whether or not Abigail had been willingly conceived.

Abigail's mother, Morgan Miceli, had been a sophomore at Harvard University. She'd gotten in on a full scholarship. And she'd been the first member of her family to go to college.

Unlike Max, Morgan did not come from money. She'd worked hard to get to Cambridge. In high school, she'd maintained a 4.5 grade point average while juggling a slew of extracurriculars and a waitressing job three nights a week.

That strong work ethic had continued at Harvard with Morgan getting a job at one of the university's graduate dining halls and an additional waitressing job off-campus on weekends. But from all reports, she didn't mind the long hours.

According to Morgan, she'd met Max at a party one night. He kept trying to get her to drink with him, but she had a test the next day and declined repeatedly. She'd only gone to the party because her friends had guilted her into it.

She'd regretted that choice almost as soon as she'd

stepped in the door. Her friends started to drink heavily. Morgan would have left, but she worried about her friends getting home safely. Finally, Max's attention grew too annoying, and she told her friends she was heading back to the dorm.

Max followed. And nine months later, Abigail appeared.

At first, Max denied that there had been any sexual activity whatsoever. But the birth and subsequent DNA test bore out Morgan's story. Then Max quickly changed his tune and declared that the encounter was consensual.

Instead of ducking his head in shame, he'd turned around and sued Morgan for full custody of Abigail.

The first court case had gone Max's way because Abigail hadn't been able to afford a lawyer. But then a guardian angel had stepped in, and she'd paid the bills for one of the top parental rights lawyers in the country. Max had been denied custody.

Then all of a sudden, little Abigail had disappeared. Morgan put her to bed at eight o'clock. When she went to check on her at ten, she was gone.

Max and his family immediately went on TV claiming that Abigail had been harmed by her mother while in her mother's care. That this was further proof that Morgan did not deserve to have custody of the child.

Through it all, Morgan shied away from the press. She made no formal statements. And only one shot of Morgan was taken: The devastated mother had been caught going for a walk outside her grandmother's home. Her tear-stained face could be seen from a distance as she placed missing posters all over the neighborhood.

It had taken Nola time, but she had tracked Abigail down. Nola wasn't worried about getting Abigail back. She was not leaving that house without the child. But she had been worried about finding a way to tie the Hannigans to the kidnapping. Without proof, they would slip through the criminal justice system's reach once again, and Morgan would still have to fight the rapist to maintain custody of her daughter.

Nola would love to think that the system would treat the girl fairly. But she knew too well how much "credit" coming from a good, i.e. wealthy, family bestowed upon a defendant. There were multiple cases where judges highlighted the defendants "good standing" as a reason for a lighter sentence or an all-out acquittal. A rape case in California was a recent high-profile example of the double standard the criminal justice system bestowed upon the "right" type of perpetrator.

A student had raped an unconscious girl on Stanford's campus. Two students witnessed the rape and intervened. There was no doubt that the girl could not consent or that he was the perpetrator. His sentence could have been up to fourteen years. Instead, the judge gave him a mere six months, only three of which were served in jail. Why such a lenient sentence? The judge worried about the impact a stronger sentence might have had on the perpetrator.

The rapist, not the victim, was his concern.

That case, sadly, was not an aberration. A New Jersey judge recently ordered leniency for a teen rapist who raped an unconscious girl, recorded it, and then released the recording with the tagline: "When your first time is rape." His reasoning? The boy came from a good family and had good grades.

But Nola knew that wasn't the worst of it. In dozens of states, a rapist could actually sue for custody of a child that resulted from their crime.

That was what had happened to Morgan. The protections for victims only happened when a rapist was convicted. And being only four out of a thousand rapists was ever convicted, that was a rather high bar to clear.

Nola didn't want Morgan having to deal with Max Hannigan for the rest of her life. But without some way of directly tying the Hannigans to the property, Max would still be given a strong legal standing in the custody fight for Morgan's daughter.

The Hannigans could simply argue they'd had no knowledge of the property. That they had too many property acquisitions to possibly know what was going on in all of them.

But now a special guest had arrived to make sure that Max Hannigan never got near Abigail again.

Nola pulled out her phone from her left pocket and checked to make sure the parabolic dish microphone she'd set up was still recording. It was. She had rented the building cross the street and set up video and audio recording devices to get everything on camera.

Of course, she would also make sure that she never appeared on camera.

Quietly, she made her way up the stairs, sliding the Taser wand from the holder at her waist. She couldn't chance a gun with Abigail there.

Once she reached the top step, she stayed flat against the wall and peered into the hallway. One guard stood outside the door, but he was looking into the room rather than out.

From her spot, she could finally make out their conversation. "What are we supposed to do with her? This is supposed to be a short-time gig," a female voice whined from inside the room.

"You'll do what you're paid to do," a man barked back.

Nola recognized that voice. Richard Hastings, the Hannigans' number one fixer. He'd been with Frederick Hannigan since they were kids. If there was a problem, Hastings fixed it.

And over the years, there'd been a lot of problems. The Hannigans had flirted with the criminal justice system for decades. But their money, connections, and Hastings always seemed to get them out of whatever jam they were in.

"How much longer are we going to have to stay here?" a deep male voice asked.

"A couple of days. Just long enough for that bitch to sign over custody or have the judge revoke it. The custody hearing's tomorrow," Hastings said. "We already took care of her lawyer, so it should be finished by three tomorrow."

Nola's ears perked up at that news. She hadn't heard anything about the lawyer being targeted. She'd have to make sure the lawyer was checked on after she got Abigail out.

Nola had no illusions that any of the Hannigans would do jail time. But she could at least make sure that Abigail wasn't caught up in the public relations reformation of their son. But if Hastings was implicated, he could trade dirt on the Hannigans to save his own hide.

That would be poetic.

Nora peeked around the corner again. It was only a short fifteen feet from the top of the stairs to the room. The second guard had moved into the doorway, his back to her. She couldn't see either Hastings or the woman. The other guy, still in the hall, kept his attention completely on his boss.

It wasn't the best situation. As soon as she made her move, the people in the room would be aware of her presence. And without a gun, it was going to take some time to take people down.

With a sigh, she rolled her shoulders, knowing there was no helping it. Sometimes you just had to deal with the situation you got.

Time to go.

She bolted from her spot. The first guard's back was still to her and his legs were spread. She didn't pause as she slammed a kick right into his groin. His knees buckled, and he let out a small cry. She yanked on the back of his shirt, pulling him out of the doorway and into the hall where he crashed into the opposite wall.

Darting past him, she jammed the Taser into the other guard, who'd turned quickly to see what was going on.

Beyond the guard, the woman stood on the far side of a bed. A playpen was positioned by the windows, wails of desperation emitting from it. Hastings, all six feet of the man with gray hair cut close and a strong build derived from years of hitting the gym—and people—stood to the right. The man her Taser had struck jolted, shaking for two seconds before he dropped to the ground.

Just inside the door, Hastings shot out with a side kick. Nola dodged to the side but hit the bed, losing her hold on the Taser. She quickly rolled over the bed and onto her feet, slamming a front kick into the chest of the woman. The woman crashed into the wall and slid down with a grunt.

Nola wasted no time. She rounded the bed as Hastings reached into his jacket pocket. Nola slammed her hand onto the gun hand while slamming her other palm into his face. Blood burst as his nose broke.

Throwing a round kick to the inside of his right knee, she followed it with a quick side kick to his left. Both of his knees buckled as she grabbed him by the back of the collar and slammed his face into her knee. His eyes rolled into the back of his head. She shoved him to the ground.

The woman moaned, getting to her feet. Nola swiped the Taser from the ground and plunged it into the woman's side. She let out a scream. Her whole body shook as she fell back down.

Nola quickly moved back to the hallway. The first guy she'd taken down was just getting to his feet. She grabbed him by the back of the head and slammed his face into the edge of the doorframe. He screamed, falling to the floor once again.

He raised his hands to his face, but Nola yanked them behind his back and zip-tied them tight. She tied up the other guard, who'd wet himself after he'd been Tased. She wrinkled her nose at the smell.

After tying up both Hastings and the nanny, she grabbed Hastings by the back of the jacket and dragged him over to the playpen. She laid them on the ground face up and then grabbed her camera. She took a picture of Richard Hastings lying next to Abigail Miceli, to whom they'd given a bottle. It lay out of the girl's grasp next to her. Her cheeks were bright red and stained with tears. Her onesie was soiled with dark marks, her diaper was obviously full.

Nola grabbed the gun Hastings had been trying to pull, cleared the chamber and removed the magazine before dropping the Glock back onto Hastings's chest. She raised the camera and started shooting the rest of the room. Once done, she remotely turned off the recording devices.

Shoving her phone into the back pocket of her pants, she stripped off her gloves and her ski mask. Her long dark blonde hair came out of the ponytail holder with the action.

Reaching down she carefully picked up Abigail, her

11

heart pounding more now than it had at any point since she stepped into the house.

As she cradled Abigail in the nook of her arm, she reached back in for the bottle. She carefully adjusted the bottle so that the little girl had better reach. "Hey there, little one. Let's get you back to your mama," she said softly.

She could feel the heaviness of the girl's diaper, but she didn't want to waste time changing it right now. She needed to get her out of this house and away from these people. She stepped back from the playpen.

Hastings let out a groan. Nola slammed the heel of her boot into the side of his face. "That's for your employer."

Quickly, she made her way down the stairs, partly to get Abigail out of this place, but also to keep herself from turning around and doing more damage to the people upstairs.

Her whole body felt hot. The little girl in her arms still whimpered as she desperately tried to drink faster than her body would allow. Nola took a lot of calming breaths as she moved. *Get Abby out. She's the priority,* she reminded herself with every step while she envisioned the injuries she wanted to inflict.

Using the edge of her jacket, she opened the front door and stepped outside. She made her way down the crumbling steps and out through the crooked chain-link fence. She made a right and hurried along the uneven sidewalk. Crossing the street she turned down the first road.

A small red four door Toyota that had seen better days stood idling at the curb. The back door flew open as soon as Nola came into view.

Morgan Miceli, her blonde hair limp and her face pale, sprinted over to Nola. "Oh my God. Oh my God."

The young woman reached for her daughter. Nola carefully handed her over. "She needs a diaper change. And she's really hungry."

Morgan nodded but didn't take her gaze from her daughter. Tears streamed down her cheeks. "Oh, Abby."

The driver of the red sedan got out and joined them. Marjorie Watson was one of the heads of an underground railroad for women in abuse cases. Nola had contacted her after she'd learned Abigail's location. Nola nodded at her. "You two need to get going."

The gray haired woman put an arm around Morgan. "Come on, sweetheart. Let's get Abby somewhere safe."

Morgan nodded again, her eyes still on her daughter as she let Marjorie pull her to the car. She was almost at the door when suddenly she turned around and sprinted back to Nola. She threw an arm around her, holding her tight. "Thank you. Thank you so much."

Nola returned the hug, her chest feeling tight. "You're welcome. Just love that little girl, okay?"

"I will. I promise," Morgan said, eyes bright with tears. Then she hurried back to the car.

Nola waited until they pulled away, with Morgan waving goodbye from the back seat. She put up the hood of her jacket and headed down the street. She pulled out her cell phone as she walked and typed. *Job's done.*

The reply came back quickly. *Any problems?*

No. I'm sending you the photos. She switched over to the photo files and quickly texted them.

Got them. Hastings showed up? That was stupid.

Grunting, Nola nodded as she typed. *My thoughts exactly. You taking a break now?*

Thinking about Morgan's face and the cries of little Abigail, her answer was easy. *No. What have you got?*

Head to the airport. I'll send you the details shortly.

Chapter Two

After collecting her recording gear from the rental house, Nola headed for the airport. She'd only been in Modesto for a few hours. It was how she liked her cases: easy in, easy out.

They were a far cry from her cases with the CIA where she'd spend months, sometimes longer, on one case. But those days were far behind her. Now, a few days at most was what she spent on each mission. Although after her initial research, she closed most in twenty-four hours.

And she liked it that way. It kept her moving.

She left the car she'd picked up in the airport parking lot. It had been purchased for two hundred dollars and never registered. Either the cops or someone else would take it off her hands.

Grabbing an Uber to the airfield, she checked her phone every few minutes along the way. She frowned. Normally, she had the destination for her next case by this point. She'd just stepped out of the Uber at the entrance of the private airfield when her phone rang. She glanced at it with another frown. Her phone never rang. Her communications were almost exclusively through texts and email.

Glancing at the screen, she expected to see a telemarketer. But she recognized the number. "Bishop?"

"Oh, hey, Nola. How are you?" Bishop said quickly.

Nola frowned, picturing twenty-five-year-old Bishop Rhodes, technology wonder kid with the CIA. With untamed light-brown hair and a pale-brown complexion dotted with freckles, she was a mix of Iranian and Nigerian heritage.

Bishop sent her the information on her cases, but she knew Nola wanted that information exclusively by electronic means. "Why are you calling?"

Nervousness rattled through Bishop's voice. "Um, I know you don't want me to, but I needed to check with you. I found you a case, but I wasn't sure if you'd take it."

In the last two years, Nola had taken on over three hundred cases. She'd never turned one down. Each case involved someone the criminal justice system had let down. And in each one, Nola found a way to bring the guilty party to justice, either legally or extralegally.

"Why would you think I would turn it down?"

Bishop hesitated. "It's about a missing girl. She was sixteen and disappeared on her way home from school. She's been gone two days now."

Nola's mind immediately went through the statistics on missing teenage girls. Thousands of kids went missing every year. The bulk of those, over ninety percent, were categorized as runaways.

But she also knew that those cold numbers hid a world of truth. Most girls who ran away ended up in prostitution, abusive relationships, or worse. It was very rarely a happy ending.

But if Bishop was contacting her about a missing girl, there was nothing normal about this situation.

"The thing is," Bishop said, "another girl went missing from the same town almost five years ago to the day. And I swear, the two of them were so similar. I need to do more digging, but I think there's something there. I have that feeling."

Bishop might be young, but her intuition was rarely wrong. And if she thought there was more to the case, then there probably was.

"I wasn't sure if it was too close to home, though . . ." Bishop said, her words drifting off.

An image of a man leaning over her, the smell of beer on his breath, shot through Nola's mind. She shoved the image away. "It's fine. Send me the details."

"I'll send you what I have. And I contacted Darius. Gave him your destination."

Darius Tahirovic was the pilot who would be shuttling Nola to her next case. "What is my destination?"

"Georgia. You're heading to Atlanta."

Chapter Three

The flight from California to Georgia was uneventful. The file from Bishop was in Nola's inbox before she boarded the private plane. But she decided not to open it right away. She'd spent the last two nights in flea-ridden hotel rooms with sagging mattresses. The private plane offered much better sleeping accommodations.

Nola spied a small bear sitting on the couch along the fuselage. She picked it up and sniffed deeply. She knew the smell had long since faded, but she still felt like she could make out the faintest hint of lavender from Molly's shampoo.

Pulling the bear to her chest, Nola curled up on the couch as soon as Darius pulled the plane door shut. There was no flight attendant. Nola didn't like being waited on. She would prefer to not even take the private plane, but her cases often required her to get to places quickly, and public transportation was generally not fast enough.

Besides, this was the one luxury she allowed herself. She hadn't even had a permanent address the last two years. This plane was the place she'd spent the most consecutive time. It was as close to a home as she got these days.

The plane began to taxi and her body pushed back against the seat. She closed her eyes, picturing Morgan's face when she saw her daughter. It had been a mixture of love, awe, disbelief, and fear. Fear that the moment wasn't real and that Abby would disappear.

Nola knew that fear well.

A tremor worked its way from Nola's fingers through her body as her heart began to pound. Her eyes flew open as she stared through the window at the landscape racing by.

No. Shut it down, Nola. Shut it down.

Taking calm, even breaths, she emptied her mind. It took a few long moments, but soon her heart slowed, her thoughts once again under her control.

Focusing on her breathing, she closed her eyes. In and out. In and out. For thirty minutes as the plane climbed and then leveled off, Nola simply breathed, calming her heart and emptying her mind.

She had planned on reviewing the file but right now the last few days were catching up to her. Exhaustion pushed down on her. She didn't sleep much but right now her body was demanding it. Letting her eyes close again, she let sleep claim her.

Images of fire and screams rolled through Nola's mind as her phone jolted her awake a few hours later.

Her breaths were shaky as she stared at the ceiling of the plane, the images receding to the back of her mind. They stayed there, though, her constant companions in sleep and wakefulness.

Turning off the alarm on her phone, she sat up, blinking

in the dark. They would touch down in another thirty minutes.

Uncurling herself from the couch, she placed the bear back on the couch next to her. She took a deep breath, picturing little Abigail and hoping that she and her mother were off to a better life.

The cabin was still dark as she made her way to the bathroom. Pulling open the door, she blinked hard at the bright lights. Leaning on the small counter, she studied her reflection in the mirror. Her hazel eyes looked tired with dark circles underneath them, not an uncommon sight.

Stripping off her jacket, she hung it on the hook on the door. Underneath, she wore her usual uniform: a black tank top and jeans. The black hid the blood, and the jeans tended to be sturdy enough for most situations.

There were a few bruises along her forearms. She didn't remember when she'd gotten them in the fight, but they were a common enough sight that she wasn't bothered by them. A quick cleanup with her toiletries and she was stepping back out of the bathroom without another glance in the mirror.

Touching the control panel for the lights as she passed, she retook her seat and pulled her tablet from her bag. A minute later, she was staring at the information Bishop had sent on the missing girl.

Anna Mae Hayes, sixteen years old and finishing up her junior year at Delford High School. Like Bishop said, she'd disappeared after school two days ago. The official police report was light on details. Her mother had reported her missing, but there was no follow-up, at least not one recorded.

Bishop had run a background on Anna Mae. There wasn't a lot there. She had a Facebook account but only fifteen friends, all of whom were family. In fact, the pictures on the website were almost exclusively family shots. Bishop left a note at the bottom of that file:

Ran a search of her online presence. No additional emails or accounts, under her name or otherwise. Every time she went online it looked like it was for some school research project. Still looking but don't think it will turn up anything.

Anna Mae had been on the school's robotics team and had already gotten scholarship offers from Georgia State University and the University of Georgia. An image scan had failed to find a picture of Anna Mae in anyone else's social media feed.

A good student, connected to family, involved in her community, she really didn't fit the runaway profile.

Nola flipped to the other police report Bishop had sent, which was from five years earlier. Tasha McNally had disappeared under similar circumstances. Both girls had been reported missing by family. There was no follow-up information listed for Tasha's case either.

Either the Haverford-Delford PD was really bad at record keeping, or no one had really been looking for these girls. She had a feeling it was the latter. Police departments across the country had been notoriously neglectful when it came to crimes against minorities, even serious ones.

The case that sprang immediately to mind was the string of child murders in Atlanta back in the 80s. From 1979 to 1981, twenty-eight children and young adults had been killed in the Atlanta area.

No one was ever convicted of the crimes, although the perpetrator was largely believed to be Wayne Williams, who was twenty-three at the time of the last murder. He was convicted of two adult murders and sentenced to consecutive life sentences. But once he was incarcerated, the murders stopped.

But what was so striking about the Atlanta murders was how little attention was paid to them. Thirty children lost their lives in two years, the youngest aged nine, and yet it received scant media attention.

If all thirty were in fact the victims of the same killer, that was four times the count of the Zodiac Killer. Yet the case was not and isn't well known.

In disappearances, there were usually two explanations. One, the person disappeared of their own volition. Or two, someone made the person disappear. Nola agreed with Bishop's assessment: Anna Mae didn't seem like the runaway type. But without further investigation, she couldn't rule that out. Her gut though was leaning more to option two—that someone made Anna Mae disappear. She'd need to talk to Anna Mae's family, friends, and acquaintances. Usually if someone was grabbed, it was by someone they knew.

The worst-case scenario would be if she was grabbed by a stranger, a random grab where Anna Mae attracted some-one's attention for reasons known only to the perpetrator. Ted Bundy had a fondness for women with long straight brown hair. Edmund Kemper liked college students. Dahmer went after young men who were on the fringes of society and whose disappearances were less likely to draw notice.

But was that the case here? Despite the public's curiosity about serial killers, they were actually a rare occurrence.

Nola stared at the image of the young girl. She had bright brown eyes and a wide smile. *Whose attention did you catch, Anna Mae?*

The seatbelt light came on. Nola slid her tablet back

into her pack and pulled on her seatbelt. Her mind mulled over the possibilities. Bishop had sent her McNally's file for a reason. She thought there was a connection between the two of them.

And without conscious intent, Nola's mind had jumped to the most likely connection for cases years apart: serial killer. Only forty were at large in the United States at any given time. But they could often go years without acting, which made it that much harder to track them.

Nola discarded the idea of a connection. She couldn't go in with preconceived notions. It was possible that the two cases were unrelated. She needed to speak with the family to get an idea of Anna Mae's routine and go from there.

Flipping open her phone, Nola stared at a photo of Anna Mae and her little brother. Both had huge smiles, their arms wrapped around one another. It was possible that both girls had, in fact, simply run away. It happened.

In her gut, though, Nola knew that wasn't what had happened here. Anna Mae hadn't run away. She understood why the case stuck out for Bishop—it just felt wrong.

Now it was up to Nola to figure out why.

Chapter Four

When the plane touched down at the private airfield in Georgia, Nola murmured her thanks to Darius as she hefted her backpack on her shoulder and headed down the stairs. She was surprised to see a familiar face waiting for her outside the plane.

Avad Tahirovic, Darius's brother, stood with his arms crossed, his legs braced. When Nola had first met him nearly thirteen years ago, he'd reminded Nola of a Viking. Nothing in the intervening years had changed that impression. A Bosnian refugee, he had a scar that cut through his left eyebrow, which had started to turn gray since she'd last seen him. As he aged, he looked more and more like Dolph Lundgren.

The fact that he talked sparingly only added to the similarity. Nola stopped in front of him, her arms crossed in front of her chest. First Bishop had called, and now Avad was here. She did not like the changes. "Why are you here?"

With a shrug, Avad spoke quietly. "She was worried. She

wanted to make sure you were all right. After all, a child was involved."

Pain stabbed at Nola's chest, her mind flashing on a small white child-sized coffin with gleaming silver handles. "I'm fine." Her voice came out harsher than she'd intended.

Avad said nothing; he simply stared at her, as if cataloguing every bruise and bump. His gaze seemed to strip past her defenses. Finally, he nodded and handed her his phone. She glanced at it in confusion. He had it open to a news page.

She scoffed as she read the account of the Modesto incident. According to the "victims," they'd been attacked by a large man who'd stolen the child, that *they* had just recovered, although they were vague on the details about how they'd managed that.

It was impossible to hold back a snort at the description they provided of their assailant: six foot four, extremely muscular, with a deep voice.

She shook her head. Nola knew that, standing at five foot six and weighing a hundred and thirty pounds, she wasn't exactly an imposing figure. And although she'd been told her voice was commanding at times, no one had ever said deep.

She handed Avad back his phone without a word. He gave her a small smile before he turned on his heel. She followed, spying the old 1978 Bronco with the two-tone blue and white exterior. Her heart gave a happy little leap. She absolutely loved this car.

She hurried past Avad and peered in at the front seat. Dark-blue interior. She tried not to swoon. Avad walked around the back of the car and opened the tailgate. Wiping the smile from her face, she followed him. A small trunk sat there.

"Everything in there?" She asked.

"Yes." He closed up the tailgate and handed her the key. "It's electric. Ileana had it converted for you."

"Tell her . . ." There were so many things to say, But finally she settled on the simple. "Tell her thank you."

He nodded. "Safe hunting."

Chapter Five

BISHOP

Bishop waited inside the terminal, watching as Avad spoke with Nola. She bit her lip, wanting more than anything to run outside and throw her arms around her. But Bishop knew that wouldn't be well received. She could tell from the phone call today that Nola wasn't ready to come back into the fold.

With a sinking heart, she watched as Nola started up the Bronco and pulled away. Her phone rang only seconds later. Bishop answered it without looking at the screen. She knew Ileana Hamilton, former DNI director, had been watching the exchange from the cameras at her estate. "Well?"

"She looked good. Healthy," Bishop said.

Exasperation ran through Ileana's voice. "I'm not worried about her medical status."

Hesitating, Bishop pictured Nola as she examined the Bronco. "She smiled. When Avad couldn't see her and she was looking into the Bronco, she smiled."

Ileana let out a breath. "Good, that's good. When are you heading back?"

Gripping the phone tight, Bishop spoke quickly. "As soon as the plane is refueled, but I could stay. Be nearby if she needs me."

"No, we've done enough for right now. We can't chance pushing her too much. And you know she would realize pretty quickly if you were in the area."

"I know. But do you think . . ." She paused, all the doubts that had crowded her mind when she'd found the Delford case running over themselves to get her attention. "Do you think this case is a good idea? Right after the Miceli case?"

Ileana didn't respond right away. When she did, her voice was heavy with concern. "It's been two years, Bishop. We need to try something. We've played it her way, but I don't think anything will change if we allow that to continue."

"I hope you're right, but . . ."

"But?" Ileana prodded.

"But I worry that maybe this case . . . it might, I don't know, do more harm than good," Bishop said.

"It's possible. But we have no other choices. We need to bring her back to the land of the living. The case before the Micelis, it was too brutal. *She* was too brutal."

With a shudder, Bishop's chest felt heavy as she answered. "I know."

Nola had taken down a pimp who was abusing his workers. She had sent him and six of his men to the hospital, two to the morgue. The pimp would never walk again. And one of the men would be eating from a straw for the foreseeable future.

But that wasn't the worst of the damage she'd inflicted.

One of the johns had been caught in the act with a four-teen-year-old. And he no longer had the physical capability of having sex. She had removed that option from his body.

"We need to do something, my dear. We need to bring her back," Ileana said pain, longing, and a hint of desperation in her voice.

"Or lose her forever," Bishop said, staring at the spot where she had last seen Nola.

Ileana's response held all of Bishop's fear and hope. "Yes."

Chapter Six

NOLA

Nola headed north out of Falcon Field. Atlanta was twenty-five miles northeast of the airfield. She needed to bypass Atlanta, as Delford, Georgia, was a little north and west of Atlanta. As she followed the I-20 west of Atlanta, she watched the city skyline.

The city of Atlanta, Georgia, had seen more than its fair share of history. Modern Atlanta had begun with the Creeks, a Native American tribe forced to sign a treaty in the early decades of the nineteenth century, giving away their land. A second tribe, the Cherokee, stayed until the 1830s, when they were forcibly removed and became part of the Trail of Tears. Settlers began to pour in, and in 1837, the railroad followed. The Civil War came along, and Atlanta was burned nearly to the ground. Following the Civil War, it became a city known for higher learning, and then in the twentieth century, it became the epicenter of the civil rights movement.

More recently, Atlanta and the wider Georgia area had been at the forefront of a Hollywood revolution, with big players like Marvel, Netflix, and AMC bringing their productions to the southern state. Perhaps the best known was *The Walking Dead*, which had been shot on location in Atlanta and Senoia, Georgia. The influx of people and money had resulted in an explosion of gentrification in small towns across the Georgia landscape. Out-of-towners, enamored with the quaint country living, had moved away from Atlanta to create their perfect home in small southern burbs. As a result, these small towns had experienced a revitalization and now rivaled some of the towns typically seen in more affluent areas of the North.

Delford, Georgia, however, had not seen any of that revitalization. Just a thirty-minute drive outside Atlanta, it was the town that time seemed to have forgotten. Or more accurately, it seemed to be a town that time had run over and left in its wake. There were no Starbucks on the street corners or small little cafés with outdoor seating. There was an old Dairy Queen that had been converted into something called Ma Bells Ice Cream, but the new name had been placed right over the old Dairy Queen sign. In fact, you could still see most of the D, and part of the Y as well as one E and the N.

According to the research material Bishop had sent, Delford had a population of 4,000 people. It had once been a thriving mill town. But when the mill had gone away, so, too, had the jobs. Now people sometimes commuted to Atlanta, although from the look of things, Nola had a feeling that anyone who commuted to Atlanta soon moved there. The majority of the Delford residents were employed in the service industry one town over in Haverford.

The main street of Delford consisted of about twenty

buildings, most of them three stories high. A third of them were boarded up. What remained included an old hardware store that had lawnmowers lined up around it and a drugstore with a small parking lot next to it. The only reason she knew it was a drugstore was the pharmacy sign.

She passed a shoe store, which was closed. A wig store, also closed. And a half dozen other nondescript business fronts. A small restaurant called Ma Bells Diner took up the middle of an entire block, with boarded-up storefronts on either side.

Delford was not exactly a thriving metropolis. Two blocks off of Main Street was a set of three two-story apartment buildings, all painted a dark, unappealing brown. Nola had been given the keys to a small house across the street from them. The house she was renting was a small Cape Cod. It definitely looked like it had seen better days. She didn't stop as she rolled by. She didn't want to go in yet, wanting to get a better feel for the town first.

She took the next right, passing a few houses with wide, deep sagging porches and a couple of double wide trailers that, from the looks of their foundation, wouldn't move until they were burned to the ground.

At the next block was the elementary school: a single-story all-brick building. There were windows by the front door and then smaller ones throughout the rest of the building. A chain-link fence in need of repair surrounded the property.

A few more turns, and Nola drove by the high school. She stopped just across the street. This was the last place Anna Mae had been seen. A long thick wall of gray brick met her eyes, unbroken except for a few small windows. The elementary school might have been depressing to look at, but it was downright cheerful compared to the high school.

It appeared the designers of the high school had only one look in mind when creating this structure intended to cultivate young minds: prison. The tall chain-link fence surrounding the building did nothing to dispel the illusion. There was a sad football field with a track surrounding it made entirely of dirt. There wasn't even a scoreboard.

Nola figured it probably wasn't necessary. No doubt the Delford football team was required to travel to other schools to play. She doubted many schools would come here.

She made her way back to the main thoroughfare, Route 27, and continued straight another two miles until she reached the city limits. An ornate sign on the side of the road announced: *Welcome to Haverford: The Picture of Southern Perfection.*

Nola had to admit the sign was not entirely inaccurate. The grass was greener and much better behaved as soon as Nola crossed over the town border. Instead of patches of brown grass, it was wide swaths of green broken up only for the occasional flowering tree or carefully placed floral spread.

Long rambling fences followed the dip and dive of the gently rolling hills, leading to ornate gates. The main business area was only five miles past the town line.

It was like crossing into a new world. Haverford was a gorgeous Southern town. Plenty of little shops and restaurants, a large modern movie theater with IMAX screens. BMWs, Mercedes, and Teslas seemed to be the cars of choice for the residents. A few McMansions, obviously new builds trying to imitate the look of a Southern plantation, dotted the landscape. Other homes were obviously renovated from the original mansions the new ones were trying to emulate.

Nola drove by a construction site where they were busy

tearing down older homes to create the Haverford Spa, a place of relaxation and tranquility according to the Coming Soon sign. And every sign or announcement seemed to be announcing events taking place at the Retreat. Nola came upon the country club after another three miles. It was a sprawling estate. She could not see the main clubhouse, and the guards at the gate discouraged any lookie-loos from wandering through.

But Nola did see a second entrance where a few cars turned. A beat-up old Honda Accord pulled in with three people inside, followed by an old Ford station wagon complete with wood paneling and a small trail of smoke coming from the exhaust pipe. These were not the typical cars she'd seen in town, which meant this was the service workers' entrance.

As she passed back into Delford, she noted a police car right at the edge of the border between the two towns. In an idealistic world, they would be there to keep people safe, but Nola had a sneaking suspicion they were trying to keep people *out* of Haverford . . . or at least the wrong kind of people.

Taking the next left, Nola headed back toward her rented house. She passed a tall white church. Although the church itself was rather small, the house attached to it looked like it belonged one town over. It was a gorgeous brick construction with dark-green trim, white shutters, a big deep white porch, and flowers cascading from giant urns on either side of the porch entryway. Apparently the reverend did pretty well for himself in this town. In fact, the church seemed to be the only place that was doing well for itself in Delford.

Nola turned back onto Magnolia Lane. She scanned the apartment complex as she drove by, catching more than a few curtains shifting to get a look at her car. Unlike Modesto, California, it appeared the residents were noting her arrival.

Nola pulled into the driveway of the small yellow house across from the complex. The row of houses on either side were identical to hers, with only color separating them—color and a very short distance. On each side, there was only about a foot between one home and the next. If someone wanted to, they could hand something to a neighbor just by leaning out a window.

After she turned off the ignition, the swampy, hot, wet air hit her as soon as she cracked open the car door. How did people live here? Sweat darted across her neck, and she felt a drop slide down her back. She glanced at the house and noted no air-conditioning units. And she wasn't naïve enough to even contemplate the possibility that there was central air.

After locking the car, she headed inside. Five minutes later, she was back down at the car. She'd searched the place. It was empty of everything except a few basic pieces of furniture: a couch, bed, one small dresser, and a kitchen table with three mismatched chairs.

It was also desperately in need of a good cleaning. She'd clean the first floor and stay down there and not even bother with the second floor.

She opened up the back of the truck. But before she reached in to grab her stuff, she glanced at the home that bordered hers at the back.

It belonged to the Hayes family.

It was a blue two-story home. No movement or sound came from inside. She glanced at her watch. She wanted to get started by talking to Anna Mae's family, but she knew the mother worked a second job at an assisted-living home over in Haverford. She didn't want to bust in on her at work. Besides, she hadn't read much on the plane, and the number of files had no doubt quadrupled by the time Nola had driven here. Bishop was always extremely thorough. Diving into all of that and setting up her board, therefore, were her priority.

So she would clean the first floor and get set up. Then she'd go speak with the Hayes family.

A chill ran up her back as she watched the house. Anna Mae had been gone for over two days. Her time was running out.

Time to get to work.

Chapter Seven

It took two hours to read through all the files. Once completed, Nola started setting up her investigation board on the wall of the bedroom. She printed out what she needed and taped it to the wall then stepped back to admire her handiwork.

There wasn't much there. It was seriously bare bones. Dates missing, other similar cases.

It was an old-school way of working a case. In the CIA, her colleagues had teased her about the benefits of computers. But Nola's work had stood for itself. And she had no intention of changing things just because other people thought she should.

Delford and the surrounding area had a higher-than-normal number of disappearances. It could be a fluke, a spike related to some unknown factor. But Nola had a niggling feeling in her stomach it was more than that. Tonight she'd go through those other cases and see if anything jumped out.

Her eyes drifted over the reports and back to the color

photo in the middle of the wall. Anna Mae smiled back at her. She had smooth brown skin, large bright brown eyes, and perfect cherub shaped lips which hinted at the stunning woman she would be one day—if she got the chance.

But right now, she still looked more child than woman. Standing at only five foot one and weighing in at around ninety pounds, her small stature only added to her childlike appearance.

"Is that the missing girl?"

Nola turned around. Her daughter, Molly, sat on top of the dresser at the end of the room. Her brown hair was in pigtails with red bows, and her eyes, hazel, just like Nola's, watched Nola with amusement.

Nola put her hands on her hips. "What are you doing here, young lady?"

Molly shrugged, a small grin appearing on her lips that showed off her dimples. "Dad said I could come."

"He knows I don't like you being here when I'm working."

"You're always working," Molly replied.

"That's still no reason for your father to just let you show up," Nola said.

Molly just smiled.

Nola sighed and nodded toward the board. "Her name's Anna Mae. She's been missing for two days now."

"That's a long time."

"A lifetime."

"*I'll* never leave you," Molly said emphatically.

Her heart squeezing, Nola's tone was light when she answered. "I'm not sure even you have the power to avoid that someday."

"Will you be able to find her?" Molly asked.

"I hope so, honey, I really hope so."

"You will. That's what you do: find people who are lost. There's no one better at it than you."

Nola felt the lump in her throat as she stared at the little girl that she and David had created. Nola was not a romantic. She loved David and would do anything for him. But she'd never believed they were destined. She just thought she was lucky.

But then she'd gotten pregnant with Molly. The minute Molly had opened up her little eyes and looked at Nola, she was hooked. Nola knew in her gut that everything that had come before that moment had led her to the amazing event of meeting her daughter. She would never, ever regret anything that happened before. All the trials, all the tribulations, all the pain, it all faded away when she looked into her daughter's eyes.

Years later, she wasn't quite as sanguine about the pain in the world, but she still felt that overwhelming love whenever she looked into her daughter's face.

"Have you eaten?" Molly asked, her hands on her hips as she hopped off the dresser and stood, echoing Nola's earlier posture.

Nola laughed. "No. I haven't."

Her daughter shook her head. "You always forget to eat. You need to take better care of yourself."

"Hey, who's the mother here?" Nola demanded.

Looking at her mother very seriously, Molly tilted her head. "*That* is a very good question."

Nola swatted at her. Laughing, Molly ducked, and moved into the doorway. "Dad said I could only stay for a little while. Maybe we can make some mac and cheese?"

Mac and cheese was by far Molly's favorite food. Nola and David had tried to break her of the habit multiple times, but her love affair with mac and cheese remained unabated. And Nola remembered seeing a box of it in one of the grocery bags that Avad had provided. "Fine. But no more showing up when I'm at work. You tell your dad I said so."

"Okay, Mom."

Rolling her eyes, Nola said, "Don't say it like that. That's your 'I'm not listening to my mother' tone."

"Okay, Mom," Molly said in the exact same way.

Laughing, Nola followed her toward the kitchen. Maybe a little break wasn't the worst thing. But she couldn't help but glance back at the board one more time. "Seriously, though, tell your dad no more visits until this case is over."

"It's a bad one?"

Nola looked at Anna Mae's smiling face. "Yeah, baby, it's a bad one."

Chapter Eight

ANNA MAE

Black. Everything was black. At first Anna Mae wasn't sure her eyes were even open, the dark was so complete.

Terror stole through her. *Oh God. I can't see. I can't see.*

She reached up and felt her face, needing to check. They were open. Were they not working? Was she blind?

Then she saw the faintest outline of her hand. No, she wasn't blind. It was just pitch black.

The air was cool, and there was a stale musty smell to it. But it didn't move. There was no window nearby. She pushed up from the ground, surprised to feel dirt under her hands. *I'm outside?*

Her brain couldn't process that possibility. If she was outside, why was the air so still? Why was it so dark? But she'd touched the damp earth. It didn't make any sense.

Her eyes began to adjust. Above her, she could see the faintest outline of light to her right. It was incredibly slim, maybe only a few centimeters wide and about a foot long. But her heart raced at the sight, and relief flowed through her. *A way out.*

She started to stand but then dropped back down to the ground as her head began to spin. She sat with her head bowed, resting on her hands and knees, waiting for the dizziness to pass. Once she felt more herself, she started to stand again, this time much more slowly. Her stomach felt hollow.

When was the last time I ate? Her heart rate ticked up as fear pounded through her.

She couldn't remember. Her face got hot as her panic started to rise. She reached out to her side and felt a wall of dirt. Recognition flooded her. *I'm in an old root cellar.*

Using the wall for support, she stood, then leaned back against it, waiting once again for another bout of dizziness to pass. Her mouth was so dry her tongue felt like sandpaper, and her throat ached. *When was the last time I had water? How long have I been here? Where am I?*

She shoved all the questions aside as her breath came out in pants. Panic crawled raged through her mind. Her chest felt tight. *Oh God, oh God, oh God.*

She lowered her head between her knees as the light-headedness returned. *I need to calm down. I need to calm down.*

She knew the words were right was true, but she was just so terrified. She shook, her arms wrapped around herself. Where was she?

It was a struggle to remember anything, the panic making it difficult to think. The light beckoned her from up ahead. *Focus on the light. Only the light.*

Slowly, she walked toward it. Her legs felt like Jell-O. She waited to collapse to the ground. Her head felt weird, like there was a vise around parts of it. *I can do this. I can do this.*

Keeping her arms in front of her, she waved them toward the side to make sure she didn't knock into anything. Inch by inch, she moved forward. Then she touched more dirt. She'd reached the other wall, only six feet away. The light was right above her.

She leaned up toward it but couldn't quite reach it. On her tippy toes, she stretched as far as she could manage. Her fingers grazed a wooden board.

Her legs finally gave out. She dropped down to the ground with a muted cry. There wasn't enough saliva in her mouth to make much more noise than that. Her shoulders ached, and light-headedness swamped her. Her hand rubbed against something on the ground next to her. She yanked it back, her heart pounding as she tried to make out the object in the dark. Horror-movie images racing through her mind, she reached out again. She touched the smooth surface and then gripped its cylindrical shape as she recognized it. Her heart leaped. *A water bottle.*

She pulled it to her and quickly unscrewed the top and downed the bottle's contents. After reaching around, she felt a second water bottle along with an apple. She started to unscrew the water bottle and then thought better of it. Wiping the apple as best she could on her shirt, she bit into its skin. The sweetness made her want to cry. There were a few mushy parts, but she didn't care, she was so hungry. And the extra juice was helping with her thirst.

Her head felt clearer after she'd eaten. She leaned back against the dirt wall, struggling to remember how she'd ended up here. But it was like there was a gaping hole in her memory. She'd finished classes. She remembered that. Then she'd gone to get Oz.

But she couldn't remember anything after that. What had happened?

There was a squeak above her, and then light blared down at her. Anna Mae lifted her arm with a cry. The brightness was too intense, too fast. Heat wafted in.

Before she could say a word, a body dropped to the ground next to her with a thud. Anna Mae scampered away with a yelp. In the light, she could make out a young girl, tiny, skinny, with skin lighter than Anna Mae's.

Two more bottles of water dropped to the ground, one hitting off the edge of the young girl's hip. A few more pieces of fruit were dropped as well before the wooden slats above were closed again.

Anna Mae scrambled to her feet. "No! No! Wait!"

No reply came from up above.

"Help! Help me, please!" She yelled herself hoarse for a few minutes, but no one appeared. She sank to the ground, tears burning in her eyes. Her hip brushed the edge of the girl's body. Anna Mae jumped back in fright.

With a shaking hand, she reached out and touched the girl's shoulder. She followed the edge of the girl's shoulder to her neck and found a pulse.

Thank God. The light had caused spots to appear before her eyes, but now they had faded, and the darkness was once again complete.

The girl was unconscious, probably the same way Anna Mae had been when she'd arrived. Anna Mae adjusted the girl so she was in a more comfortable position and then leaned against the dirt wall. She took the girl's small hand in hers. She really was tiny. Anna Mae didn't think she could be any older than eleven. Anna Mae wanted more of the water, her throat parched again from all the yelling, but she only took a few sips and then put the cap back on. She was going to need to conserve it.

She squeezed the small girl's hand in hers and whispered, "It's okay. I'm here."

Chapter Nine

NOLA

The mac and cheese had been good. Nola realized that she hadn't eaten in close to twenty-four hours. Her body needed the nutrients, if mac and cheese offered any. She and Molly had laughed and talked, but then Nola had to send her back to her dad, because it was time to go speak with the Hayeses.

Molly hugged her tight. Nola felt the warmth of her daughter's body against her, and the cold space in her heart filled for just a moment before her daughter stepped away. "Dad's waiting."

Nola nodded. "No coming back until after the case."

Her daughter glanced back down the hall to where Nola's crime board was. "Are you going to be okay?"

"I'll be fine. You don't have to worry about me."

"We do, Daddy and me. And Grandma's worried too."

"Did she tell you that?"

Molly shrugged. "I heard her talking to Bishop."

Sighing, Nola knew there was no way to get her to quit listening in, but she didn't have the heart to tell her to stop. "Well, I'll be fine. And I need to go."

Wrapping her arms around Nola, Molly hugged her one more time. "Love you, Mommy."

"Love you too," Nola said.

Grinning, Molly skipped out of the kitchen. Walking more slowly, Nola followed and watched her step out of the house.

David stood at the end of the path. He had the same dark wavy hair that she had once loved to run her hands through. His skin was darker than Nola's, a gift from his Afghani mother. His blue eyes came from his father. Together with the high cheekbones, they created an image that had set Nola's heart racing the first time she had seen him.

And every time since.

Today, her heart rate still ticked up a notch, but Nola kept her face neutral. She glanced around the street. No one was around. David raised his hand in greeting, his smile sad.

Nola took a breath and waved back. Molly joined him on the sidewalk. Nola turned and headed back inside. She never watched them leave. They were a life she wanted more than anything and one she could never have again.

Slipping into the bedroom, she scanned the board again, letting her defenses build back up. Seeing David and Molly always shook her. It was why she didn't want Molly to visit her when she was on a case. It took her mind off the task at hand.

She closed her eyes, focusing on her breath. Five minutes later, she opened them, her emotions locked back down.

And that was how they would stay until this case was over.

She headed for the front door. It was time to visit Anna Mae's family.

———

Nola walked around the block to reach the Hayeses. Technically she could have just cut through the backyard, but she didn't think that would help ingratiate her to Anna Mae's mother.

Anna Mae's home was a blue ranch house with white shutters. Abandoned window boxes hung beneath the windows on the first floor. The windows were open to allow some air into the house. But the air felt so heavy that Nola didn't think it offered any relief.

A car in need of a muffler turned onto the street. It slowed as it approached Nola. She turned, her arms crossed, as the car drove by. Four young men stared straight at her. They made no pretense of looking anywhere else. They wanted her to know they saw her. They wanted her to know she wasn't welcome.

She waited until the car had turned the corner, aware of the press of her gun at the small of her back. But she'd made no move for it. A warning was all the young men had wanted to give her.

Nola took her gaze from the receding car, aware now of other eyes on her. Across the street, a curtain shifted as a head ducked out of view. Two houses down from that, two small children on bikes stood on the sidewalk watching her unabashedly. On her side of the street, a woman stepped outside and walked to the mailbox, slowly watching Nola from the corner of her eye.

This neighborhood kept an eye on its people. And it definitely kept an eye on the people who shouldn't be here. So if Anna Mae disappeared from here, someone would've seen something. Which meant she hadn't been grabbed from here. The neighbors might not have told the cops, but they would've told somebody.

Careful on the uneven boards, Nola walked up the three steps to the porch. She knocked on the edge of the door-frame. A small boy who seemed younger than his eight years appeared behind the screen door. He looked up at her with big brown eyes. "Are you with the church? Because my mom doesn't like when people come talking to her about God. She says she's got all the God she needs."

Nola smiled in spite of herself. "No, I'm not here to talk to your mom about God. Is your mama home?"

The boy nodded and then turned to look behind him. "Mom!"

A woman in nursing scrubs appeared from beyond the living room. "Oz! How many times have I told you not to yell for me like that?"

Oz shrugged. "There's a woman who wants to talk to you."

Martha walked to the door, and Nola got her first good look at her. She was a little shorter than Nola, standing at maybe 5 5". She was softly built and didn't have any lines in her face, but her eyes looked tired, or maybe sad. Her dark hair was pulled back into a small bun on the back of her head. Little duckies dotted her lime-green scrub top. She wore blue scrub pants, and on her feet were pink crocs. She peered up at Nola with light-brown eyes. "If you're from some church, I am not interested."

Nola shook her head. "No, I'm not from a church. I'm here to speak with you about Anna Mae."

Martha scanned Nola from head to toe. "Are you a cop?"

"Not exactly. More of a private investigator."

"I can't afford to pay for a private investigator," Martha said with a shake of her head.

"I'm not asking you to. I was just hoping I could ask you some questions about Anna Mae that might help me find her."

Anna Mae's mother crossed her arms over her chest. "Why are you looking for her?"

"It's what I do. I look for people, help people out when the system doesn't."

Martha scoffed. "And you do it for free?"

"I will never ask you for money. I have a backer who covers my expenses. Your daughter's case was flagged as one I might be able to help with."

As Martha hesitated, Nola could practically hear the war inside her head:

I don't know this woman.

But I need help and I miss my girl.

Finally, she pushed open the screen door. "Come on in."

Nola stepped into the living room. The house was only a degree or two cooler from the outside. Well-worn but clean wooden floors lined the front room. A leather couch with matching chairs sat around a fireplace. Above the fireplace, a small TV hung in a frame.

Martha gestured to one of the chairs. "Can I get you anything? Water, sweet tea?"

Shaking her head, Nola took a seat in one of the chairs. The leather was warm, but the seat was soft and comfortable. Obviously it was well used. "No, I'm fine."

Sitting down opposite her, Nola got her first good look at the other occupant of the room. An older woman sat on a small chair beyond the couch against the wall. Nola met her gaze and gave her a brief nod. The woman nodded back with a small smile. She was an older version of Martha. She had to be her mother.

"So really, who hired you?" Martha asked.

Nola redirected her attention to Martha. She was used to this response. "No one, really. I heard about the case and thought I might be able to help."

Martha pursed her lips. "You're not a reporter or something, are you?"

"No, nothing like that. I used to work for the government. I used to track down really bad people. Now I do the same thing, just not for the government." Nola pulled out a small notepad and a pen. "What can you tell me about the last time you saw Anna Mae?"

Taking a breath, Martha hesitated for a moment, her skepticism obvious. But desperation to find her daughter won out. "It was just a normal day. There's nothing about it that stood out. I had the early shift that morning. I leave by six. I made sure Anna Mae and Oz were up before I left. She takes Oz to school and then goes on to her own. I didn't have time to make them breakfast because I slept through my alarm. So when I left, Anna Mae was standing at the stove making Oz pancakes."

"According to the report, she made it to school?" Nola asked.

Martha nodded. "I went and spoke with all her teachers myself. She was there. And then she walked home to pick Oz up from his school. He had soccer practice. But she never showed up. Oz walked home by himself. I got home at around six thirty, and she still wasn't here. We called around, and I drove back to the school. There was a basketball game going on, and I spoke with a bunch of the teachers and the principal. But no one had seen her. I waited all night. But she never showed."

"When did you report her missing to the cops?"

Curling her lip, Martha said, "The cops. I called them that first night. They told me she just ran off. That girls her age did that. But Anna Mae, she wouldn't do that. She would never leave Oz on his own. She would never make him walk home by himself."

Nola's gaze strayed to where Oz stood peeking from of the kitchen doorway.

"The cops aren't even trying to find her. They told me I should just wait, that she'd come back. But Anna Mae isn't like that. She doesn't date. She knows what happens to girls who make boys a priority over school."

Nola noted her mother's use of the present tense.

Wiping a tear away from the corner of her eye, Martha said, "She saw how hard I worked. How hard her grandma worked. She told me once that she's going to be successful. That she's going to get me a big house so I never have to work again. Her plan is to get out of Delford and make a life for herself and for us, where we don't have to work all the time. Where we can put our feet up some of the time. She doesn't have a boyfriend. She doesn't have a lot of friends. She is quiet, shy but determined. She's top of her class. She'll be valedictorian next year, I know it. And then she's going to college. She already has offers. She's getting out of here."

Stopping, she took a deep breath. Her words had rushed out in a torrent, like she had been building them up. And she probably had. She wanted to tell someone who her daughter was and get them to understand that she needed help. But she hadn't been able to get anyone in a position to do something about it to listen.

Martha grabbed a tissue from the box on the coffee table and wiped the edge of her eyes before crushing the tissue in her fist. "Um, can you hold on a second?"

"Sure."

With a nod, Martha stood up and disappeared down the hallway. She reappeared a minute later with a large trophy in her hands. She placed it on the coffee table in front of Nola. "Anna Mae won this a few months back. She was so proud she came home floating and started looking up engineering schools. This is my daughter."

The engraved plaque faced Nola and read:

1st Place
2nd Annual Robotics Championship
The Retreat

"This is who my daughter is. She is a good girl, a great student. She doesn't bother with boys; she has other goals. We don't even have a computer for her to go online and get in trouble."

"Phone?" Nola asked.

"She doesn't have one," Martha said with a shake of her head.

That made her a rather unusual teenager, although Nola had expected the answer. "What about friends? Did anyone see her walking home that day?"

"I spoke with Susie and Siobhan, but neither of them saw her."

"What about Charlene?" Oz yelled from the kitchen doorway.

Turned, Martha speared him with a glare. "I thought I told you go to your room."

Oz's head peeked around the corner of the kitchen doorway. "But I want to help find Anna Mae."

"Go to your room, Oz," Martha ordered in a tone laced with fatigue.

"Fine," he grumbled before disappearing from the doorway.

"Charlene?" Nola prodded when Martha turned back to her.

Sighing, Martha folded her hands in her lap before she sighed again and looked up at Nola. "Charlene Hudson. Her and Anna Mae have been tight ever since they were little. And then something changed last year. Charlene started hanging with a rougher crowd. She started using. I don't know what happened, really. The two of them were both committed to going to college, and then poof. For Charlene, all those thoughts were gone."

"Did her and Anna Mae stay friends?" Nola asked.

Martha shook her head. "Anna Mae tried. She tried to get her to talk to her, to explain what was going on. But Charlene just pushed her away. I doubt Charlene would know what was happening with her, but I know Anna Mae never stopped trying to reach out to her."

"Where does Charlene live?" Nola asked.

"Just three doors down. At least, her family does. Charlene doesn't stay there very much. She's usually at a place over on Crenshaw." Martha glanced over her shoulder, scanning the kitchen doorway. She tilted her head, listening. Finally satisfied, she turned back to Nola. "It's a drug house."

That was not a surprise. Nola had been thinking that's what Martha was hinting around. "Do you have addresses for Siobhan and Susie?"

Grabbing her phone, Martha looked them up and gave Nola the addresses, as well as their phone numbers.

"Would you mind if I looked at Anna Mae's room?"

Although Martha hesitated, she finally nodded. "Follow me."

Nola followed Martha down the short hallway off the living room. Anna Mae's room was the first door on the right. Oz's room was directly across from it. He looked up from his bed, where he was sprawled out, reading a comic book. "What are you doing?" he asked.

"Nothing." His mother reached in and pulled on the handle, closing his door. Then she nodded toward Anna Mae's room. "I haven't touched anything."

The room was neat. There was a twin bed against the right wall. A desk and corkboard sat on the opposite wall. A closet was to her right, and there was a window straight ahead. A poster of some TV show Nola was familiar with hung above her bed, and a picture of Anna Mae, her brother, mom, and grandmother sat on her side table.

She wandered over to the corkboard. Everything on it was related to school: article ideas, deadlines for classwork, a few brochures for colleges. Martha stood in the doorway as Nola read each piece of paper. She gestured to the desk. "Do you mind . . .?"

"No, go ahead," Martha said making no move to step inside.

Rifling though, there was nothing that stuck out to her. Kneeling down on the floor, she knocked on the wood, but there didn't seem to be any hollow spots. She checked the closet, but nothing there stood out either. And an examination of the floor and walls revealed no little hidey-holes.

Finally, Nola stood in the center of the room, looking around. All of Anna Mae's priorities were in front of her:

family and school. There was nothing that indicated she was thinking of running away. In fact, the calendar on the corkboard had Oz's birthday, two weeks away, circled in bright-red marker. Anna Mae had drawn balloons inside the calendar's square. Plus, she'd noted an article on the marching band she needed to finish up by Monday. And there was a college fair coming up that she seemed to be counting the days until.

Martha noted Nola's interest. "She's really excited about the college fair. She wants to talk to some of the Ivy League representatives. She knows it's a long shot, but she wants to see what they think her chances are of getting in."

Nola glanced around the room one more time. It hadn't provided any clues as to where Anna Mae had gone, but it did provide a better picture of the young woman.

With one last scan of the room, Nola followed Martha back to the living room. She handed Martha her card. "If you think of anything else, give me a call."

Staring down at the card, Martha asked, "You don't have a business name?"

"No." Nola headed for the door.

"Where are you headed now?" Anna Mae's mother asked.

"I'll speak with Siobhan and Susie. Then I'll head over to the Hudsons to see if Charlene's there. If she's not, I'll head to Crenshaw to see if maybe Charlene knows something. Any chance you have a picture of her?"

"Hold on a sec." Martha disappeared into the kitchen.

Flicking a gaze at the doorway where Martha disappeared, Nola looked at the older woman sitting along the back of the room. She spoke quietly. "Hello, ma'am."

The woman gave her a nod. "You'll find my granddaughter."

"I hope so."

"No, you will. She's waiting for you to find her," the woman said.

Before Nola could reply, Martha hustled back into the room. "This is the most recent picture I have of Anna Mae, at least printed out. It's from last year. It was after the school play. Anna Mae's on the right. That's Charlene with her. They were both in the chorus." She handed it to Nola.

It was shot outside the school on a sunny day. Two African-American girls stood there with their arms wrapped around one another, beaming. Both had their hair in tight ringlets. They looked a lot alike. They could pass for sisters. They were the same height with the same bright smiles. Charlene's eyes were a little smaller than Anna Mae's, her cheekbones a little higher, but they had that same look of happiness. Two girls: one missing and one had been missing from her life for a year now. How did it go from such happiness to such sorrow?

But she knew the answer to that question. She knew what humans could do to one another and could do to themselves.

Charlene's life had gone off the rails a year ago. Now Nola needed to find out if the reason for her life turn was related to Anna Mae's disappearance.

Chapter Ten

Nola walked around the block back to her rented house. None of the friends Martha had mentioned had appeared in any of Anna Mae's limited social media footprint. She wanted to do a quick online search for them. Nola didn't like going into an interview without having done her due diligence. By the time she reached the rented house, however, she knew her research was going to have to wait at least a little bit.

Because she had a visitor.

Oz was at the end of her driveway, sitting on the back bumper of her Bronco. He watched her as she walked up the drive toward him. Finally, when she was a few feet away, he pushed himself off the Bronco and crossed his arms in front of his chest. He was a very small tough guy.

Putting her hands into her pockets, she gave him a grave nod. "Oz. You need to speak with me about something?"

He nodded, his face just as serious. "I don't want you getting my mom's hopes up."

"I wouldn't do that."

Oz blew a raspberry. "Yeah, right. We've already had three different people call and offer to 'help'." He used air quotes. "All they were looking for was money. So if you're not here for money, why are you here? And how'd you hear about her, anyway?"

"One of my people found your website."

Hidden in Bishop's file was the reason that Anna Mae's disappearance had attracted her attention. It was a simple website that had been set up about Anna Mae. Anyone who knew anything about her disappearance was told to call the Haverford-Delford PD. Bishop had traced it back to Oz's elementary school.

His eyes went wide. "You did?"

Nola nodded. "It was pretty good. Did you make it by yourself?"

With a shrug, he said, "Most of it. My teacher wrote up some stuff for me."

"Well, you did good. It brought me down here. And I'm going to try my best to find Anna Mae."

Taking a deep breath, he darted a glance back at his house before he spoke. "Each time my mama talked to those other people . . . She knew they weren't telling the truth, but she still got sad when they left."

He took another deep breath, his chest and chin trembling. It was taking a lot of effort for the poor kid to maintain his tough façade. Nola's respect for him went up a few more notches.

"I don't want my mom to cry anymore," he said in a small voice.

"I do hope I can find your sister. I can't promise that I will. But I can promise that I will try my hardest to bring her back home."

Oz stared up at her.

Nola kept her face without expression. She had a feeling that Oz was coming to a decision and that it was important he made it on his own.

"Have you found a lot of missing people?" he asked.

An image of Abby Miceli floated through Nola's mind. "Yes."

She didn't tell him about the dozens and dozens of people she'd tracked down over the years.

Oz seemed to like the fact that she didn't explain herself. "Do you think my sister is still alive?"

The question pulled Nola up short. Her first impulse was to say of course. Because who told a little kid that his sister could be dead? But she could see in his eyes that he wasn't looking to be placated. He knew that there was a very good chance that Anna Mae wasn't going to come back.

"I don't know, Oz. But I can promise that I will find out what happened to her."

The boy's gaze shifted down to his feet, his shoulders slumping and his feet shifting on the gravel drive. "Yeah, I don't know if she is either."

A tear rolled down his cheek. He wiped it away quickly, darting a look at Nola to see if she had caught it. She made a point of looking away and not mentioning it. "Do you have any ideas? Was there anybody that was bugging your sister or paying too much attention to her?"

He shook his head. "No. Anna Mae, she just went to school and came home with me. Unless she was going to one of her clubs or something."

"What about her friends, Susie and Siobhan?"

Oz's mouth turned into a snarl. "Susie and Siobhan aren't really her friends. I mean, they hang out, but they're not friends with her the way Charlene was. Charlene would come over and hang out and sleep over sometimes. Anna Mae hangs out with Susie and Siobhan at school and has lunch with them, but they're not really good friends."

"Okay. That's good to know."

Kicking at a rock on the drive, Oz asked, "What are you going to do now?"

"Now I need to go speak with Susie, Siobhan, and Charlene. Sometimes people see things they don't realize they've seen."

"Okay. But . . ." He paused, glancing over his shoulder at his house and then dropping his voice. "Don't get my mama's hopes up. Just don't make her hope . . . well, just don't."

Turning, he walked slowly back toward his house. His head was down, his shoulders hunched. He had way too many worries on those young shoulders.

Nola watched him go, feeling the lid she had carefully placed on top of her emotions sliding open just a little.

Poor kid. She shook away the thought and the empathy that came with it. Empathy wasn't going to help him.

Focusing on the task at hand and tracking down every lead, that's how she would help Oz. She turned up the path toward the house. But she couldn't help but glance over at the heartbroken boy who, instead of going into his own house, took a seat on the back porch and wiped away the tears that he didn't want his mama to see.

Chapter Eleven

Unlike Anna Mae and Charlene, Siobhan and Susie had social media profiles on dozens of sites. Each was a frequent user of Instagram, Snapchat, and TikTok. Both shared way too much information about themselves and their activities. Sadly, instead of that being a red flag, it indicated they were normal teenagers.

Nola lucked out and caught both of them at Susie's house. That's where her luck ended, because it looked like Oz was right: they weren't really close.

Neither Siobhan nor Susie had much to share about Anna Mae. They were concerned about her, but they didn't really talk outside of school. Charlene had apparently been the one that had linked them together. And once Charlene drifted away, they hadn't really spent as much time together.

"I wish we had walked with her that day," Susie said, "but we were talking to Mrs. Fields about our English paper."

"Anna Mae couldn't wait because she had to get Oz . . . We should have gone with her," Siobhan added.

"Was Anna Mae dating anyone?" Nola asked.

Siobhan shook her head. "No. I mean, I don't think she even had a crush on anyone. Well, except for Cole Sprouse."

Nola started to write the name down. "Cole Sprouse?"

"Oh, no," Siobhan said, her eyes on Nola's notepad. "He's an actor. He plays Jughead in *Riverdale*, and he was in *The Suite Life of Zach & Cody*. She's had a crush on him since we were kids."

Scratching out the name, Nola tried to hide her annoyance. "What about Charlene? Do you think she might have some idea where Anna Mae's gone?"

Siobhan and Susie exchanged a look before Susie spoke. "I doubt it. Charlene . . . she's not really been around much."

"Is there any chance Anna Mae might have gone to speak with Charlene, maybe down on Crenshaw?" Nola asked.

Her eyes growing wide, Siobhan shook her head. "Anna Mae would never go down to Crenshaw. No way."

Susie nodded her agreement. Nola spoke with them for another fifteen minutes but didn't get any more information that might help find Anna Mae. Then she headed over to the high school. There was a basketball game on, and she hoped she might be able to speak with some of Anna Mae's teachers. She managed to find her English, math, and social studies teachers, as well as the principal, who were all helping out at the game. She even spoke with a few students the teachers had suggested might be able to shed some light on Anna Mae.

But no one added anything of value. What Nola did get, though, was a better picture of what Anna Mae was like: smart and nice to everyone. She was one of those people who everybody liked but that no one really knew well. Charlene had been the one Anna Mae had confided in. But once Charlene was gone, it seemed Anna Mae had kept her confidences to herself.

After meeting with Susie and Siobhan, Nola stopped by the Hudson home, but there was no answer, so she headed toward Tasha McNally's family home, the other missing girl Bishop had mentioned. But as good as she was at tracking people down, Nola had no illusions about being able to find Tasha. She had disappeared without a trace five years earlier.

The family of Tasha McNally still lived in Delford. In fact, Tasha's parents still lived in the same home that Tasha had grown up in. And it was only six blocks away from Anna Mae's house.

Nola decided to walk over to Field Street. She needed to stretch her legs, needed to feel the air on her face, and she needed to get a better feel for the small southern town.

Those six blocks provided a world of insight into Delford. She passed homes that had window boxes meticulously planted and yards perfectly mowed. The homes and lots were small, but the paint was fresh, and it was obvious the owners took a great deal of pride in their home. A block away, homes still had a well-kept appearance, although new paint was rarer and the window boxes were a little sparser.

Another block was another step down the poverty ladder. Homes were in a sad state of disrepair, with abandoned homes in between houses, sometimes with a swing set out front or a bike leaning against an old wooden porch.

The one thing all the streets had in common were the people: They were everywhere. People sat on porches chatting with one another. Others sat rocking alone, a pitcher of iced tea or some other cool drink next to them. Kids rode by on bicycles or ran by chasing one another. Cars were less prevalent, although all those that went by had the windows down to let in some air.

The air itself felt like it wasn't moving at all. It was just heavy and weighted. Nola's tank top was sticking to her by the time she turned onto Tasha's old street. This street was once again a mix of homes, although fewer of them had the abandoned look. It was more of a mix of the incredibly well-taken-care-of home with the not-quite-able-to-afford-some-paint ones of the other blocks.

Only a few of the homes had house numbers on them. Tasha's house was missing the numbers, but luckily the houses on either side provided them. Nola approached 67, noting the bright white daisies in the window boxes and the well-watered lawn. The house could use a paint job, but the picket fence had been painted recently, as had the mailbox.

As she approached, she could see a clothesline out back, shirts and pants hanging on it without any movement. Today would be a tough drying day with the complete lack of wind and all the humidity in the air. A small Hyundai sedan was in the gravel drive, which was in need of more gravel. Grass had begun to sprout up through the rocks.

A *Beware of Dog* sign hung on the chain-link fence. But as Nola opened the gate, there was no telltale sign of the watchdog. Nola walked up the few steps to the porch and found the ferocious beast. The old mastiff's tail wagged slowly when he spied her. He lay sprawled in the shade, a large bowl of water next to him and an ignored large bone on his other side. The dog was brown with big soulful eyes and gray working its way through his snout.

She crouched down next to him, reaching out a hand for him to sniff. "Hey there, boy. How you doing today?"

As she scratched behind his ears, he closed his eyes in

response, leaning into her hand. She smiled at the gentleness of the canine. This was no watchdog. It was a good size, and maybe in his earlier days that alone would scare someone off, but right now he was more of a giant teddy bear than a giant warning.

With one last pat, Nola stood up. The dog let out a small whine. He stretched back, raising his butt in the air and then slowly got his back legs underneath him. It was painful to watch as he walked with a limp to the front door to join Nola.

The dog stood next to her, leaning against her leg as she rapped on the edge of the screen door. She gave him one last pet before someone appeared. It was a young man in his mid-twenties. He had on a blue button-down shirt and khakis. A tie was unwrapped around his neck. Nola guessed he was Darrell McNally, Tasha's big brother. He frowned when he saw Nola. "Can I help you?"

"I'm looking for Clyde and Michelle McNally," she said.

Darrell crossed his arms over his chest. "What do you want to speak with them for?"

His posture was defensive but not aggressive. He was protecting his parents. She understood that. She appreciated that. "I don't know if you've heard, but another young woman has gone missing in Delford. She's only sixteen years old. I'm looking into her disappearance. I was hoping I could speak with your parents about Tasha's disappearance."

The man's eyes flashed with pain for a moment before he shook his head. "I'm sorry. I really am. But that's just too difficult for my parents to talk about. They've been through enough. They've finally been able to put it aside and live again. I don't want to bring that back up for them."

"I understand that, Mr. McNally, but, like I said,

another girl is missing. And maybe there was something about your sister's disappearance that can help us find her."

Anger laced his words along with frustration. "Why? My sister's been gone for five years. There's no trace of her. She just disappeared. I don't see how—"

"That's enough, Darrell." A tall African-American gentleman with dark hair stepped out of the kitchen. He made his way toward the front door. Standing next to Darrell, the two of them could've been mistaken for brothers in the dim light. It was only when the sunlight touched Clyde McNally's face that the gray hairs and lines became apparent.

"Dad, you don't need to go through this again. How many people have we talked to about Tasha? It's never helped," Darrell said as he turned to his dad.

Clyde patted his son on the shoulder. "No, it's never helped Tasha. But maybe we could help this other girl."

"But Mom shouldn't have to go through this again," Darrell countered.

With compassion in his eyes, it was clear Clyde knew it wasn't only his wife who bringing up Tasha's disappearance was hard for. "I know. She should be home from Edith's any minute now. Why don't you keep an eye out for her, and I'll talk to this nice young lady?"

Darrell sighed before shaking his head. "Okay, Dad. But I don't want Mom to get upset."

The elder McNally smiled. "Oh, trust me, son, none of us wants your mother upset."

A few minutes later, Darrell was positioned outside on the porch with a pitcher of iced tea, waiting for his mother along with Snuffles, the giant dog with the incongruously cute name.

Clyde led Nola through the house and out to the back

patio. A retractable awning extended from the house, providing some shade. There was a small seating area along with a patio set for eating. And a mister had been set up along one of the poles to provide a cool, damp breeze. It was actually a nice little setup.

Nola took a seat in the chair that Clyde indicated. "As I explained to your son, I'm investigating Anna Mae Hayes's disappearance."

Sitting back, Clyde nodded. "I heard about that. Seemed like a nice girl. I saw her at church every weekend. She reminded me of Tasha."

"How so?"

Clyde shrugged. "I can't really say for sure. I didn't actually know her. Sometimes when you see someone, you just kind to get a feeling about them, you know?"

Nola nodded. "Yeah, I know that very well."

"Well, I got the impression that Anna Mae was quiet and shy but smart. Tasha was the same way. She never had a lot of friends, but she did incredibly well at school. And if you ever asked for help, she was the first one to volunteer. She was a really good girl."

Unlike Martha, Clyde did not speak about his daughter in the present tense. "And there was never any clue, any hint, as to where she went?"

For the first time, Clyde's face shifted to one of anger. "Not with the little help we got. The cops, they did little to nothing in looking for her. It was me, a few of the neighbors, some of the kids from school, members of the church —we were the ones out looking for her. But the cops kept telling us she'd run off. That girls her age did that all the time. And that we just needed to accept it."

"But you never did," Nola said. It wasn't a question.

"No," he said softly. "Tasha . . . I mean, I know some

girls get wrapped up in boys or in a bad situation and make poor decisions. I understand that. But Tasha, she was just too shy for any of that. At the first sign of trouble, her instinct was to run back *to* us, not away from us. If there was any trouble, she would have come to us."

"But you don't think that maybe there was a boy or . . ."

He gave Nola a small smile. "No, there was never a boy. From a very early age, we knew Tasha wasn't interested in boys. But explaining that to the cops would only have made them *less* likely to look into her disappearance than more. Times are changing, but not that fast."

Nola pulled out her notepad. "Can you tell me about Tasha? Her hobbies, her activities?"

"She worked on the school newspaper. She was the features editor. She was real proud of that. She thought that the next year, she might actually have a chance of being editor-in-chief. She probably would've. By the end of her junior year, she was practically running the paper by herself anyway. The seniors didn't care at that point.

"But she didn't really do much else, at the school, at least. She was very active in the church, though. Singing in the choir, volunteering for all activities, helping lead the youth group. The rest of the time she spent studying, reading, helping her mom and me. She sometimes took some catering jobs up at the Retreat when they had big parties."

Nola perked up at the mention of the Retreat, the same place Anna Mae had won the robotics competition. It was a small connection, but sometimes small led to much, much bigger.

Clyde continued. "That was about it. She was just a good girl. A good girl who loved her family and helping people."

Nola could tell from his tone of voice that Mr. McNally

held no hope that Tasha was still alive. He'd accepted her death and moved on past the pain to remembering her with a smile. Nola hated to be the one to step in and possibly ruin that peace for him. She hoped he stayed on this path that he was on after she was gone.

"What about Anna Mae? Was she like Tasha?" he asked.

"I don't know about the girl thing," Nola said, "but otherwise, they sound like they had parallel lives. Anna Mae did have one good friend, but she got lost in drugs and other stuff about a year ago, and they'd grown apart. She took care of her little brother every day while her mama worked."

Clyde sighed. "It's hard on the brothers. Darrell was only a few years older than Tasha when it happened. He was taking classes at the community college. He put his classes on hold to look for her. But after a month with no sign and no movement by the police, we knew we weren't going to find her. Darrell's never really been the same since then. He's been a little quieter, a little more protective."

Glancing back at the house with a wistful look, Clyde said, "When he was younger, he kept talking about moving out and starting out on his own, but here he is with a good job. He can afford to move out, but he's never mentioned it once in the last five years. And neither have we. When you lose one member of the family, it's hard to let the other ones out of your sight."

Nola felt a lump forming in her throat. She took a few breaths, trying to keep them quiet so that Clyde didn't notice. But his eyes were sharp. "You understand," he said knowingly. "Perhaps a little too well, I think."

Not trusting herself to talk, she simply nodded.

He reached out and squeezed her hand. "It gets better,

child. One day you look back, and it's not with pain or anger; it's with a smile. It's with joy as you remember them and thank God that they were part of your life, at least for a little while."

Nola cleared her throat, latching on to another topic, anything that would let her get a little distance between herself and the pain that Clyde had unintentionally brought to the surface. "You said she volunteered at the church? Is that the First Baptist?"

As Clyde released her head, he said, "Only church in these here parts that anybody goes to. Well, I suppose there's the Protestant church over in Haverford, but no one from Delford goes over there."

"And how many times did she work over at the Retreat?"

His hand on his chin, Clyde frowned. "Oh, not real sure about that. A dozen at most, I think. I'd drive her up there and then pick her up afterwards."

"And there weren't any problems?"

He shook his head. "Not that she talked to me about. A few times she seemed a little upset, she said that some people had said some things, but she never really went into detail, and the next day she seemed fine. I figured it was just some idiot boys hitting on her."

They spoke for another few minutes, but there wasn't really much else that Clyde could add. As Nola stood, she handed him her card. "If you think of anything else that might help, please give me a call."

Clyde nodded. "I sure will. And if there's anything I can do to help out Anna Mae's family, will you please give me a call? I know what it's like, and I'd like to help if I can. I'm retired and don't have much on my plate."

Nola promised she would. She took her leave, walking

down the driveway instead of through the house. She waved at Darrell and Snuffles on the porch. She'd just crossed the road when another car pulled into the driveway. A thin African-American woman stepped out. Her hair was pulled back in a bun, and she grabbed a blue handbag that matched her skirt, top, and shoes before closing the door.

Darrell smiled, walking down from the porch, his arms outstretched. Mrs. McNally laughed and hugged him tight.

The family had been through a lot with Tasha's disappearance, but they seemed to be in a good place now. But as happy as the McNallys now seemed, Nola really hoped that this wasn't the future that the Hayeses were destined for.

Chapter Twelve

ANNA MAE

The young girl's name was Natalie, and that was all that Anna Mae managed to get out of her before the girl latched on to the bottle of water Anna Mae handed her and drank greedily.

"Slow down. You don't want to upset your stomach."

Anna Mae knew that from experience. Her stomach had cramped painfully for about an hour after she'd guzzled down her own water.

Natalie slowed her drinking. She wiped her mouth with the back of her hand when she was done. "Where are we?"

"I don't know," Anna Mae said with a shake of her head. "I only woke up a few minutes before you got here. No one's come by since then."

The young girl gripped the bottle to her chest in a protective measure that Anna Mae recognized. She had done the same thing as she sat next to Natalie, waiting for her to wake up. "I . . . who are you?"

"My name's Anna Mae Hayes."

"How'd you get here?" Natalie asked.

Anna Mae shrugged. "I don't know. I don't remember. I was heading home from school and— I just don't know."

"I was biking back from soccer practice. I remember there was a strange car, but . . ." Natalie shook her head. "I don't remember anything else either."

Studying her, Anna Mae's concern grew. "How old are you, Natalie?"

"Twelve. It was just my birthday last month."

So she was a little older than Anna Mae had thought but not by much. "Are you from Delford?"

Natalie shook her head. "No, Spalding."

Anna Mae frowned. Spalding was twenty minutes away from Delford.

"Do you know why they took us?" Natalie asked.

"No. I really don't."

The two spoke for a few more minutes, but neither had any information that explained their current predicament. And Natalie's eyes kept closing.

"It's okay. I'll watch out for you. Sleep," Anna Mae said.

"You won't leave me?" The girl asked sounding way too young.

Forcing a smile to her lips, Anna Mae promised. "Nope, I'll be right here."

While Natalie slept, Anna Mae's mind raced. There was not a single good reason she could come up with explaining why they had been taken. But there were dozens and dozens of horrible ones that could explain what was going on.

Yet when Natalie woke, even though the young girl was right here with her in this experience, Anna Mae didn't want to share any of those horrible possibilities with her. She knew it was silly, but it made her feel better to think that maybe she could at least protect Natalie a little bit from the horror of what was going on.

"Will anybody be looking for you?" Anna Mae asked.

"My aunt, if she notices. My parents . . . they're locked up. I've been living with my aunt for the last six months."

"My dad's gone too," Anna Mae said, her chest tightening. "But my mom and my brother, they'll be looking for me, so we just have to wait until they find us."

Anna Mae handed Natalie the apple. Natalie wiped it on her shirt and took a deep bite. Even in the darkness, Anna Mae could feel Natalie's gaze on her. Her voice was whisper soft and sounded so incredibly young. "Do you think so? Do you think they'll find us?"

It was an effort but Anna Mae thought she did a good job of keeping all of the fear out of her voice. "Absolutely. It's only a matter of time."

The younger girl seemed to accept her answer and busily munched away at the apple. Anna Mae's gaze drifted toward the wooden door covering the hole. Her stomach clenched harder and her heart pounded. *Oh God, please let someone find us.*

Chapter Thirteen

NOLA

Clyde McNally's eyes seemed to take up residence in the back of Nola's mind as she walked back to her rental. He'd loved his daughter, understood her. And he didn't believe she'd run away. If his description of her was accurate, she sounded a lot like Anna Mae. And they had two things in common: the church choir and the Retreat.

Nola swung by Charlene's home on the way back, but there still wasn't anyone home. She let herself into the rental and pulled up the websites for both the First Baptist Church and the Retreat. There was a service starting soon at the church, followed by two weddings. She'd have to hold off on that visit. She didn't want to get rushed out the door in between activities.

Which left the Retreat.

It wasn't a strong connection between the two. But being she had little to no leads to work with, it was worth a shot. And you never knew what small thread would unravel a whole case. So she hopped in her Bronco and turned it toward Haverford.

Fifteen minutes later, she pulled into the servants entrance of the Retreat, following a long line of cars. She wasn't sure how much of a hassle they'd give her at the front gate. Being the servants' entrance had a steady stream of cars, she figured it would be easier slipping through that way. And it was. As she pulled up to the guard hut, he simply waved her through.

The Retreat at Haverford was a sprawling two-hundred-acre estate. Flowers lined the servants' driveway, which wound through about two acres of the estate before the first building came into view. It was the barn for all of the estate's landscaping needs. A group of three men were unloading a riding mower from the back of a flatbed as Nola passed.

It was another half mile before she reached the back of the main house. From the website, she'd known what to expect: a sprawling Southern plantation-style mansion that had ballooned over the years to 20,000 square feet. It looked like the White House on steroids.

The main building dated back to the end of the Civil War. According to what Nola had been able to find online, it had been one of the first buildings resurrected after the Northern destruction. It hadn't been called the Retreat then. In fact, it had been the main house of the Haverford family. In 1902, it and the land surrounding it had been converted into the Haverford Country Club. A place for genteel white Southerners to escape the toils of their life while being waited on by the people the government had forced them to free just a few decades earlier.

The estate had remained a country club until 2000, when it had been converted to a high-end retreat center by the Haverford family. According to Honoria Haverford, the matriarch of the family, it was time to provide an escape for people from all walks of life. The move worked, expanding the membership of the Retreat. Of course, the prices for those escapes made sure that the expansion simply included wealthy people from other parts of the country.

Nola broke away from the cars and headed around the back of the main house and into the parking area in front. Flowers cascaded from planters everywhere she looked.

The estate was busy. Catering vans, florists, and other work vehicles dotted the front of the building. According to the banner strewn across the front entrance tonight was the Gala for Children, with all proceeds going to help children's poverty.

With raised eyebrows, Nola eyed a giant ice carving that was being carefully wheeled toward the front steps of the main building. The carving was five feet tall and about seven feet wide. That alone had to cost hundreds if not thousands of dollars. If they had skipped that, they could have helped quite a few poverty-stricken children.

She knew that most of these high-end charitable causes didn't actually raise much money. People felt good because they said they were going to a gala for a good cause. But the galas themselves were so extravagant that in the end, very little money was left over for the charity itself.

Stepping out of the car, she took a good look around. The scent of lilac drifted through the air. She wasn't sure if it was the result of lilac bushes, which she hadn't seen on her drive in, or if the fragrance was somehow being pumped into the air. She stared up at the main building, trying to figure out if it was possible that this place was actually linked to a string of girls' abductions. It seemed unlikely. But she had very few leads, and this was one of the only ones she had, so she would follow it until she could cross it off.

It didn't mean she was looking forward to this. Rich people creeped her out. They seemed so foreign compared to regular people. They didn't talk the same or view the world the same. There was even research indicating that they were unable to identify emotions in the same way their less-well-off counterparts could. Apparently when you didn't have a boss whose mood you had to worry about, you didn't really pick up the subtle clues of negative or positive emotions.

And she had no reason to think the Haverfords would be any different. They came from very old money. In fact, the Haverfords had founded the town in 1824. The current generation consisted of William Beauregard Haverford V; his second wife, Honoria; his son from his first marriage, William Beauregard Haverford VI; daughter Catherine May Grundy; and sixteen-year-old son, Teddy Haverford, son of William and Honoria. Catherine had married Jackson Grundy, a state senator for the great state of Louisiana and according to the scuttlebutt, hopeful gubernatorial candidate in the next election race. William Junior and Honoria were the exact same age. There was over a thirty-year age difference between the eldest Haverford and his second wife, the current matriarch of the Haverford dynasty.

And I'm sure that's a true love match, Nora thought.

The pictures Nola had seen of the family made them all look like Southern royalty. In each one, the Haverfords smiled brightly into the camera, shoulders back, gaze strong.

All except the youngest Haverford. Teddy always seemed to look uncomfortable in his family photos. Shoulders hunched, a good distance between him and the person in the photo next to him. Nola wasn't sure if it was because of his age or if he really didn't like his family. Maybe both.

She picked up her pace so she could skirt around the sculpture. She didn't want to get stuck behind them trying to get that monstrosity in the front door. As she stepped into the front foyer, the temperature immediately dropped by twenty degrees. In addition to the air-conditioning, rattan ceiling fans stirred the air, providing a much-needed contrast to the heavy, humid air outside.

White shadow boxes lined the large foyer, which extended along the entire front of the building. Small tables with four deep-seated leather chairs had been placed by each window. The windows were large and offered an incredible view of the well-manicured estate.

In front of her, the foyer continued into a large hall. To the right of the hall was a lounge area. A bar the length of the lounge was along the back wall. Heavy drapes hung from the floor-to-ceiling windows. Leather couches and sitting areas dotted the area.

A few groups of men sat at the couches, most with a drink in hand, a few with a cigar. Boisterous laughter erupted from one group. A waiter stood ten feet away, trying to be available for the group while not paying too much attention to what they were saying. But the grimace on his face indicated that he'd heard whatever had set the rest of them off into peals of laughter.

To the right was a series of ten doors, all thrown wide to reveal an immense banquet hall. Ornate carpeting lined the area with a wooden dance floor toward the back of the room and a small stage.

Nola headed into the room, sidestepping to avoid being overrun by a harassed-looking woman pushing a dolly lined with hangers and two unused tablecloths. More workers moved in and out at a rapid pace, carrying trays of glasses, pulling carts of flowers, and generally looking like very busy worker bees.

The reception room was actually stunning. Tall ceilings stretched thirty feet above them with chandeliers dripping with crystals every twenty feet or so. The walls were panels of deep, rich wallpaper in reds and greens with the slightest hint of gold. The carpeting was an intricate pattern with the Haverford initials in the middle of each ornate construction.

Tables set for ten were scattered across the room with gold silk tablecloths covering them. Workers in black pants and white shirts were carefully arranging place settings. High-backed chairs with ivory-and-blue fabric sat at each table, tied with a gold bow. Ornate silverware was being put out at each place setting. And in the middle of each table was a seven-foot-tall floral creation. Each floral display was set on a three-foot-tall ornate pillar, a mix of dozens of roses, orchids, calla lilies, and a few other flowers that Nola couldn't identify. All were done in pale pink and white. A ring of additional roses was wrapped around the pedestal, leading to a small wreath that encircled the base.

Yup, this charity isn't going to see a dime.

A quick head count revealed there were about two dozen people in the room, all of them busily seeing to different tasks. Nola quickly dismissed the worker bees, homing in on the queen bee, who moved from detail to detail within the room, providing instructions, and from the look on her face, more than a few scoldings.

Honoria Haverford was much younger than her seventy-one-year-old husband, who was in a rehab resting. Only thirty-seven, she was a tall, slim, stately looking woman. Her blonde hair was carefully coiffed in a chignon. Diamonds sparkled in her ears and at her throat, contrasting with a navy-blue dress that revealed the shape of a woman who could not possibly eat much. She strode across the dance floor. The click of her high heels was consistent and steady. This was not a woman who wobbled in her heels, not even the five-inch Louboutins she currently wore. A young woman moved quickly with her, holding a clipboard and carefully taking notes.

Nola made her way toward the pair, noting how the staff did not smile in the woman's presence and tried to avoid making eye contact. Apparently Honoria was not exactly a beloved boss.

"Honoria Haverford?" Nola called.

Turning, Honoria frowned as she caught sight of Nola. Her lip curled as she scanned Nola from top to bottom. "It is *Mrs.* Haverford. And help is supposed to come in through the kitchen." She started to turn away.

Nola gave her a smile that held no warmth. "I am *not* the help. I have some questions about Anna Mae Hayes."

Honoria's well-manicured eyebrows dipped before she looked past Nola. "I have no idea who that is. Now as you can see I am quite busy so—"

"She was the winner of the robotics competition two months ago. And she's disappeared," Nola said.

Throwing up her hands, Honoria rolled her eyes. "Well, these girls sometimes do that. I don't see what that has to do with me."

"These girls?" Nola asked.

Honoria waved her hand in a dismissive manner, and the young woman with her quickly scurried away. "Yes, yes. You know what I mean. No father figure, a mother who's barely there, no prospects for a respectable future. Some good-looking boy comes along, and they just take off with them."

"Anna Mae wasn't that type of girl."

"They're *all* that type of girl," Honoria said, finally making eye contact.

Nola had to bite back the retort wanting to escape her lips. "I'll need to speak with the people who were at the competition. See if any of them know anything about Anna Mae."

Tucking her tongue into the side of her mouth, Honoria tilted her head. "Who did you say you were with again?"

"I didn't. I'm looking into Anna Mae's disappearance on behalf of her family." Not entirely a lie. After all, Oz did ask her to look.

"Well, unless you have some sort of warrant, I won't be providing you with any information. And if you don't leave right now, I will be calling the police to have you removed." Honoria waved her hand again. Two men stationed by the far doors hustled over. "Please escort *her* off the premises."

"So let me get this straight, a young girl is missing, and you are refusing to help," Nola said.

Fixing Nola was a frigid look, Honoria's tone was just as glacial. "Whatever happened to that girl has nothing to do with me or our competition. And as you can tell, we are little busy right now, trying to help children who *deserve* our help. If the *police* want to ask us about the girl's disappearance, we will be more than happy to comply."

One of the men moved in as if to grab Nola's arm, but a quick look from Nola stopped him. His hand hung in the air for a few seconds before it dropped back to his side.

Nola knew she wasn't going to get a scrap of information on Anna Mae's visit. To be perfectly honest, she hadn't expected to get any help at all. But she had wanted to get an idea of how the Haverford Retreat felt about its charitable causes. From the looks of the dining room and Honoria, she had a very good idea about that now. Nola headed for the exit, her two shadows trailing behind her. They escorted her all the way to the front door but then stayed at the top of the staircase, watching her walk across the parking lot.

Getting into her car, Nola immediately rolled down the windows as she turned it on. It was amazing how fast a car could heat up in this weather. The two security guards stood at the top of the stairs, watching her.

Well, this was a big waste of time. All she'd gotten was confirmation that Haverford's country club was just as uptight and prejudiced as she'd thought it was going to be. She put the car into gear knowing that it was going to take a little bit of time before the AC kicked in.

As soon as she'd pulled away from the main building, the two security guards headed back inside. Apparently their loyalty only went as far as the air-conditioning. Her eyes on the rearview mirror, she nearly missed the figure bolting out from the side of the road and into her path. She slammed on the brakes, yanking the wheel to the right, and still barely missed hitting the boy.

Taking a deep breath, she looked up at the boy, who stood with his hands up, his heart obviously beating hard through his chest. Blue eyes, blond hair—he looked a lot like his mother.

And unlike his mother, apparently Teddy Haverford wanted to have a conversation.

Chapter Fourteen

Stepping slowly from the car, Nola cast a glance around to make sure there wasn't anyone else nearby.

The teenager hustled over to the passenger door. He tried the handle, then looked over at her above the car roof, his eyes pleading. "I don't want anyone to see us. Can you open the door?"

Nola wasn't sure what young Teddy wanted, but she got absolutely no sense of threat from him. She unlocked the car door, and Teddy shot inside.

Getting back into the car, Nola turned to face him. "Teddy Haverford?"

He nodded, nervously glancing at the road both ahead and behind them. "Um, can we go? If my mom sees . . ." His words drifted off.

Nola shrugged. "I'm not really interested in being accused of kidnapping."

"No, no, nothing like that. There's an old lake house that nobody uses. It's on the estate. We can talk there."

Nervousness wafted off the boy in waves. He looked

completely terrified. He turned his deep eyes toward Nola. "Please, it's about Anna Mae. I heard you talking to my mom. Please."

He knew Anna Mae. Nola put the car into gear. "Okay. Where am I going?"

———

A few minutes later, Nola pulled up in front of the old lake house. The lake sparkled in the afternoon sun. A few water cranes took flight as they drove up. The house itself was small, made of rock and wood. It was not impressive by Haverford standards.

But there was something about it that was incredibly appealing. It had to be at least a hundred years old, with thick, unfinished wooden beams outlining the windows and doors. An old porch that was level with the ground held two rocking chairs positioned toward the lake.

Tall trees towered over the area, leaving the ground largely without grass. But along the water's edge were water lilies and cattails. All things considered, Nola thought it was way more beautiful than the manufactured perfection of the rest of the estate.

Teddy got out quickly when Nola brought the car to a stop. Nola got out a little more slowly, scanning the area. It appeared deserted. And the road leading to it was a dirt road, not paved. It didn't look like many people came out here. "What is this place?"

"It's the old servants' quarters from I don't know, maybe a hundred years ago? No one comes out here anymore. I don't think people have used it in fifty years or so. But I like it. It's quiet. No one bothers me here."

The statement was telling. In the short car ride, Nola got

the impression Teddy was nothing like his mother. He was definitely a Haverford in looks, even more so up close. His bright-blue eyes were fringed with dark lashes, set above prominent cheekbones. His hair was nearly white in spots although Nola had a feeling that was from being outside rather than from a salon.

He was tall but extremely thin. Less of a football player like his father's old pictures and more of a cross country runner. He was dressed in shorts and a simple T-shirt that hung off his frame.

He was a good-looking kid. But while he might have the looks of a model, he did not have the confidence. He also seemed to have none of his mother's haughtiness. He seemed uncomfortable, jittery. He stood next to the car, shifting from foot to foot. His eyes scanned the area almost as closely as Nola did. He obviously didn't want to be here and was afraid of being found out.

Which made Nola all the more curious as to why he had sought her out in such a dramatic fashion. "So, what did you want to tell me?"

Teddy gestured toward the building. "Do you think we could go up on the porch? The house is probably still too warm. The windows have been shut, but maybe we could go up there?" He glanced around again.

From the porch, it would be hard for anyone to see them, even someone who drove up along the drive. Nola nodded. "All right."

The relief across the boy's face was palpable. He gave her a smile that convinced her that he had probably set quite a few hearts fluttering in his young life.

He hurried toward the porch. He stepped up and dusted some leaves off of one of the rocking chairs before gesturing for Nola to sit. He did the same for another one across from it and took a seat himself.

Another telling gesture.

While Nola had a feeling Mother Haverford would never come here to begin with, she definitely would have waited for someone else to clean off a chair for her. Teddy had automatically cleaned one for Nola before taking care of his own needs. Somehow this kid had escaped that Haverford arrogance.

Nola took a seat and settled back in the deep chair. Then she waited.

Drumming his fingers along the edge of his armrest, his feet similarly shifted along the ground. Nola scanned him for track marks but saw nothing. And his eyes gave no evidence of drug use. It was just plain old nervousness. "Teddy?"

He jumped and turned back to her. "Sorry. I just . . . I'm trying to figure out where to start."

"How about how you know Anna Mae?" She asked.

A smile drifted across his face as his hand movements slowed. "We met about six years ago. Nana was running errands with me in Haverford."

"Your nana?" Nola prodded.

He shook his head slightly. "She was my nanny. She was with my family practically since the day I was born. I called her Nana." There was a world of emotion in Teddy's voice when he said her name.

And a world of pain.

Clearing his throat, he began. "One day, she'd forgotten something at her house. So I went with her over to Delford."

"Do you get to Delford very much?" Nola asked when he paused.

87

"That was the first time I'd ever been there. It's crazy, right? I mean, it's right next us, and in my entire life I had never crossed the boundary between this town and Delford until I was ten years old."

"What did you think?"

A genuine smile of warmth crossed Teddy's face. "I loved it. People were real. I mean, I know people struggle there. Obviously it's a lot poorer than Haverford. But the people smile. People know each other's names. People laugh. And when I was with Nana, I was just kind of part of it. That first time I went over there, we went to Ma Bell's Diner. Ma Bell was there. She gave Nana a big hug and ruffled my hair. No one had ever ruffled my hair before. And she gave me this giant serving of ice cream and told me to come back whenever I wanted. And she meant it."

Nola, who'd done a good job of locking her emotions away since Oz had tapped into them earlier, felt another little crack in that armor. Teddy was another lonely kid. Despite all of his privilege, despite being surrounded by people, it sounded like young Teddy had had a very lonely life. Like he'd been on the outside looking in.

"And Anna Mae?" She asked.

"I met her when Nana took me to choir practice. Anna Mae has the most amazing voice. I've never heard anyone sing like her. She was tiny. She's always been small, but her voice filled up the church. I go to church with my family, but I'd never heard anyone sing like her."

"You two became friends?" Nola asked.

He nodded. "Yeah. I begged Nana to take me to choir practice each week. There was something about being there, I don't know. It just felt good. And so she did. I even started singing in the choir, at least for practices. But Nana managed to take me to a few services on Sunday when my parents were out of town. I loved it.

"But it was meeting Anna Mae that made everything better. Anna Mae and I, we just clicked, you know? She understood me like I understood her. I could tell her anything and she . . . she just understood." He looked up, wiping tears from his eyes.

"Was there something romantic between you two?" Nola asked.

Shaking his head, Teddy sat back. "No. It was nothing like that. She's not my . . . type. You know what I mean?" He didn't look away, locking her gaze with his. He wasn't being racist. He wasn't being elitist. Anna Mae was simply the wrong gender to attract him.

"But that was the thing. She was one of the first people I came out to. And it was nothing but love. We couldn't see each other very often, but she became my best friend. She's *still* my best friend. When we were younger we wrote letters, and Nana would carry them back and forth. I told her everything. She told me everything. When we got older, I got her a cell phone so that we could text each other."

Nola leaned forward. "You gave Anna Mae a cell phone?"

Teddy nodded. "Yeah. Years ago."

"Does her family know?" Nola asked.

He shrugged. "I don't think so. It was just kind of something between us, you know? And her family, her mom, she really didn't like Haverford. Something happened when she was younger, and she never really forgave the town, so I doubt Anna Mae ever told her."

Nola sat back. Anna Mae had a cell phone. "Do you have the number?"

Teddy rattled off the seven-digit number. "I've tried to

call her every day since she went missing. That first day, I called her practically every hour and sent texts. She never replied to any of them. That isn't like her. If she could reply, she would."

"When was the last time you tried?"

"This morning," Teddy said immediately. "I tried right after I woke up. But there was no response."

"What about a boyfriend? Or someone else she was close to?"

Teddy shook his head. "She's not into boys. I mean, not that, like, she likes girls. But she's just too shy. I keep telling her she shouldn't be. She's amazing. Any guy would be lucky to call her their girlfriend. But she doesn't see it."

"Does she have any other close friends?"

"No. I mean, she has friends at school, but she's not close with any of them. She was close with Charlene, but that friendship ended last year."

Charlene again. "Why?" Nola asked.

Teddy shrugged. "Anna Mae never figured it out. One day, Charlene just stopped talking to her. She stopped going to school a short time later. It really hurt Anna Mae. They'd been friends since they'd been in diapers."

Studying the boy, who'd grown less guarded in his expressions as he spoke, Nola asked. "Did you know Charlene?"

"A little. She was in the choir too. She was nice, funny. She did *not* suffer from a lack of confidence. But she kind of changed a little, even before she stopped talking to Anna Mae."

"Changed how?"

"She was quieter, which was *not* Charlene. And then she dropped out of the choir, and I haven't seen her since. I got the feeling . . ." He broke off.

"What?" Nola prodded.

"I don't know. Now I kind of wonder if something happened to her, you know? Now that I'm telling you about her, the changes in her were too fast, you know?"

"Yeah," Nola said, agreeing with Teddy that it sounded like something had happened to Anna Mae's friend. Although Nola doubted it had anything to do with Anna Mae's disappearance. After all, it happened a year ago, and Charlene was still around.

She stood up. "Thanks, Teddy. This'll help."

Hands clasped together, he stood up quickly. "Find her. Please find her. I can't lose her. If you need anything, any money, any information, just ask. I'll find a way to get it. Did you need something from the club today?"

"I was looking for information on the robotics championship," she said.

A smile crossed his face. "Yeah, Anna Mae, she won that. The design was so awesome. She was so proud. Pierce was so pissed when he lost. He'd had some special Swiss engineer come in to help him, and he lost to Anna Mae. God, that was so great."

"Can you get me a list of people that work at the Retreat? The list of the people that were there that night?"

Teddy nodded. "What about the security footage? Do you want that?"

"Oh, I definitely want that." Nola handed him a card with her email address on it. "Send everything you have to this address. I have some people who will go through it."

"You have people?" Teddy asked his eyes widening in surprise.

Nola tried not to take it personally. With the car, and her less-than-designer duds, she obviously didn't look like she had any sort of backing. "Yeah, I've got people. If there's anything there, we'll find it."

"Okay. I'll get it to you right away. As soon as I get back to the Retreat, I'll pull it up and get it over to your people."

Nola could tell that he felt better, that he felt like he was actually doing something. She knew how helpless it felt when the people you loved were in danger and there was nothing you could do. "If you think of anything else, write it down and get it over to me. Anything at all, even something small."

He nodded quickly. "I will. I'll write down everything I can think of, even if it's silly."

Studying him again, Nola tilted her head. He was a good kid. And he desperately wanted Anna Mae back. She had a feeling he didn't have many people in his life. "What happened to Nana?"

Teddy grimaced. "When I turned fourteen, my mom decided I didn't need her anymore, so they fired her. Then somehow they found out about my trips to Delford. They made sure that nobody else hired her as a nanny. She died about a year ago."

"I'm sorry."

His bottom lip trembling, Teddy looked out over the water. "She was a really good person, you know?" He said softly.

"Yeah, I know." Nola paused, giving him a moment. "You want me to give you a ride back to the main house?"

Teddy shook his head. "It's better if they don't see me with you. But I'll get you all this stuff as soon as I get back there, okay?"

"Okay. And call if you think of anything else," Nola said.

Once he'd nodded, she headed for her car. She glanced

back over her shoulder. Teddy stood at the edge of the porch, watching the water. He reached up and wiped the corner of his eye. He looked so alone. But one day, he would make it out from under his family's thumb, and he would be the better for it. He was a good person, and the world needed more people like him out there.

She slid back into her Bronco, thinking of his mother. Apparently the apple had fallen very far from the tree when it came to Teddy Haverford. And Nola had a feeling that was a very good thing indeed.

Chapter Fifteen

The youngest Haverford had not been what Nola had been expecting. He seemed really torn up about Anna Mae's disappearance. And as much as she felt for him, she had learned the hard way that she couldn't take people at face value. She stopped by Ma Bell's Diner on the way back. Teddy had mentioned coming here with Nana, and Nola wanted to check out his story.

The bell jingled above the door as she pushed through. There were only four patrons in the diner, but it was only three o'clock, well before the evening rush. All four patrons sat along the back in red booths, two by themselves and two together. They glanced up at Nola as she stepped in but quickly went back to their conversations. Ma Bell, however, straightened up from behind the counter with a big smile. "How you doing, honey? What can I get you?"

Nola took a seat at the counter. "Some sweet tea would be great."

"Sounds just about perfect today," Ma Bell said, her smile widening before she made her way over to the pitcher behind the counter. She poured two glasses of sweet tea into cups overfilled with ice. Bringing one back to Nola, she's slid it across the counter toward her. "Just made it fresh."

Taking a long drink, Nola closed her eyes, and sighed. When she opened them, Ma Bell stood leaning against the counter, sipping from the other glass. She smiled. "Looks like you needed that."

"I most definitely did." Nola took another sip and then placed the glass back down on the counter. "I was wondering if you wouldn't mind answering a couple of questions."

Leaning forward, Ma Bell nodded. "I heard you been looking into Anna Mae."

At Nola's raised eyebrow, Ma smiled. "Martha's a good friend of mine. Anything I can do to help. That girl has the voice of an angel, an absolute sweetheart. Have you had any luck?"

"Not yet. I was just over at the Retreat asking about her."

Ma's lip curled up.

"I take it you're not a fan?" Nola asked.

"Not of the hoity-toity do-nothings over there. Talking about their 'charitable good works.' I ain't seen no charity head this way. They even closed the road between the towns on the day of the Fourth of July celebration. Guess they don't want any of us *undesirables* over there."

Nola didn't doubt that was true. She remembered St. Louis got into a lot of trouble for doing the same thing not that long ago.

"They actually tell you anything?" Ma asked.

"Not really," Nola said with a shake of her head. "It seems I caught them just as they were setting up for a big gala. I spoke with Honoria Haverford, though."

Ma Bell looked like she'd just sucked on a lemon. "Now that is a woman who got way too big for her britches. Did you know she grew up in Delford?"

Nola's mouth fell open. She had been able to find very little on Honoria's background. According to the Retreat's website, though, she'd been raised in Atlanta and sent to the best boarding schools. "That's not what her bio on the Retreat site says."

Chuckling, Ma Bell nodded. "Oh, yeah, all those fancy Swiss boarding schools. Well, apparently I was sitting right next to her during those boarding school days because she and I came up in school together. She was always striving to get over to Haverford. She finally did when she was seventeen. And she got herself knocked up real quick. Then one, two, three, she was Mrs. Haverford and had an illustrious background."

Doing the math, Nola frowned. "They had another child?"

Ma shook her head. "Lost her that first year. Poor child. Teddy was born three years later. Honoria had a bunch of pregnancies in between, but none of them took. But we all knew she was desperate to make sure she had a claim to the Haverford name. And there's no better claim than an heir or three."

A thought flitted through Nola's mind. "Any of the people from Haverford come around here?"

"Oh, you know how it is, the rich folk want to take a little walk on the wild side. That's actually how Honoria met Daddy Haverford. Through Junior."

"She was friends with the son?"

Ma laughed again. "Oh, they were friendly all right. But I wouldn't exactly call them friends, if you know what I mean. To be honest, when I heard she got knocked up, I figured it was the son that had done the deed, not the father."

Nola felt a little sick at the thought. Were father and son knowingly sharing?

"But I haven't seen either of them since then. Got to be close to twenty years."

"What about Teddy Haverford?"

Ma smiled for the first time since Nola had mentioned Haverford. "Now that's one Haverford that does *not* fit into that group. Luanne used to bring him by while she was the nanny for them. He's a sweet kid and has a great voice. Him and Anna Mae singing together in the choir, why that was just—"

Narrowing her eyes, Ma cut herself off. "Now you're not thinking he's got anything to do with Anna Mae's disappearance, are you? Because let me tell you, that boy wouldn't hurt a fly. And if you're thinking there was anything romantic between him and Anna Mae, well, you're just barking up the wrong tree. That boy is not interested in girls."

Nola put up her hands. "I wasn't thinking anything like that. I actually spoke with him today. He and Anna Mae stayed tight over the years. He seemed really distraught over her going missing."

Ma nodded. "Like I said, he's a sweet boy. When his parents fired Luanne without so much as a by-your-leave, that poor kid was beside himself. He showed up here one day after she'd been fired. Biked the whole way here. He was beyond a mess. Luanne took him, cleaned him up, and rocked him like he was a baby. No, that boy doesn't have a mean bone in his body. When Luanne had to leave for Chicago, she struggled trying to find a job. But then, every month like clockwork, money would show up in her account. No one ever claimed it. No one ever said it was from them. No note. Just money every single month. Luanne knew it was Teddy."

Continuing, Ma smiled. "He's a good kid, but he isn't very good at being sneaky. It was always the exact same amount that he got for allowance from his parents. He sent her every single dime."

"When Luanne died, the funeral was back here. Teddy showed up. He stayed at the grave long after everyone had left. Anna Mae stayed with him." Ma's eyes teared up. "Still gets me, picturing the two of them there, side by side. Luanne was his mama in every way that was possible. I think that's why he's such a good kid, unlike the rest of that family."

Nola was struck by the image of the two teens leaning on each other. Both lost in their own way. But there was a third lost child related to Anna Mae.

"Do you know anything about Charlene Hudson?"

Her mouth turned down, Ma shook her head. "Sad case, that one. Her daddy died a few years back. He took good care of her. Loved her something fierce. Her mama, well, she wasn't much into being a mama, and she definitely wasn't when she was the only parent."

"I heard Charlene spends some time down on Crenshaw."

Ma's mouth shrunk into a tight line. "I don't care how much you don't want to be a parent, you don't let your kid spend time down there." Ma eyed Nola. "You going to talk to Charlene?"

"Yeah. I've been trying her home, but no one's been there. I'm going to try again after I leave here. If no luck, I'll head down to Crenshaw. Any idea where to look down there?"

"Only one place: 216 Crenshaw. But you won't need the number. You won't be able to miss it." She eyed Nola. "You going down there by yourself?"

Nola smiled. "I can handle myself."

"I hope you're right, because Crenshaw isn't a place you seek out. It's a place that you avoid."

Nola stood up. "What do I owe you?"

Ma waved her away. "Nothing. It's on the house. Just be careful. It's not a good place. And if Charlene's going down there regularly, well, she's probably already lost."

"What do you mean?"

"Once Crenshaw's got its clutches in you, there's only two ways out: the jail or the morgue."

Chapter Sixteen

Nola stopped by the Hudsons'. This time, Charlene's mom was home. Charlene was not. Charlene's mother, however, made it clear that her daughter was no longer welcome there. She offered no further information and showed zero concern about where her daughter was.

So Nola went out in search of her.

Ma Bell was right about the house on Crenshaw. She didn't need the number. The house stood out amongst the other beaten-down houses on the block. Unlike the Hayeses' house, which, while not rich, was well taken care of. On Crenshaw, nobody seemed to take care of their homes. Most of the houses had an abandoned look to them. A few were even boarded up.

The street itself had a few people walking on it. None of them looked like they were going anywhere in particular. And no one was walking in groups. Everyone seemed to be ambling down the street on their own. Nola had to swerve to avoid one man who was taken by some unknown impulse to sprint across the street before disappearing into the space between two houses on the other side of the road.

Nola pulled up across the street from 216 Crenshaw. There were four people outside the house. A man with long dirty-blond hair, a pair of torn jeans, no shoes, and no shirt leaned against the mailbox. An emaciated woman with long stringy brown hair paced along the side of the house, having an argument with an invisible foe. And two men sat on the front lawn, or what should have been the front lawn. There wasn't any grass left. It was just dirt and weeds. The men both stared intently at their fingers, a look of absolute awe on their dirt-streaked faces.

Nola could make out feet sticking out from behind the porch wall. She hoped that the owner of them was still alive. She wanted to talk to Charlene and not get caught up in any overdose drama.

She got out of the car. A man who'd been eyeing her from down the street hurried over. "Hey, hey there, pretty lady. This isn't a good neighborhood. You should leave. A nice car like that stands out here."

"I've got business here."

The man tutted as if disappointed in her response. "Tell you what, you give me fifty bucks, and I'll make sure that nobody touches your car."

Nola eyed the man. "I tell *you* what. If I come out here and there is so much as a scratch on my car, I'll take it out of your hide."

The man laughed, but his laughter died away when he looked into Nola's face.

Nola leaned closer. "Not. A. Scratch."

The man nodded quickly. "Yup, not a scratch."

Nola crossed the street, scanning in both directions as she did so. She didn't have faith in her erstwhile car guardian. In neighborhoods like this, people grabbed what they could, sold what they could, and then snorted or injected what they could from that.

Nola paused for only a second at the sidewalk in front of 216. The house was an old Victorian. Back in its day, it must have been stunning. The stained-glass transom was still intact above the front door. The sidelights on either side of the door, however, were cracked and missing pieces. On the second floor, there was a hexagon-shaped window in the middle.

Floor-to-ceiling windows were also in evidence on the first floor. But they, too, had fallen into a sad state. There were cracks in the windows that had been taped over with plastic, and one of the concrete steps leading to the front porch had completely crumbled to dust.

How the hell has this place not been condemned? She wondered. But she was guessing that Delford didn't have the money to go around condemning all the properties that needed it. She felt the cool presence of her knife up her sleeve as she walked to the front door. She wasn't sure what exactly to expect inside, but she knew it wasn't going to be pleasant.

As she walked up the path, one of the men staring at his fingers toppled over to the side, his eyes rolling back in his head. The man leaning against the mailbox ambled into the street, weaving from side to side.

Keeping an eye on the agitated pacing woman, whose arguing had only increased, Nola stayed to the right of the cement steps, avoiding the crumbled disaster on the left. The feet that she'd seen from the road did indeed belong to a young man who was breathing. His chest rose and fell, one arm flung over his face.

Two more individuals were curled up on the couch

below the porch wall. Neither of them even looked up at Nola. And neither was Charlene.

One was an older woman, probably in her late fifties, although it was possible the drugs had aged her prematurely. The other was a younger man in his twenties. Neither had shoes on their feet, and their clothes had seen better days. Both were white with the same shade of chestnut-brown hair. Nola wondered if they were mother and son. She shuddered at the thought.

Carefully Nola eased open the front door and slipped inside. Dark wooden floors, stained and scarred, lined the front hall and the rooms off to each side. What had once been a parlor to the left now held eight bodies, all sprawled in different locations. One large individual hung dangerously off a very dainty-looking brown Victorian couch. Another individual lay half off an old folding chair. The rest were strewn on the ground on a threadbare rug.

To the right was a living room, and it was the same type of scene. Nola walked through to check each person, but none of them was Charlene. She walked to the back of the first floor where the small kitchen was located. Two women sat at a metal card table, the vinyl top shredded. There was no food between them, but there was a shared ashtray overflowing with butts. They glanced up at Nola and then looked away, completely unconcerned with her appearance.

Nola headed back to the front room and up the stairs. She held on to the banister and then pulled her hand back, grimacing at the unknown substance now on it. Up the stairs, she could hear the sounds of people having sex. She glanced into one room and saw two individuals, both in their late twenties, in the middle of a sexual act that she was pretty sure was illegal in Georgia.

She moved down the hall toward a second door that was

cracked open. A young African-American girl lay on the bed in underwear and a T-shirt. A white man who had to be close to fifty lay on the bed next to her snoring.

Nola narrowed her eyes, anger crawling up her throat as she stared at the man. He wore only boxers and a wifebeater with a rip over the heart. It had probably been created when his heart had escaped his chest.

Because it was obvious he didn't have one if he was in bed with a child.

Nola opened the door with her foot to get a better look, already knowing what she was going to see.

The girl on the bed was Charlene.

Chapter Seventeen

Nola stepped into the room, her hands in tight fists. She had to practically bite her tongue in two to keep the anger boiling inside of her from spilling out. The man on the bed was old enough to be Charlene's father. She was only sixteen years old. Hell, he could even be her grandfather.

She took a few deep breaths and then quickly regretted it. She could practically taste the unwashed bodies, the lingering stench of sex, and the complete abandonment of hope in the air.

Nola strode over to the bed. Flicking a glance at the man, she leaned down, gently touching the teenager's shoulder. "Charlene?"

No response, except for a slight frown marring the girl's face.

Nola tried again, a little louder this time. "Charlene?"

Charlene's eyes flickered open, confusion in her gaze as her deep-brown eyes peered into Nola's. "What—"

"I need to talk to you about Anna Mae."

Charlene blinked a few times. "What?"

"Anna Mae," Nola repeated. "I need to talk to you about Anna Mae Hayes."

Some of the confusion cleared from Charlene's face. She frowned as she struggled to sit up. "Anna Mae? What about her?"

"She's missing."

Charlene's gaze shot to Nola. "Missing?"

The man on the bed next to Charlene stirred. "Shut up!" His hand lashed out. Charlene cringed.

Nola's arm darted out. She snatched the man's wrist before it could crash into Charlene's face as she pulled Charlene from the bed with her other hand. "Move."

The man started speaking before his eyes were even completely open. "You bitch. You think you can—" His eyes widened. He caught sight of Nola, his wrist still in her hand. "Who the hell are you?"

Nola didn't answer, at least not verbally. She took the man's wrist and wrenched it to a ninety-degree angle.

"Ow, ow, ow, ow!" The man contorted himself, trying to relieve the pain, his chest practically touching his knees. Nola switched her grip and pushed down on his elbow, keeping his wrist locked as she walked around the bed, dragging him with her.

He cried out again, but she didn't give a damn. She yanked him forward. He landed face first off the bed. His arm was still up in the air, held in a viselike grip by Nola.

"Get up," she ordered through gritted teeth.

She released the pressure only enough for him to get to his knees and then to his feet. He tried to take a swing at Nola. She simply ran him face first into the wall.

"You bitch," he mumbled

Keeping one hand on his wrist and the other on the

back of his head, she slammed his head into the edge of the closet frame. Blood burst from his nose.

She stepped toward him, her nose wrinkling at the stench. Images of violence flashed through her mind. "She's. A. Child," Nola seethed.

The man mumbled something, but Nola didn't understand it. With the blood pouring into his mouth from his nose and the tooth she'd apparently knocked out, it wasn't a surprise. With a look of disgust, she marched him to the door and flung him out into the hallway before she slammed the door shut behind him.

Charlene sat on the edge of the bed, her arms wrapped around her knees as she watched Nola with nervous attention. Her dark curly hair hung limp around her face, making her look even younger than her sixteen years.

Nola tried to calm the anger down inside of her. Men abusing girls was one of those issues that was sure to rile her up.

It cut a little too close to home.

She took a deep breath. "I need to speak with you about Anna Mae."

Her neck stretching, Charlene looked up at her, Her pale-pink T-shirt hung off her tiny frame. Her eyes looked incredibly large, in part due to her sunken cheeks. Her legs and arms were barely more than sticks.

Charlene Hudson was a girl desperately in need of a good meal. She was a far cry from the happy girl she'd seen in the photo at Anna Mae's house. The anger drained out of Nola, replaced by a need to do something to make the poor girl's life better, if only for a short while.

"How about you get changed and we go get something to eat?"

Chapter Eighteen

Once Nola had gotten Charlene out of the flophouse and into her car, she headed for Main Street and Ma Bell's Diner.

Charlene sat quietly in the passenger seat. Her hands nervously twitched in her lap. Her nails had chipped pink nail polish, and it was clear she had bitten them. Her shoulders hunched forward as if expecting a blow and being resigned to it. There was no fight left in the girl.

She didn't say anything as they drove. Nola wasn't entirely sure that Charlene had come down from whatever she'd been on. As Nola approached a stop sign, she reached into the side pocket on her car door. She pulled out a bottled water and handed it over to Charlene.

Charlene took it without a word. By the time Nola reached the next stop sign, the girl had finished it.

The water seemed to revive her a little bit. Charlene looked around. "Wait. Where we going?"

"To get something to eat."

Her eyes grew larger as she stared down the street.

Charlene started to shake her head as she grabbed for the handle of the car. "No. No. Not Ma Bell's. I can't go there."

Nola slammed on the brakes. "Whoa, whoa. It's okay. We don't have to go there. There's a diner out by the interstate. Will that be all right?"

Charlene's fingers melted off the door handle. She nodded slightly, her voice young and scared. "Yeah, that would be all right."

Nola took the next left and headed toward the highway. Charlene didn't say a word as they drove. It was about a twenty-minute drive to the other diner. From the look of the parking lot, it was frequented by truckers and other people just passing through.

Nola picked a parking spot close to the door, away from the four sixteen-wheelers that were parked in the back of the lot. When she pulled the key from the ignition, Charlene spoke. "Is Anna Mae really missing?"

"Yes. Her mom and brother are really worried. They don't know where she's gone."

"She wouldn't just leave. She wouldn't do that to them."

Before Nola could reply, Charlene was out of the car.

Nola followed the young girl into the diner. The diner was like a million others Nola had been to in her lifetime. Directly across from the door was a long counter with a dozen stools attached to the floor. Booths lined the windows, with another few along the side walls. Another half dozen wooden tables had been placed in between the counter and the booths.

There were only about a dozen people scattered throughout the diner. There were a few couples, but most people sat by themselves. One waitress was off to the left, taking an order while another stood behind the counter. Both wore uniforms only a shade lighter than the sky blue of the booth seats. The tile floor was an ivory color flecked with brown, popular back in the 1960s, and gold trim edged the tables and counter. Wood paneling lined each of the walls.

The waitress behind the counter gave Charlene a hard look when she stepped into the diner. Charlene was wearing threadbare jeans, her T-shirt had a few holes in it, and she wore flip-flops on her feet. Her hair was unwashed.

Nola gave the waitress a hard stare in return. The woman quickly averted her eyes.

Charlene paused, unsure.

Nola nudged her chin toward a booth against the back wall. "How about back there?"

Nodding quickly, Charlene made her way to the booth, staying on the opposite side of the path from any of the truckers.

Charlene slid into the booth with her back to the room. Nola was surprised by the choice. She thought that Charlene would take the spot with her back to the wall, giving her a view of the room. That was where Nola liked to sit. She wasn't comfortable giving her back to people.

But then she realized that Charlene wasn't worried about someone attacking her. No, she was more worried about judgmental eyes watching her. *That* was what she was trying to avoid. Physical attacks, those, Nola had a sad feeling the girl had accepted.

The waitress who'd been taking orders when they walked in hustled over, giving them a distracted smile. "What can I get you, ladies?"

Charlene looked over at Nola. "You're paying, right?"

Nola nodded. "Order whatever you like. It's on me. I'll take a coffee."

"Could I get . . . do you have egg creams?"

The woman's voice softened, her eyes full of under-standing as she took her first full look at Charlene. "Sure do, honey. I'll bring it right over. Menus are against the window."

Nola reached for the menus as the waitress headed back for the counter. She handed one to Charlene, who took it with trembling hands. Nola pretended not to notice. Neither of them spoke as they perused the menu.

There was no need for Nola to look at it. Diners pretty much had the same fare no matter where you went, with a little bit of cultural flair. Up north, it was cheese fries or gyros that were added to the menu. Down here, it was grits. She closed the menu as the waitress reappeared and placed their drinks on the table in front of them. "You two ready to order?"

"Charlene?" Nola asked.

Shooting a nervous look at Nola, the girl nodded. "I'll take a cheeseburger and fries, please."

"Sure thing, sweetie. And for you?"

Nola closed her menu. "I'll take the same. That sounds good."

"All right. That'll be just a few minutes."

Nola took a sip of the coffee. She should have ordered something cold. "So I hear you and Anna Mae were close friends."

Charlene gripped her cup, not looking up. "Yeah. We were best friends. Our mamas had us at about the same time. I don't really remember much of my life without Anna Mae in it."

"You don't think she'd run off? Maybe take off with some guy?"

Charlene shook her head. "No. The only guy she spent

time with—" Charlene cut herself off, darting a look at Nola.

"It's okay. I already spoke with Teddy."

The girl's shoulders sagged. "Then you know it wasn't like that between them. And he's a good guy. He wouldn't hurt her."

"I know," Nola said, touched by Charlene's defense of the poor little rich boy.

"Anyway, besides Teddy, she didn't hang out with guys. I mean, we both were crushing on Cole Sprouse last year, but that's kind of her thing. Guys on TV or in movies, not guys in the neighborhood. She knows that comes to no good. That's not Anna Mae. She was a good girl. She *is* a good girl." Charlene looked up and met Nola's gaze for the first time, her gaze fierce.

Nola nodded her agreement. Some of the fight seemed to leave Charlene. Her shoulders drooped. She leaned forward, her elbows on the table. "She was always good. I was the one who got us in trouble. She was the one who was always helping people make the right choices."

"I heard you were doing pretty well in school yourself until last year."

Charlene's head jerked up, her eyes growing wide before she shook her head, her chin trembling. "I don't want to talk about that."

Nola let the silence stretch between them, giving the girl a chance to pull her emotions back. Then she spoke slowly. "I get that. But something's happened to Anna Mae. And being you and her were so alike not that long ago, I can't help but wonder if what happened to you might have happened to her as well."

Charlene was shaking her head before Nola was even

finished speaking. "No. Anna Mae would never do anything wrong. She's not like me."

Nola leaned forward, dropping her voice. "I have a feeling you two *are* a lot alike. And I don't think you did anything wrong. I've got a feeling somebody did something wrong to you."

Charlene's chin trembled again. She turned her head, her hair covering her face. She stared out the window, her chest heaving.

The waitress appeared, placing their plates in front of them. Pulling a ketchup bottle out of the pocket of her apron, she placed it close to Charlene's plate. "There you go, sweetheart. You need anything else, you just holler, you hear me?"

The waitress gave Nola a hard look, obviously blaming her for Charlene's upset state. And Nola couldn't blame the woman.

Nola nodded. "Thanks. I think we'll be all right."

With one last glance at Charlene, the waitress headed for another table.

Nola took a bite of one of the fries on her plate. "These are good."

Reaching out Charlene grabbed one of the fries from her plate as well, and then she was shoveling them in two at a time. When she was done, she turned her attention to the cheeseburger and devoured it just as quickly. When she finished, she looked up at Nola in shock, her cheeks reddening. "I, I—"

Nola waved off her stammering. "You're hungry. Nothing wrong with that. If you're still hungry, order something else. I was thinking I might get myself a shake." Nola caught the eye of the waitress, who held up one finger.

After finishing stacking the coffee cups behind the counter, she hurried over. "Can I get y'all something?"

"I was hoping for a vanilla shake." She looked at Charlene. "What about you?"

Charlene looked up, biting her bottom lip. "Maybe some mozzarella sticks?"

"Sounds good. Do you want a shake with it?"

Charlene nodded. "Chocolate, please."

"Sure thing, honey." The waitress headed back for the counter.

Nola didn't press Charlene on what had happened last year that had changed her life so dramatically. But she did manage to get her talking about some of the things that she and Anna Mae had done together. Nola got Charlene to order a little more food, which the girl devoured. They sat there for close to an hour, and by the end of it, Charlene almost sounded like any other teenage girl.

But when the waitress came over with the bill, Charlene's face fell. Nola knew that she'd just remembered that this wasn't her life, and that this little reprieve was about to come to an end.

Nola pulled out two twenties and left them on the table. Despair written across her body, Charlene scooted out of her side of the booth a little more slowly than Nola did. Her gaze darted to the twenties, but she left them where they were.

Once they stepped outside, they headed for Nola's Bronco. Nola walked around to Charlene's door and unlocked it, holding it open. "Is there somewhere else I can take you, Charlene? Somewhere you'd rather go? I could take you home if you like."

"No," Charlene said quickly. "I don't want to go there. My mom, she—" She shook her head. "No."

"Is there anywhere else?"

"I, I . . . I don't have anyone, except my meemaw. But she lives all the way in Clarkson."

"Would she take you in?"

Charlene shrugged. "Yeah, but I mean, I can't get there. I don't have money for a bus, and I don't even know what bus I could take to get there."

"Well, hop in. I'll run you out to your grandma's."

Charlene's head jerked up, hope springing in her eyes. "Really?"

Nola nodded. "Really."

Charlene scrambled in the door, and Nola closed the door behind her. If she couldn't find Anna Mae today, at least she could help Charlene get her life back.

Chapter Nineteen

The drive out to Clarkson was actually peaceful. Charlene's fear and despair seemed to drift away the closer they got. But as Nola took the exit for her grandmother's house, Charlene sat up in her seat, her feet tapping on the floor in a steady rhythm. "Maybe this wasn't a good idea. I don't know that my meemaw will take me in. What if she doesn't want to see me?"

"Well, at least then you'll know. But there's a reason you mentioned her, and I'm betting she'll be happy to see you."

Her voice barely above a whisper, Charlene shook her head,. "You don't know what I've done. No one could ever—"

"You're not defined by things you did when you were a teenager. We've all done bad things. We've all done things we're ashamed of. But right now, it seems like there's a chance you could step out of that life and into a different one. Shouldn't we at least see if that's an option?"

Her mouth tight, Charlene nodded. She looked out the

window, her fists opening and closing repeatedly while her feet tapped away.

Charlene's grandmother's house was only a short three-minute drive from the highway exit. Nola pulled up in front of the house. It was another single-story bright-blue ranch like the Hayeses'. But unlike the Hayeses', this one was brimming with color. There were pots by the front door that held sunflowers and cascading petunias. The shutters had been painted with black and white checkerboards, as had the mailbox.

Turning off the car, Nola shifted to face the young girl. "You ready?"

Charlene shook her head. "I can't do this. She won't want to see me. I can't. Let's just go."

"Hey, we're here. Let's at least find out."

"Can you go? Can you ask and see if . . ." Charlene's chin trembled as her words seemed to fail her.

The poor girl had been through so much. Humanity had let her down in a major way. And now she thought that all of humanity would. Nola prayed she was wrong. She prayed her grandmother would take her in and would be happy to do so. Because there was no way Nola was taking Charlene back to that house on Crenshaw.

And she had no idea what she would do with her if this didn't work out. But she kept all those fears and concerns out of her voice as she answered Charlene. "I'll go speak with her. You stay here."

Exiting the car, Nola strode across the street. A black cat with white on its paws and nose sat curled up in the window of Charlene's grandmother's home. It watched lazily as Nola made her way to the front door.

Through the screen door, she could see a welcome sign

on the wooden front door, two cats holding it. Nola knocked loudly.

"Hold on. Hold on. I'm coming." An African-American woman in her midfifties hustled into view, wiping her hands on a dishtowel. She looked up at Nola in confusion. "Can I help you?"

"My name's Nola James. Are you Chantilly Hudson?"

"That's me," the woman said slowly, "but if you're selling anything—"

"No, no, nothing like that. Charlene asked if I could—"

The screen door flew open. Nola had to jump back to avoid getting hit.

Chantilly stepped through. "Charlene? You know Charlene? Is she all right?"

"She's all right. In fact, she's right—"

"Meemaw!" Charlene's cry came from across the street as Charlene sprinted toward her grandmother. Chantilly let out her own cry as she raced forward, gathering her granddaughter in her arms as she sobbed.

Nola watched the reunion with a catch in her own throat. Charlene had been through hell. But it looked like she'd finally made it home.

Chantilly got Charlene, whose legs seemed to have stopped working, to the front door. It was as if everything that had happened had crashed down on the poor girl at once. Nola helped get her through the door, and then Chantilly hustled her into the bathroom, putting on the shower and leaving Charlene to get herself cleaned up with some of the clothes that she'd left behind on her last visit. Nola had started to leave, but Chantilly stopped her, insisting she sit down at the dining room table for some sweet tea.

Nola sat across from Chantilly, waiting for the interrogation to begin. She didn't have to wait long. "How do you know my granddaughter?"

"I just met her today. I'm looking for Anna Mae."

"Anna Mae?"

"She's been missing for a few days."

"Lord have mercy. What is this world coming to? Those are two good girls. Anna Mae, that poor child. Her mama must be beside herself."

Nola knew there wasn't a correct response to that statement, so she just took a sip of her tea.

"How did you find my granddaughter?"

Nola knew that wasn't her story to tell. Charlene would tell her grandmother in her own way what she had been through, or she might hide it under a mountain of shame. But either way, it was Charlene's decision. So instead of answering, she asked, "Have you been looking for her?"

Her face screwing up in anger, Chantilly nodded. "She's my oldest son's daughter. He died five years ago, an accident at work. Charlene's mama, well, she isn't the greatest. And she made it real hard to see Charlene. But I managed to get her out here for a couple weeks in the summer and for a couple of weekends during the year. But then last year, Charlene was just *gone*. Her mom wouldn't tell me anything, just that she had left. I went over to Delford for two months every weekend looking for her. But I couldn't find her. I don't think she wanted to be found."

"I think you're probably right about that."

Wrapping her hands around her glass the same way her granddaughter had not that long ago, Chantilly said, "You bring children into the world, and you try to protect them from all the ugliness. But you can't. The ugliness finds a way in. It broke my heart when Charlene disappeared. And now you're saying Anna Mae is missing too?"

Nola nodded.

Chantilly shook her head. "The world is a hard, cruel place at times. But for young black girls, it's even crueler."

Nola had no argument against that statement. Everything she'd seen and read bore it out. Recent research indicated that people believed young black girls needed less nurturing, protection, and support than white girls. Young black girls were believed to be more adult than their white counterparts. But the truth was, girls were girls. Skin color didn't change that. And for young black girls, this mistaken belief that they were more independent could result in them being overlooked in the school environment in favor of their male counterparts, which of course made them less attached to their schools. Black girls received more severe sentences when they entered the juvenile justice system than did members of any other group of girls.

It did not get better as they aged. Black women disproportionately experienced violence at home, at school, on the job, and in their neighborhoods. In the workforce, black women earned only sixty-one cents to every dollar of a white man.

So Nola knew Chantilly was right: The world was especially cruel to black girls. She tilted her head, hearing the shower stop as Chantilly disappeared into the kitchen. She reappeared with a plate of homemade biscuits and some jam. She offered Nola one, but Nola turned it down. She handed Chantilly her card. "If Charlene says anything or remembers anything that might help find Anna Mae, would you give me a call?"

"I sure will." Chantilly wrapped her arms around Nola. "Thank you for bringing my baby back."

Returning the hug, Nola felt the warmth of it all the way to her toes. Charlene was in good hands with her meemaw.

With a nervous step, Charlene appeared out of the hallway from the bathroom just as Chantilly released Nola. Chantilly wiped at her eyes. "You are a sight for sore eyes, baby doll. Now come eat some biscuits. You need some fattening up."

The older woman hustled over to Charlene as she hesitated in the doorway and ushered her to the table.

"I think you're in good hands now. Take care, Charlene," Nola said as she stepped back.

Chantilly made a move for the door, but Nola waved her back. "No, no. I'll see myself out. You've got something more important to take care of."

There was a tightness in her chest as Nola made her way outside. Charlene was in for a long road back. Even with Chantilly's support, there was a chance she wouldn't be able to get out from underneath whatever darkness had pressed down upon her. The memories of what she'd done and what she'd seen would haunt her. Nola prayed that she was able to find some peace somewhere in the future.

She'd reached the edge of the sidewalk and paused to wait for a minivan to pass when the screen door behind her slapped open. "Nola!"

Charlene sprinted down the path toward her, her hair wild around her face. She panted a little as she stopped next to Nola.

Nola looked back at the house. "Everything okay?"

Charlene nodded, shifting from foot to foot. "Yes. I

just . . . I never said thank you. Thank you for bringing me here."

"You're welcome. Just remember our past doesn't define us."

Charlene looked into Nola's eyes, and a sense of recognition passed between them. Charlene nodded. "I'll remember."

"And if you think of anything that might help Anna Mae, give me a call, okay? I gave your grandmother my card. Call me anytime." Nola paused, studying the young girl. "Is there something else you want to tell me now?"

Charlene looked up and then away. "No, nothing."

"Okay." Nola placed a hand on Charlene's shoulder. "Take care of yourself, Charlene. Let yourself be happy."

"Are you? Happy?" Charlene asked looking up into Nola's eyes, once again she knew Charlene was looking for an answer beyond her words.

Avoiding her gaze, Nola started across the street. "I'm working on it," she said softly.

Chapter Twenty

The sky was growing dark as Nola left Clarkson. It matched her mood. She felt agitated, unsettled. And she didn't know why. Probably because she didn't have any new leads on Anna Mae.

But in her heart she knew it was more than that. The image of that man lying in that bed with Charlene was branded in her brain. Predators like that got under Nola's skin like nothing else. They preyed on the weak and defenseless. They preyed on the vulnerable.

Nola gripped the steering wheel, knowing that she needed to release some of what she was feeling before she released it at the wrong person. As she headed back to Delford, she caught sight of a sign for a boxing gym. She pulled off the highway and into the parking lot.

It was a new gym. The parking lot was about half full, even though it was before most people got out of work. Nola grabbed the bag she always kept in her car and headed inside. Ten minutes later, she'd signed the waiver, paid the fee, and gotten changed. Pulling on her gloves she headed for the heavy bag in the corner of the gym, ignoring the looks she got from some of the gym's other patrons. She wasn't interested in making friends. She wasn't interested in male companionship. Right now she was only interested in hitting something.

She lined herself up in front of the bag and rolled her neck. She pulled out her interval timer and set it for two minutes. When the timer beeped, she began to hit. Dancing around the bag, she threw jabs, hooks, and straights. Then she added combinations, including kicks and knees. She didn't stop for two minutes.

When her timer beeped, she stepped back from the bag and took a long swallow of water. Stretching her neck again, she lined up in front of the bag again before hitting the timer. For an hour, she wailed away at the bag, taking a minute in between sets.

By the time sixty minutes had passed, her arms felt like spaghetti. But her anger had lost a bit of its bite. She grabbed a towel and her water bottle and headed for the locker room while taking off her gloves.

A muscle-bound gym rat who'd been watching her for the last twenty minutes stepped in her path. "Hey, saw you over there. How about you and I—"

"No." She kept walking, and the man had to jump out of the way or she would have plowed him over.

Long ago, she had given up on the idea of stepping out of the way for men. If she had the right of way, she kept going. She'd read an article when she was a teenager, talking about how women stepping out of the way of men when they were walking toward one another was what helped give men their sense of entitlement in the world. Then and there, Nola had decided that she would never do anything that helped enable that entitlement.

Twenty minutes later, she'd finished with her shower and was back in the truck after a quick stop at the sandwich shop next door for a turkey sub. As she pulled out of the gym's parking lot, she took a bite of the sandwich, her mind rolling through everything she had found so far.

She had to admit it wasn't very much. She still didn't have any idea who would have taken Anna Mae. She tried Anna Mae's cell again, but once again the phone went right to voicemail. Wherever it was, it was dead.

Damn it.

If she had known about the cell phone earlier, she might have been able to use it to pinpoint Anna Mae's location. But it had been days now. No cell phone lasted that long. Like Teddy, though, she couldn't help but keep trying.

She paused for a moment, wondering if maybe Bishop could do something about the cell phone. Hearing her voice earlier had been . . . difficult. There'd been a time when Bishop had been family. Truth was, she was still family.

Nola just couldn't be around family right now.

Today was the first time she'd heard her voice in two long years. Maybe that was what had made her so unsettled for the last day.

But even as she thought it, she knew that wasn't entirely the case. It was Charlene. It was Anna Mae. And it was the powerlessness she felt right now with no possible leads.

That was when she realized she didn't have the right to let her baggage get in the way of finding Anna Mae. She pulled over to the side of the road and pulled out her cell phone.

She quickly sent a text to Bishop, typing in the phone number and a quick message: *I need you to keep an eye on the cell phone number. Let me know if it goes active.*

It only took a few seconds and Bishop replied. *Sure, no problem.*

Nola paused, debating how to reply. *Honoria's face flashed through her mind. And I need you to check out a place called the Retreat in Haverford.*

Anything you're looking for? Bishop asked.

There was no hesitation in Nola's response: *Anything that might get them in trouble.*

Some of the tension in Nola's chest eased away at the quick reply. She didn't want to dwell too long on that feeling. She pulled back onto the road, her mind trying to figure out what the best next step was.

Her mind spun with possible lines of investigation, disregarding each of them. God, she had nothing. She'd been here a full day, and she now had less than when the day began.

Her phone beeped just as she was pulling across the Delford line. It was a text from Teddy: *I sent the footage to your email. Let me know what else you need.*

Nola quickly texted the kid back. *Will do.*

Only a few minutes later, she pulled into the drive and turned off the engine. She'd been looking for an avenue of investigating, and now it looked like she'd found it.

Chapter Twenty-One

Nola wiped at her eyes, which stung from staring at the monitors. Darkness had fallen a few hours ago, but she still sat, going through the recordings Teddy had sent of the robotics competition. Most of it wasn't related to Anna Mae or the Haverfords or anything of interest.

But she had seen Anna Mae on the tapes. Anna Mae had beamed when she'd been announced the winner. After, of course, a look of complete shock crossed her face.

And Nola had been able to easily pick out the Pierce kid who Teddy had mentioned. He'd stormed out of the room when he'd been announced as second place. He hadn't even bothered to go pick up his trophy.

When all the hubbub had died down, Teddy and Anna Mae slipped out of the ballroom to a small spot off the kitchen. They hugged and talked excitedly. Even with the poor quality of the image, it was easy to see both their faces light up with joy as they looked at the trophy. It made Nola's heart ache just a little bit to watch. Normally when she went on these cases, she was in and out. She barely had time to unpack. For the Miceli case, she hadn't even met Morgan until she handed Abigail to her.

This one, though, was taking longer. This one required her to get to know the people involved.

She didn't like how much she was coming to feel for those people, both good and bad. Honoria Haverford had elicited a huge negative reaction from Nola. She just didn't like the woman. And Teddy, it was hard not to feel for poor Teddy, stuck in a world where he didn't belong. Then there was Oz, his mother, the McNallys, Charlene. How had she gotten so involved so quickly?

Everything worked out better if emotions weren't part of the process. But this case

just wasn't following her carefully laid out plan. Nola felt like she'd stepped into a world of despair. With a sigh, she reviewed the tapes again, but there was nothing there.

Damn it.

This was the first time in two years that she had floundered on a case. And she didn't like it. She reviewed all her notes, but nothing jumped out at her. The only lead she had, if you could even call it that, was the First Baptist Church. But a check of the church's website indicated the reverend wouldn't be back until tomorrow evening.

She rubbed her eyes again as she yawned. It was early, at least for her. But she hadn't slept much in the last two days. Maybe the lack of sleep was why she was uncharacteristically distracted. Maybe she just needed a little more sleep and a pattern would appear in the data.

Pushing the papers aside, she crawled into bed. She'd been in Delford for less than twenty-four hours, and it felt like she'd been here for days. She'd spoken with Anna Mae's family, friends, teachers, the McNally family, and what did she have to show for it? Nothing. She felt no closer to finding Anna Mae.

Some people might think that twenty-four hours wasn't very long. But if Anna Mae was still alive, she was willing to bet that twenty-four hours felt like years.

The heat pressed down on her, and the bed felt hot. But her exhaustion took over, and she slipped into the black.

Chapter Twenty-Two

ANNA MAE

The dream was good. Anna Mae was in her kitchen making pancakes for Oz. Her mom had the day off and wandered in with her robe over her pajamas, a smile on her face. The three of them sat down at the table and dug in, laughing as Oscar imitated his teacher.

Although Anna Mae felt a stirring of consciousness at the back of her mind, she refused to give in to it. She was happy in the dream. Her family was happy in the dream. She didn't want to leave.

"Anna Mae. Anna Mae, wake up!" Natalie shook Anna Mae's shoulder, her voice a frantic whisper.

Enjoying the warmth in the dream, Anna Mae came back to consciousness slowly and then jerked awake, remembering where she was. "What? What is it?"

"I heard voices. I think someone's—"

The door above them opened. Anna Mae braced for the sunlight, but none appeared. A dark night sky was above them, twinkling with stars. Flashlights speared the darkness down at them. "Get on the other side," a voice ordered.

Anna Mae scrambled to her feet, Natalie helping her. Together, the two of them moved to the other side of the hole.

A ladder lowered to the ground. "Climb up."

Her voice trembling, Natalie gripped Anna Mae's hand tightly. "Anna Mae?"

Anna Mae squeezed her hand back in response. "It will be all right. We're together. It will be all right."

Even as she said them, Anna Mae knew her words didn't make any sense. Nothing about this was all right. But Natalie nodded and let Anna Mae pull her over to the ladder. Anna Mae had to release Natalie's hand to climb up. The young girl let out a little whimper of fear. Anna Mae wanted to let out her own whimper, but she needed to stay strong for Natalie. She gripped the sides of the ladder and then began to climb. The ladder shook with each step she took. Her own shaking wasn't helping stabilize it. When she reached the surface, an arm grabbed her bicep and yanked her onto the grass.

This time she did let out a little cry, her arm aching painfully where the man held her.

"Shut up," he growled.

Biting her lip, Anna Mae tried to hold back her cry, but she couldn't keep the single tear from dripping down her cheek. She wiped it away, not wanting Natalie to see it. She glanced around.

They were on some sort of old farm. She could see a stable in the distance and an old farmhouse as well.

Six cars were parked haphazardly across the grass along the back of the house. About a dozen people surrounded the hole. But in the dark, she couldn't make out their faces.

Somehow that made them even more terrifying. She forced her gaze from the faceless men to her surroundings.

There didn't seem to be any other houses nearby. Wherever they were, it was definitely remote.

As Natalie appeared at the top rung of the ladder, Anna Mae got her first good look at her. She had long dark-brown hair and big brown eyes. She didn't look like she was even five feet tall, and she was extremely thin. God, she looked so much younger than her twelve years. Another man reached over and grabbed her, pulling her onto the grass as well. But he pulled too tightly.

Natalie's right leg caught on the edge of the ladder. She tripped, stumbling forward to the ground, the man still holding on to her arm. Natalie cried out.

"Get up!" The man shook her arm roughly.

Anna Mae stepped forward, but the man holding her yanked her back. "What the hell you think you're going to do?"

"Looks like we got a hero here." One of the other men stepped forward, the moonlight giving her enough to see his face. He had black hair and skin scarred by acne. He stared at her with a sneer.

She'd never seen him before. He was slimmer than the other men and an inch or two shorter than all of them. Yet she knew without a doubt that this was the guy that she needed to be the most wary of; everything about him screamed predator.

He walked up to Anna Mae slowly, stopping when he was only two inches away from her face, and then he leaned down, whispering, "Are you, sweetheart? Are you a hero?"

Anna Mae kept her head down and shook her head.

"I can't hear you," he said his voice laced with threat.

"No," Anna Mae said, her voice soft.

The man lifted her chin. "That's what I thought." He shoved her back. "Get them in the van."

The man who'd yanked her from the hole pushed her forward. Another set of hands caught her, these ones much less calloused.

"Don't say anything. Just walk, Anna Mae," a voice whispered.

She looked up into a set of brown eyes in a face that seemed only slightly familiar. "Who—"

He pulled her upright, much more gently than anyone else. "You need to walk," he said, urging her forward.

Natalie was just in front of her. She turned back to look at Anna Mae, her dark eyes full of fear.

Anna Mae tried to give her a smile, but she wasn't sure if she managed it. She was pulled past the hole. Anna Mae's gaze strayed to it for a moment. At that moment, she realized that as horrible as the hole was, it was probably infinitely better than whatever was in store for them now.

Chapter Twenty-Three

DEREK

Derek Rivers glanced over at the van. Anna Mae and the other girl had been loaded in, the doors closing behind them with a resounding thud.

"What the hell you waiting for? Get in," Derek's cousin Devante said as he slid behind the steering wheel.

As Derek pulled open the door of the old blue Mustang. Devante grinned at him. "You're in the big leagues now, little cousin."

Derek didn't say anything in response. But Devante was fiddling with the radio and didn't seem to notice. The van pulled out first, and Devante followed.

But Derek couldn't take his eyes off the back door. Anna Mae was in there. He'd had the biggest crush on her in sixth grade. He'd liked her so much that he couldn't even bring himself to talk to her. He got completely tongue-tied.

Yet she'd always smiled at him as if she understood that he couldn't quite get the words out. He flashed back to the last time he'd seen her. It had been four years ago, just after his dad died. Anna Mae had come to the funeral. A lot of kids from his class had come, but Anna Mae, she had sat with him the whole day. She had just been there.

He'd moved schools the next week. They'd moved in with his grandmother on the eastern side of Atlanta. His mom had moved for a job, and then two years ago she'd lost it. She'd picked up some waitressing shifts. He'd picked up a few odd jobs here and there as well, trying to balance it with school.

But it wasn't enough. He'd seen the eviction notice last month.

So he'd asked his cousin Devante if he had any work. Devante always had money. He'd been pestering Derek for years to come work for him. But Derek had never taken him up on the offers. He didn't know exactly what Devante did, but he knew it was illegal.

He'd thought it was selling drugs. And he did do that. He'd put Derek to work as a runner. But then yesterday, he told Derek he was bringing him along on a new business venture, one that would make them lots of money.

Derek had tried to talk his way out of it. Being a runner was bad enough; he didn't want to get in any deeper. But the look in Devante's eyes stopped his protests. Devante had a trigger temper, and there was no telling what would set it off.

So here he was. He'd thought Devante was maybe selling guns. Or that maybe it was a big drug shipment.

But he'd never imagined his cousin was so far gone that he was selling *girls*. One looked like she couldn't be any older than ten. And the other . . .

He swallowed. He couldn't let this happen to Anna Mae. She was a good person. And what kind of person would he be if he let this happen? If he let his cousin sell girls?

But even if it hadn't been Anna Mae in that goddamned hole, Derek couldn't go through with this. There was no way he was trading his soul to make a couple of bucks. But now he just had to figure out a way to get out of this without getting himself killed. And he also needed to figure out a way to get Anna Mae out of this without getting her killed either, because if both of them got killed, well, that wouldn't help any of the other girls, now would it?

He watched his cousin from the corner of his eye. He bobbed his head in time with the music, a smile on his face. Devante looked over at him and grinned. "Big time, boy. We are in the big time."

Derek nodded, turning his gaze back to the van in front of them. What the hell was he going to do?

Chapter Twenty-Four

NOLA

The man's hand reached for her, the smell of spilled beer on it.

Her hands out in front of her, Nola cringed away. "No, I don't—"

Nola's eyes flew open as she yanked herself from the dream. Her heart pounded, and she sat up in bed, her hand wrapping around the handle of the Beretta on her side table.

Pausing, she listened to see if something had pulled her from the dream. But no, all was quiet. She had pulled herself from the dream.

She released the gun and ran a hand through her hair. Damn nightmares. She supposed she should have expected them. With everything going on, her old ghosts were destined to appear.

Placing her bare feet on the floor, she walked to the kitchen while pulling her hair back into a ponytail. She grabbed a container of water from the fridge and drank deep.

Ever since she'd come to Georgia, she felt like she was losing gallons of water by the hour. She wasn't sure how people weren't just dropping in the streets with all this humidity. She'd read that the people of Nepal had developed a genetic marker that allowed them to survive at higher elevations. Most humans wouldn't be able to because of the lowered oxygen content in the air. Idly, she wondered if maybe Georgians had somehow managed their own genetic adaptation to survive the fact that there was too much humidity in the air.

The cold water felt good as it slipped down her throat. She wiped her mouth with the back of her hand. Placing the container back in the fridge, she stood in the open doorway, letting the cool air run over her. When the sweat on her body had dried, she headed back to the bedroom. She'd only slept two hours. Even she needed more than that.

She lay back down on the bed, her eyes open wide. The night was quiet. The air barely moved. The fan in her bedroom seemed to only push the hot air around. She tossed and turned for forty minutes before giving up and lying on the floor. It was cooler, just not cool enough.

With a growl, Nola got to her feet. She slipped on her jeans and boots. She felt unsettled. She wasn't sure why. Probably the case and the lack of movement on it. But as she pulled out of her drive, she knew it wasn't that, or at least not just that.

It was Charlene and the long road ahead of her.

It was Oz and the sadness that clung to him.

It was Darrell McNally and a future put on hold.

It was Teddy, seeming so lost and alone.

So many lives, desperate and wounded. Their emotions pulled at Nola. She felt like she was drowning under them.

For two years, she had kept people away, holding herself together by pure force of will. But now it felt like all those carefully created boundaries were under siege.

She felt helpless, powerless.

And she did not do powerless.

Now she was looking for something to make the feeling go away. Not even Molly's visit earlier helped.

Normally, seeing Molly eased the ache in her heart. She wished she could see her more. She wished she could see her every day. But that wasn't an option. But every time Molly left, a crater-sized hole developed in Nola's chest. She wasn't sure how much longer she could handle this lifestyle. She dreaded the day when Molly no longer wanted to visit her.

Which led her to thinking about Anna Mae and the fact that her mother couldn't see her daughter at all. It had to be tearing her up inside.

To add to the churn of emotions, she'd gotten a text earlier about Abigail Miceli's case. The little girl and her mother still hadn't been found, which was good. And legal action had been started against the Hannigans. The Hannigans denied all knowledge of Hastings's activities in Modesto. But Hastings was singing like a canary for the police, and it was believed that the Hannigan dynasty was about to collapse.

Max Hannigan had taken himself off to the Maldives, a non-extradition country. Nola wasn't sure what Hastings had on him, but apparently it was big enough to get the kid to skip town. Rumor had it that Hastings had recorded all of his interactions with the Hannigans. His own little insurance policy.

Nola couldn't really blame him. The Hannigans had turned on him faster than their defense attorneys could say "incarceration." As far as Nola was concerned, they all deserved one another. The only two people in that whole mess that didn't deserve to be there were Morgan and Abby. And hopefully now they were far away from any of that ugliness.

The injustice of the years of the Hannigans abusing their power weighed heavily on the media reports. Abuse of power always weighed heavily on Nola. Ever since she was a kid, she felt righteous anger whenever someone was treated unfairly, be it aimed at herself or anyone else.

And she'd had a lifetime of experience with that righteous anger. For the last two years, she'd been delving into that anger and helping those the criminal justice system couldn't or wouldn't help.

Anna Mae's case, though, was different. Normally when she swooped into a town, she knew exactly who she was going after and exactly how she was going to make them pay. Here, everything was still cloaked in darkness. She didn't know who had taken Anna Mae. She didn't know who was even related to Anna Mae's disappearance.

It was frustrating the hell out of her.

And what she wanted right now was to take that frustration out on someone else.

At the same time, she knew that was a dangerous mindset. Dangerous for her because the last thing she needed was to attract the attention of the police, but it was also dangerous for someone else.

Because an angry Nola was a lethal Nola.

Without conscious thought, she headed back to Crenshaw Street. There were just as many people out tonight as there had been during the day. She wasn't surprised.

Central air was definitely not an attribute of any of the houses on the street. She wasn't sure standing fans were even an option. The heat would have built up all day long until it would be like sleeping in an oven. Outside was most definitely cooler.

A few people were actually lying on the grass. Nola wasn't sure if they had passed out, were trying to sleep, or had overdosed. She didn't slow down to find out. She turned off of Crenshaw and made her way into the part of Delford she hadn't explored yet. It looked the same as Crenshaw. Too many people, too many vices.

She decided to head back home just as a familiar shape lumbered out into the street. She hit the brakes and watched in the rearview mirror as the man that she'd seen in bed with Charlene hoisted himself into an old Buick Le Sabre.

The Buick rattled as the man's weight settled in on the driver's side. She pulled over to the side of the road and waited. Minutes later, the Buick drove past, weaving a little over the center line.

Nola pulled in behind him, keeping a few car lengths between them. She followed the Buick through the streets of Delford, almost right to the edge of Haverford. The man pulled into a dirt drive next to a small ranch house. Nola pulled over to the side of the road in front of the house.

The light was on over the door. A rusted swing set stood silent in the side yard. A bike lay on its side in the path leading to the front door. The man stayed in the car for a few minutes before he hoisted himself out. He swayed in the doorway for a minute, holding on to the car door before he stabilized. He slammed the door shut behind him and walked unsteadily toward the front path.

Nola turned off the interior light of her car and slipped

outside. She crossed the street, staying in the shadow of the trees along the drive. The man continued to lumber forward, his gait unsteady.

Nola could see what was about to happen, clear as day. The man stepped onto the path and shuffled forward. His foot caught the edge of the handlebars of the bike. He screeched as he went tumbling down hard. He landed on his knees and rolled over to his side.

Nola stayed where she was, slipping a little farther into the shadows. The man stood up. Even in the dim light, she could see the large cut in the knee of his pants. He grabbed the bike and flung it across the yard before he stormed toward the house. "Shirley! Shirley!"

He yanked the screen door wide. It slammed back into the house and stayed open. "Shirley!"

Nola quickly walked toward the front door.

"Damn bike! Where the hell is he?"

A voice answered him. Nola had to ease forward to catch the response. " . . . sleeping. Just let him sleep. He didn't mean any—"

The sound of a hand meeting flesh echoed through the night. "Shut the hell up. I don't need you babying him."

Nola moved to the window. It looked into the living room. Shirley was crouched on the floor, holding the side of her face. The man had disappeared from view. Seconds later, screams came from farther in the house. "No! Daddy, no!"

Nola had seen and heard enough. She bolted through the front door. Shirley was just getting to her feet. She looked at Nola with a dazed expression. "Wh—"

Nola didn't stop. She sprinted down the hallway, stopping at the second room on the right. Bunk beds had been set against the back wall. A small child was curled up on the bottom bunk, yelling for her father to stop. She was only about four years old. The man stood at the edge of the bottom bunk so he could tower over his son in the top bunk.

He had a hold of the boy with one arm while he punched him with the other.

Nola darted into the room and slammed a sidekick into the small of the man's back. He released the child as he was flung forward, his chest crashing into the edge of the top bunk bed. Nola threw a hook to the man's kidneys and then stomped on the back of his right knee. She grabbed the back of his shirt and yanked him away from the beds. The man let out a scream as he stumbled onto the floor.

Nola placed herself between the children and the man, who now blocked the door. "Stay away from them," she said.

The man pushed off against the desk he'd crashed into, his gaze focused on Nola. His nose was a mass of color, and a nasty bruise appeared underneath his left eye. Gifts from their earlier encounter. "You. You're that bitch from earlier. Someone needs to teach you a lesson."

Nola smiled. "I assure you, that person is *not* you."

With a yell, the man ran for her. Nola easily ducked the wild punch. She grabbed his forearm as she redirected the punch away from her face and slammed her palm into his face. He let out a scream as she hit his already-damaged nose. Shifting her grip to his wrist, she ran her right hand down to his elbow and then yanked his wrist back to his shoulder. Keeping pressure toward his shoulder, she spun him off his feet. The satisfying pop she heard was his shoulder coming out of its socket.

With a shout of pain, he crashed into the wall. He crumpled to the ground again and started to cry. "Bitch. You bitch. You dislocated my shoulder."

Nola ignored him and looked at the boy on the top bunk. His cheek had started to swell on the left side of his face. His right eye had begun to close as well. He couldn't be more than five or six. She held out her arms. "It's okay. I won't hurt you."

He reared back from her for a moment before leaping forward, wrapping his arms around her neck. She squeezed him delicately, his little body shaking. He was so light.

Anger spiked through her. She wanted to beat his father all over again.

She knelt down and looked at the little girl. Without even waiting for an invitation, the girl launched herself at Nola, wrapping her arms around her waist.

Nola picked up the little girl and carried both of them from the room, leaving their screaming father on the floor.

Chapter Twenty-Five

ANNA MAE

The ride was long. They were in an old paint van. It smelled of chemicals, and there was dried paint splashed along the floor of the back. There weren't any seats, and every time they went over a bump or took a corner, Anna Mae had to brace herself to keep from being flung to the ground. Natalie sat next to her, curled into her side, as if somehow she could make herself disappear if she curled up tight enough. There were two men in the van with them. Anna Mae wasn't sure if the other ten men were following them.

Not that it really made a difference. One man, a dozen men, she was no fighter, even on her best of days. And right now she felt weak from hunger and a little dizzy from dehydration. She wasn't even sure how long she'd been in the hole. There'd only been two drops of food and water. The last time it had only been a single apple that had been dropped down and one small bottle of water. She and Natalie had shared both.

Anna Mae had her arm around Natalie's shaking shoulders. As they turned another corner, Anna Mae held on to her, but the giant pothole they hit made it impossible to stay upright. She was flung to the hard metal floor. Natalie fell with her, slamming her forehead into Anna Mae's elbow. Anna Mae winced. Natalie backed up quickly. "I'm sorry. I'm sorry."

Anna Mae shook her head, keeping her voice low. "There's nothing to be sorry for. None of this is your fault. None of it's my fault either."

Natalie's eyes, which always seemed to be shining with tears, looked up into Anna Mae's face. "Where are they taking us?"

Anna Mae shook her head but didn't answer. She'd been trying not to think about that.

Because she knew it was nowhere good.

At the same time, she couldn't figure out how this had happened. She had been a good girl. She got good grades. In fact, she'd been first in her class. At the beginning of the year, teachers had started talking to her about scholarships and colleges. She'd floated home from school that first day. Her mother had been over the moon when she'd mentioned it to her. She'd taken her and Oz out for a celebratory dinner at Pizza Hut over in Haverford. Oz had gobbled up a pie all by himself.

God, I would give anything for a pizza right now.

Anna Mae's heart clenched at the thought of Oz. A lot of people didn't like their little brothers. They complained about them and said what brats they were. But that had never been her and Oz. Their mother worked so much that it had been her and Oz most of the time. They had become a team.

She didn't know when she made a point of trying to

protect him from the ugliness in the world. She turned off the TV when there was news that she thought would upset him. She taught him how to look on the bright side of things rather than the bad side. There was no way she would be able to protect him from this, though. And if she never came home . . .

Anna Mae didn't even want to think about how his life was going to change because of it. Would he join a gang like so many other kids in their neighborhood? Would he end up down on Crenshaw Street, just lost in that world?

Maybe it would make him stronger. Maybe it would encourage him to stay the path and fight the good fight.

Even as she thought it, she knew that was crazy. This was going to change his life forever. And the only lesson he would learn was that fighting the good fight got you nowhere. So many other people had taken the easier path. Not that their lives had ended up much better. But she wasn't sure that Oz would be able to see that, not at such a young age. And by the time he was old enough to see it, he would be too entangled to get himself out.

"Anna Mae?"

Anna Mae started. She'd gotten lost in her mind there for a moment. And as troubling as her thoughts about Oz were, being lost in her mind was a much more pleasant option than being fully aware in her present circumstances.

"I'm right here, Natalie."

Natalie leaned into her and wrapped her arms around her. Anna Mae wrapped her arms around the young girl in return. She told herself she was doing it to comfort the girl. But the truth was, she needed a little of that comfort as well.

God, if you're listening, please help. Please, please help.

Chapter Twenty-Six

NOLA

Nola normally didn't like dealing with the police. But in this situation, she didn't really feel like she had a choice. The young boy needed medical care, and the mother, she was out of it. Nola was afraid that the hit the man had given her had left her with a concussion. Only the little girl was unharmed.

And she was talking up a storm.

"My daddy gets real mean when he comes home late. It's my mama he hits, my brother, and he hits me too." She stood glaring at Nola, waiting for a response, an angry angel in pink pajamas and pigtails.

Nola adjusted the ice pack she'd placed on Devon's eye as he lay on the couch, his eyes closed. "That's not right. He shouldn't do that."

The girl nodded her agreement before her eyes filled with tears. "Is Devon going to be all right? And Mama?"

"I think they'll both be all right," Nola said. "They just need to get checked out at the hospital."

She was saved from having to make more small talk with the righteous four-year-old when the ambulance siren wailed from down the street. Nola moved to the door as lights sprayed across the yard. The ambulance pulled into the drive. A few people craned their necks from across the street. Lights popped on in a few more houses.

A woman hurried past the ambulance, beating even the EMTs to the door. She bustled in. Anger flashed across her face as she took in Nola holding the door open. "Who the hell are you?"

"Aunt Caroline!" The little girl threw herself at Aunt Caroline's legs.

"Aisha, baby." Caroline reached down and patted her back. "You all right, sweetheart?"

"Nu-uh." Then Aisha went into a blow-by-blow accounting. Caroline's eyes grew wider as Aisha spoke. The little girl hadn't missed a thing. She had the makings of a top-notch intelligence agent.

When Aisha paused to take a breath, Caroline reached down and pulled the little girl into her arms, hugging her tight. She gave Nola a tight nod, then hurried over to Shirley, who sat with a bag of ice pressed to her face. "Shirley, you swore you were going to leave that man."

Shirley just looked at her, dazed, as if trying to figure out which Caroline she should focus on. Her eyes finally focused on the one in the middle.

The paramedics stopped at the door, taking in the scene. Nola explained what had happened, nodding to Shirley and Devon.

A strangled cry came from down the hall. One of the

paramedics, a young woman with close-cropped hair, looked at Nola. "Is there another victim down there?"

"No. He's the perpetrator. He can wait until his family is seen to," Nola said.

The EMT met her gaze and nodded. A second set of lights appeared at the end of the driveway as the paramedics moved toward Shirley and Devon. The little girl was now curled up with her mother's friend, adding to Shirley's recounting of events in detail.

A single African-American police officer stepped from the car and moved down the drive. She looked like she'd just gotten out of the academy. She couldn't have been older than twenty-two. As she reached the doorway, she took in the scene in a glance and then zeroed in on Nola.

Nola couldn't blame her.

If this room was one of those kids' puzzles, Nola was most definitely the one piece that didn't belong. And while the officer was young, she read Nola's intentions correctly, because she said, "I need you to stay around until I get a chance to speak with you."

Nola nodded her acquiescence and stepped aside as the officer walked up to Shirley. She lowered her voice, leaning in. "Shirley, did you get that restraining order?"

Shirley nodded slowly.

Nola stepped outside and made her way through the crowd that had now gathered at the end of the drive to her car. She got more than a few curious looks. She opened her Bronco door, rolled down the windows, and took a seat, pushing the seat back so she could stretch her legs. She had a feeling she'd be here for a while. She wanted to just leave, but she didn't want to cause the young officer any more problems than she had to.

A car pulled in behind her. It was a Jeep Cherokee, a few years old. Nola sighed.

Through the rearview mirror, she watched as its occupants stepped into the street. The man was extremely slim, and even with just the streetlight, the lighter complexion of his brown skin was apparent, as was the detective badge clipped to his belt. He reached back into the car and placed a hat on his head.

Great.

Nola was tempted to just drive away. But that would make the detective a lot more suspicious than if she just answered a few questions and then left.

The detective glanced at the house and then at Nola's Bronco. He hesitated for a second and then headed toward Nola.

She stepped out of the car before he reached it. "Evening, Detective."

The man paused, studying her face. "It seems you have me at a disadvantage. I don't recall us meeting."

"That's because we haven't. How can I help you this evening?" She asked, her tone making it clear he needed to keep it short.

"Well, the station got a call from Deacon Baker. He says some woman came in and stomped on his family."

Nola struggled not to roll her eyes. She should have checked the idiot for a cell phone.

The detective continued, his gaze unwavering. "I'm guessing that someone would be you."

"I believe he has taken some liberties with the truth in that explanation," Nola said crossing her arms over his chest.

"I figured as much. We've been called out here a dozen times over the years. It's always the same: Deacon claiming nothing happened while one or more members of his family looked like they ran into a door . . . repeatedly." The detective paused. "But tonight, you're the new cast member to this little family drama. You want to tell me how you happened to be here?"

Nola shrugged. "Right time, right place, I guess."

"I'm going to need a little more than that."

"I was walking by. I heard him yelling. I went to go see if I could help. And I did."

The detective glanced at her Bronco. "Just walking by, huh?"

Unflinching, she met his gaze. "Yup."

The detective pulled a notepad and pen out of his jacket pocket. "You got a name?"

"Yes."

The detective rolled his eyes. "Could you *tell* me your name?"

"Nola James."

"I haven't seen you around Delford before, Ms. James. New to town?"

Shrugging, Nola said, "I've been here a little while."

"And you've already met the police."

Nola leaned back against the car. "Well, I guess I could have let the man beat his family. But . . ." She shrugged again.

The detective gave her a hard look. "So you're just walking by and happened to hear Deacon hitting his kids?"

"That's what I said," she replied.

"I'm going to need a detailed account of what you said, did, and heard."

Nola sighed but then complied. She gave him a rundown of the last hour, starting with her walking across the street. She didn't bother mentioning following Deacon from Crenshaw. She offered nothing more than what was absolutely necessary. When she was done, the detective looked at her, arching an eyebrow. "That everything?"

She gave him one more shrug. "Yep."

The man closed his notebook. "Well, thank you, Ms. James. I'm sure everyone appreciates what you did here tonight."

Not so sure about Mr. Baker, she thought, but she just nodded and didn't say anything. The detective pulled a business card from his inside coat pocket and handed it to her.

Taking it, she turned it slightly so she could read it under the streetlight. Detective Rascal Nealon. Now it was her turn to raise an eyebrow. "Rascal? Is that a nickname?"

"No," he said with a slight edge to his voice. Apparently his name was a bit of a touchy subject.

"Huh." Nola nodded toward the house. "Is there a reason a detective is out here for a domestic violence case? My understanding is that would normally be handled by a uniform."

"The Baker family is of special interest to the mayor of Delford."

"Meaning Mr. Baker knows somebody in the mayor's office? The mayor himself?" She asked.

"No. Mr. Baker went to school with the deputy mayor."

"Ah, so what are the chances Deacon is actually going to do some time for assaulting his wife and child?"

This time Rascal didn't meet her gaze. "Well, I guess that's up to the courts."

"Yeah," Nola drawled. "I'm sure that's *entirely* up to the courts."

The detective tipped the edge of his hat toward Nola. "You have yourself a good evening, Ms. James."

Saying nothing, Nola just slipped the detective's business

card into the back pocket of her jeans. The crowd at the edge of the driveway parted as Rascal approached. He nodded at a few people, who nodded back.

Nola waited until he stepped into the house before she climbed back into the Bronco and readjusted her seat. The father had connections, which even in a small town meant something.

She'd gone out tonight looking to lose some of the pent-up rage from the injustices of the day. But now it looked like she had more to add to the injustice pile.

Chapter Twenty-Seven

ANNA MAE

The van came to a stop, jerking Anna Mae awake. Luckily, this time she had been lying down so she wasn't thrown to the ground. But she did roll into Natalie. On instinct, her arms wrapped protectively around the girl, even though she knew there was nothing she could do to protect her from the real horror awaiting them.

When they'd first gotten in the van, Anna Mae had told herself she needed to stay awake. She needed to prepare herself for whatever they were about to face. But once they hit the highway, the drive seemed to go on forever. Natalie had fallen asleep first, and the steady rocking of the van had proved too much to resist.

As she sat up, Anna Mae glanced out the front windshield. It was still dark out, but she felt like she'd been asleep for hours. She had a feeling they had traveled pretty far.

A feeling of despair welled up in her chest, stronger than it had been before. Being in that hole had been horrible. But she was pretty sure she had still been in Delford, which meant she could cling to the hope that maybe, just maybe, someone might find her.

But now? Now she could be anywhere. No one would be looking for her this far away. As slim as her chances of being found had been in that stupid god-awful hole, they were even worse now.

The men at the front of the van got out without saying a word to her or Natalie.

Leaning down, Anna Mae whispered into Natalie's ear as she shook her shoulder gently. "Natalie. Natalie. You need to wake up."

Natalie squirmed in her sleep, her eyes opening slowly. Even in the dim light, she could see the moment Natalie realized that she was still in the nightmare. Her mouth fell open slightly, and her eyes grew larger as her head jerked up to stare into Anna Mae's face.

Anna Mae put on a smile that she didn't feel and pushed back Natalie's hair. "The van's stopped."

She didn't say anything else. She wasn't sure what else to say. She strained her ears, listening for voices, but she couldn't hear anything through the walls of the van. She had a feeling that meant they were in another isolated location. When the trip had started, she could hear cars driving by, the occasional honk of a horn or the sound of a car radio. But now there was nothing. There was no sound of traffic going by and no lights indicating they'd stopped at a highway exit to refuel.

Natalie pushed herself up, rubbing at her eyes. "Where are we?"

"I don't know. I fell asleep too."

Natalie reached out and took Anna Mae's hand, scooting a little closer to her so that their hips touched.

They sat in silence, hand in hand, hoping that this little reprieve would continue. That by some miracle those men would completely forget that they even existed.

But Anna Mae added that thought to the pile of unanswered prayers that had grown large since all of this had begun. Laughing voices reached her first before the van door was pulled open. She covered her eyes against the glare of the flashlight.

"Just two?"

"That's all they gave us."

The first man who had spoken sighed deeply. "Fine, fine, get them inside before somebody sees them."

Anna Mae's heart lurched, and her head jerked up. Before someone saw them? A rough hand reached in and pulled her from the van. Her knees banged onto the van floor. She tripped as she tried to get her feet underneath her. But she didn't care about any of that. "Help! Help us!" she screamed, pulling the sound deep from within her body. "Help!"

The punch caught her on the side of her cheek. Her head whipped to the side as pain radiated from her cheek to her jaw.

A man dragged her roughly by the front of her shirt, pulling her toward him. His spit sprayed in her face as he leaned close. "Do that again and I'll dump your body in the river." He shook her violently.

Her head snapped back, more pain now cutting through her neck. Her vision swam for a moment as she trembled in a combination of pain and fear.

She was shoved forward. "Take her."

Rough hands grabbed her and jerked her forward.

As she straightened, her vision blurred in and out, so she could barely take in what was around her. She could feel concrete under her feet. She could see tall looming structures. But they were all dark. No lights emanated from the walls. Ahead, the sound of metal screeching reached her ears.

But it seemed like it was a delayed response. Because it felt like she had just heard it in the distance, and yet she was now stumbling over a metal entrance and being pushed forward. Her knees and palms slammed painfully into a metal floor. A warm body crashed on top of her. She turned automatically and pulled Natalie to her. She looked up, her eyes adjusting to the dim light just in time to see a large metal door being closed and blocking out all light. The darkness was complete.

She swallowed hard, holding a trembling Natalie to her, but she didn't have any words. Because the sight that she had seen before the darkness had been thrust upon them again had taken her breath away.

Instead of a hole in the ground, they were in some sort of metal box.

And they weren't alone. Twelve other girls sat in the dark with them.

Chapter Twenty-Eight

NOLA

Nola didn't get much sleep after the incident at the Bakers. She went home and reviewed the evidence board before closing her eyes again. Sometimes, if she focused on a problem before drifting off, her subconscious would work on it while she slept.

When her eyes popped open at 5:30 the next morning, she had nothing new, so she headed to the gym over in Haverford. There wasn't one in Delford.

She lifted weights for twenty minutes and then ran hard on the treadmill for forty-five minutes. She preferred to run outside. There was something about expanding your gait to eat up the road that really made a woman feel powerful. But with the humidity, it would be like running through soup. She'd be dehydrated before she reached the end of the first block. So she'd had to settle for cranking up the treadmill.

She ignored the looks from a few of the men who appreciated her work ethic. One had started to approach her, but with a glare from Nola, he quickly changed directions. She had no interest in establishing a relationship, even a short one that might release some of her angst. Not right now. Right now she'd destroy any man that came near her.

By nine a.m., she was back at her house, after picking up some breakfast to go from Ma Bell's. She'd just finished it when there was a knock on the front door. Nola wiped her mouth, then stood up to answer the door. She'd been expecting this, although she thought it might happen a little later in the day.

She stopped by her bedroom and closed the door, making sure that her guest had no view of what she was working on. Luckily, with the heat, everyone had their blinds down to keep out the brutal sun. Therefore, the fact that all of the blinds were down in her house did not make her stand out.

She placed her sweet tea on the small table next to the couch before making her way to the front door. She opened it and gave Detective Rascal Nealon a nod. "Morning, Detective."

He tipped his hat toward her, reminiscent of an old Southern gentleman. "Ms. James, I do hope you don't mind the interruption, but I was hoping we could speak for a few minutes."

Nola closed the front door behind her and gestured to the two old plastic Adirondack chairs on the porch. "By all means."

Rascal hesitated, glancing toward the door. "Wouldn't it be more comfortable inside?"

"Not for me." She walked toward one of the chairs and took a seat.

With a sigh, Rascal took off his hat, running a hand

through his hair, and then took the other seat. "It's a might hot this morning."

Nola shrugged but didn't say anything.

"I just wanted to stop by to let you know that Shirley and her son were released from the hospital about an hour ago. Shirley has a mild concussion, and Devon has a few bruises that will heal in a few days."

Nola reined in her snort. The physical bruises for that boy were going to be the least of his problems. "And the father?"

Rascal met her gaze as he spoke. "There was a restraining order out for him. Shirley had taken it out just a week earlier. He wasn't allowed within 500 yards of her or any of the kids. He violated it. So he's locked up until he sees the judge."

Nola raised an eyebrow. "And what will the judge say?"

Rascal stretched his legs out in front of him, crossing them at the ankles. "Hard to say. But being both Shirley and Devon have documented injuries, it'll be hard to ignore. Don't suppose you'd be willing to come to court and give your eyewitness testimony?"

"No."

"I had a feeling you'd say that. I did a little research on you last night when I got back to the station to write up my report. Apparently you used to work for the Department of Agriculture in DC." Rascal stared at her for another few moments before realizing she wasn't going to answer. "Is that a yes?"

"Was that a question?"

The smallest amount of annoyance crossed Rascal's face. "Yes. It was a question."

"I did indeed work in DC."

"For the Department of Agriculture?" He pressed

Nola nodded.

"What exactly did you do for them?"

"What exact business is it of yours?"

Rascal looked taken aback by the response. "Just making conversation."

"No, you're not. You're doing the old-fashioned country-western 'there's a stranger in town' bit. Look, I helped that family last night, and I'm glad I did. But I'm not interested in having people digging through my life."

He studied her and gave a nod. "Fair enough. How about if I take you out for breakfast as an apology?"

The offer made Nola want to smile; it was so transparent. Unlike young Aisha Baker, he would never make it in intelligence work. Nola stood. "I already ate. Perhaps another time."

Rascal stood as well. "Of course," he said smoothly, placing his hat back on his head. He extended his hand. "Well, thank you for helping Shirley and her kids last night. And welcome to Delford. If there's anything I can do to be of service, please don't hesitate to call."

Nola shook his hand, surprised to find that he had a strong grip. Perhaps there were hidden depths to this detective. "Thank you, Detective. I'll keep that in mind."

Her phone rang as she watched Rascal pull out of the drive. She glanced at the number as she headed back up the stairs and into the house. She didn't recognize it. "Hello?"

"Um, Nola? It's . . . it's Charlene."

"Oh, hey. Charlene. How are you? Is everything okay?"

"Yeah, I'm okay. My meemaw . . . Yeah, I'm good."

"Well, I'm glad to hear that." Nola didn't say anything for a few beats. Instead she let the silence play out. "Is there something you needed?"

"I, um, you told me to call if I thought of anything that

might help find Anna Mae. I should have told you yesterday but I . . . I didn't."

The pain and shame in the girl's voice were palpable. "It's okay, Charlene," Nola said softly. "I understand. What did you want to tell me?"

Charlene sniffed. "I . . . my meemaw and I talked last night. She told me I should call you. She told me it wasn't my fault."

I'm betting she's right, Nola thought but didn't say anything. She could tell Charlene was on the edge, and one wrong word from Nola would spook her into silence.

Charlene's next words were so low that Nola couldn't make them out. Charlene cleared her throat and tried again. "Reverend Cornelius. He's the reason I left home." Her voice softened to barely a whisper. "He likes girls."

Nola's gut clenched.

Charlene's voice took on a stronger tone, an edge of anger lacing it. "If Anna Mae's missing, he might be the reason."

Chapter Twenty-Nine

After hanging up with Charlene, Nola sat at her small kitchen table with her laptop in front of her. She'd pulled her damp hair up into a messy bun on top of her head, a few strands of hair sticking to her neck.

He likes girls.

The words had seared themselves into Nola's brain. Charlene hadn't said much beyond that. She'd hung up after getting Nola to promise to look into the reverend.

Now Nola was doing just that. On the monitor, she pulled up the website for the First Baptist Church of Delford. Reverend Cornelius, the man Charlene had mentioned, was the pastor.

The picture on the website of the church was professionally done. There was even the barest trace of a rainbow in the air above the church. Nola wasn't sure if that was an actual rainbow or photoshopped, but it had the desired effect: It made the church appear to be blessed. The pictures of smiling congregants, many of the shots with children, added to the appearance of a happy, joyous church.

She rolled her hands into fists. As she sat at the monitor, she remembered the hopelessness that surrounded Charlene when Nola had found her. And it looked like all of that stemmed from a man she thought she could trust.

Nola pictured Deacon Baker in the bed next to her. She liked to think he'd get what he deserved now that the criminal justice system was involved. But apparently they'd known about his domestic abuse for years and hadn't done anything to help his family. She didn't think that Charlene as a victim would engender much more compassion.

At the same time, she knew that drugs were a disease. She knew that, but she couldn't help but want to beat that man into a bloody pulp for taking advantage of Charlene. She was a poor lost girl. He might be in the throes of a disease, but he should still be able to tell the girl was young enough to be his daughter, if not his granddaughter.

But she turned her attention from that to the immediate issue: Reverend Cornelius Matthews. The website announced that the reverend was out of town for a family event and wouldn't return until this evening, leaving Nola with no one to aim her rage at.

He was easy enough to find. His name was the first one to pop up on a Google search. He ran the only church in Delford, the one she had driven by and wondered at its affluence. It stuck out like a sore thumb in the middle of all the poverty surrounding it.

The picture of Cornelius on the website did nothing to erase the idea of a man who embraced affluence, even at the expense of his flock. He stood with his arms spread wide in a pure white suit that contrasted with his dark-colored skin. His round head was fleshy, and he had gray streaking his dark hair even though he was only forty-six years old. Standing in the front of the church with a giant smile, he'd been caught in the middle of a sermon.

According to his bio, he'd been with the church for fifteen years. He claimed to have been called to God after seeing the hardship and pain that his deceased wife had gone through before her death. The bio went into detail about how she had sunk into a world of drugs and prostitution. According to the site, Cornelius had done everything in his power to save her, but the vice had proven too strong. Which was when Cornelius turned to God, desperate for answers as to what had happened.

Cornelius claimed that God came to him and told him to help the others in his flock. Feeling lost and alone, he made his way to Delford and established the First Baptist Church. According to the website, his son also worked for the church, running the business aspect of it. Young Cornelius looked just like his father, except in his picture, his suit was a bright blue. He looked to be about twenty-six or twenty-seven. The quote attributed to him was an uninspired "God is great." In a short post, he went on to explain how God, through the example of his father, had called him to serve the church and the people of Delford in whatever way he could.

Nola flipped through the different pages describing the outreach of the church and its services, along with information about the dates and times of the services.

And at the bottom of each and every page, in bold colors, was a donation form.

Sitting back, Nola placed her hands behind her head as she stared at the picture of Cornelius. *So what did you do to Charlene, you bastard? And did you do the same to Anna Mae?*

She switched away from the public face of Cornelius and decided it was time to look at the hidden face. She switched over to a closed system that Bishop had developed for her and went to the dark web. It tapped into federal and state databases without leaving a trace.

Nola entered her username and password. Sipping water, she waited for the security protocols to be enacted. When the cursor appeared, she typed in Cornelius's name and hit enter.

A minute later, the real Cornelius appeared on her screen. Apparently he'd been quite an active teenager. He had juvenile arrests going back to the age of thirteen. He'd been part of a gang on the eastern side of New Orleans. He'd spent some time in juvie for battery and had even spent a few years in an adult facility for armed robbery and involuntary manslaughter. Later, there'd been some domestic violence allegations against him by his "beloved" wife, but none of the charges had made it to court.

In fact, when his wife finally left him, she was going to take the charges to court, but then she died. It wasn't drugs that killed her. She'd been found in an alley, beaten to death. The cops suspected Cornelius but had no proof.

Not exactly the stuff of romance novels.

But since Cornelius had moved to Delford, there was nothing in his file. No indications of violence. No indications of anything. Apparently he'd decided to walk the straight and narrow.

Or he was getting better at covering up his misdeeds. Nola knew the vestiges of religion were often a good cover in and of themselves. Victims were hesitant to come forward against such a well-respected individual.

But if Charlene was right, then there would be a trail of

victims. If Cornelius was targeting young girls, then Charlene would not be the only one.

And maybe Anna Mae had been the latest.

Nola flipped back to the church's website. It looked like the reverend would be at choir practice tonight. That was good. After practice, she and the reverend would have a little chat.

Chapter Thirty

To kill time until she met with the reverend, Nola did a search of missing girls in the surrounding area. And she didn't like what she found.

Nola had just finished the files. There were too many missing girls in Georgia and the surrounding states. They came in all races, all ages, all sizes. Finally, an aspect of America that had become a true melting pot.

But she noticed a disturbing pattern. The girls that had gone missing from the western side of Atlanta, which included Delford, all seemed to be between the ages of eleven and sixteen. And none of them had been found again.

Unlike the other girls who'd gone missing in Georgia, there were no indications of a problem at home or in school. All seemed to be pretty good students. None had gotten into trouble. There were no previous reports of delinquent behavior or running away. Some of them had some pretty horrific personal stories such as patterns of abuse, but overall they were really good kids. Nola sat back, staring at the monitor. *So where did you all go?*

Nola's stomach rumbled. She pushed away from the desk. She needed something to eat. She needed something to drink.

And she needed something to hit.

Maybe she'd do some drills. She didn't have a heavy bag to hit in the house, but there were other ways to get the frustration out. An image of Charlene floated through her mind as well as one of that pile of human waste who'd taken advantage of her.

She laughed in her mind. Taken advantage of. What a stupid phrase. Charlene had turned sixteen a week ago. She'd been legally able to consent for seven days. But she was pretty sure that guy and others like him hadn't waited until last week.

Which made them all rapists.

Maybe she should go back down to Crenshaw Street and see if there were any other men she could have a little "chat" with. But she shook her head as soon as she had the thought. She wasn't a one-woman lynching crew, at least not where it was undeserved.

Most of those men had likely fallen on hard times themselves. Many of them probably had lost their way and had just ended up down there because they had one small injury that had led to an addiction that they couldn't control. In the United States, more people abused prescription drugs than those that used cocaine, hallucinogens, inhalants, and heroin combined. And most of those new addicts took the prescription on a doctor's orders.

So Nola knew she needed to stay away. That didn't mean it was going to be easy.

She walked into the kitchen and pulled open the fridge.

There wasn't much, but she would be able to rustle up something. Avad had put a couple of staples into her supplies. She could make an egg and tomato omelet with some toast. She really didn't want to go out, so it looked like it would have to do.

She'd just placed the ingredients on the counter when she turned her head, listening. Quick footsteps headed up her back stairs, followed by frantic knocking. "Help! Help!"

Nola recognized the voice immediately. She hurried to the back door and pulled it open. Oz stood there. Tears streamed down his face, dirt streaked across his knees, and there was a small amount of blood.

"Oz, what's going on?"

"I need you to come. I was trying to make dinner—and fire!" Oz sprinted away.

Nola ran after him, her gaze shooting to the back window of Oz's house. She could see smoke and flames through the window. "Oz! Wait!"

Movement on the back porch drew her attention. His grandmother sat quietly on the back porch just rocking, her expression peaceful.

Oz darted through the back door. Nola was only a few steps behind him. She glanced at his grandmother, who met her gaze. Nola glared back at her before following Oz inside.

The fire had started on the stove. A spark must have spread to the curtains above the kitchen window.

"Get back!" Nola grabbed Oz's shoulder and pulled him away from the flames. Grabbing a kitchen towel from the counter, she pulled the pan from the stovetop. Macaroni was seared to the bottom of the pan. She tossed it into the sink and flipped on the water immediately.

As the water hit, steam shot toward the ceiling with a

loud sizzle, Nola stepped back to avoid an involuntary facial. Then she grabbed the sprayer and aimed it at the curtains. She reached up and yanked the curtain rod from the wall, letting it drop into the sink as well.

In another two minutes, she had the fire under control, and then it was gone. But the smell of smoke hung heavily in the air.

Oz stood in the doorway, his hands clasped tightly together as he shifted from foot to foot. His chin trembled, his eyes bright with tears. "I just . . . I was hungry."

"Where's your mom?"

"She-she's at work."

"Who's watching you?"

"No one. Anna Mae used to but . . ." He shrugged, looking away as a tear rolled down his cheek.

Nola let out a breath. "So you're on your own."

He nodded.

"Mom said if there were any problems, I was supposed to go over to Mrs. Johnson next door. But she's not home today. And I didn't know who else to go to. I'm sorry. Mom's going to be so mad, and I just . . ." Oz dropped his face into his hands, his shoulders shaking.

Nola didn't know what to do. Her first instinct was to comfort the boy, but she fought against it. She needed to stay detached. She needed to stay in control. When you got attached, it made everything so much more difficult. But Oz looked so heartbroken.

Nola took a step toward him, and that was all the encouragement he needed. He flew at her, his arms sliding around her as his whole body shook with sobs. Nola didn't say anything, just held the little boy clasped to her.

Tears pressed against the back of her own eyes, his raw

pain a palpable thing. She looked up at the ceiling, took some calming breaths, and willed her own tears back.

But slowly the warmth of Oz seeped through, touching a spot in Nola's heart that she thought she had shut down a long time ago. "It's okay, Oz."

"I miss her," he said softly.

"I know."

The two stayed clasped together until Oz's tears subsided. He stepped back, wiping at his tears. "Mom's going to be so mad."

"Hey," she said, "it's going to be all right. No harm done."

Oz's jaw dropped as his gaze locked on the destroyed curtains in the sink. "The wall and the curtains," he wailed.

Nola grimaced, looking at the damage done. "Okay. So some harm done. But you weren't hurt. That's what's important."

"It wouldn't have happened if Anna Mae was still here. She takes care of me when my mom's at work. But she's not coming home, is she?"

Nola didn't know what to say. She didn't want to lie to the boy. But she also didn't think telling him the stats on young girls missing was the best approach either. "I don't know. But I'm looking. And I hope I'll find her."

Oz just nodded as he wiped the tears on his cheeks with the back of his hand, which only served to push around some of the soot. Nola looked back at the kitchen. The house was so quiet. It was no place for a little kid. Especially not a kid who was essentially in mourning. "Tell you what, why don't I help you clean all this up, and then we go down to Ma Bell's Diner and get a bite to eat?"

"I don't have any money. And Mom said I can't get in the car with anyone that's a stranger."

Nola nodded. "That is some good advice. Well, how about if we walk down, and I'll pay for dinner, because I don't feel like eating by myself, and you'd be doing me a huge favor if you came with me."

Oz looked at her, skepticism scrawled across his raised eyebrows. "Really?"

Nola had to bite back her smile. This was a kid who didn't put up with BS. But at this moment, she did want some company. She wanted to sit down across from this little kid and have dinner and maybe buy him a milkshake to make him smile. She didn't look too deeply at those feelings. She just accepted that they were there. "Actually, really. I like spending time alone, but right now I would kind of like some company. So what do you say?"

He nodded. "Okay."

And Nola took the acceptance as a sign of what it was: two lonely people who just wanted to not feel so alone for a little while.

Chapter Thirty-One

The last few notes of "Glory Hallelujah" hung suspended in the air for a few moments after the chorus brought the song to a pitch-perfect conclusion. Nola sat in her car at the back of the church's parking lot. She had reversed into a spot at the back, in case she needed to make a quick exit.

After the fire, Nola had called Oz's mom and explained what had happened. Martha had been upset, but Nola promised Oz was fine. After assuring her that it wasn't necessary for her to come home, she got her permission to take Oz to the diner.

While on the phone, she asked about Anna Mae and the choir. According to Martha, Anna Mae lost interest after Charlene stopped going. Martha hadn't thought anything about it at the time.

After hanging up, she and Oz had gone to the diner for dinner. Then they'd taken the long way home. Oz had talked almost nonstop, giving his version of a Delford tour.

He pointed out the hole in the wooden fence behind the

grocer, where the neighborhood dogs snuck in and out to go through the dumpster. He indicated to the empty storefront that used to be a candy shop. In his retelling, candy lined the walls up to the ceiling, and towers of chocolate and sour balls stood in the middle of the store. He made it sound like Willy Wonka's Chocolate Factory minus the Oompa Loompas.

Nola knew that as a small child, that was probably how he actually remembered it. Molly often spoke of things in much more magical terms than Nola recalled them.

But there was one difference between Molly's and Oz's stories: In Oz's stories, Anna Mae was always a central character. She was always the one accompanying him on his adventures. She was a good sister.

After they returned to Oz's home, Nola washed down the wall. She even found some paint in the garage and managed to touch up the few scorch marks. There was nothing she could do about the curtains, but otherwise it didn't look bad, even if the air still stunk of smoke.

Afterwards, she and Oz sat outside, watching the sun drop toward the horizon. Nola couldn't remember the last time she'd sat down with nothing to do. It was strange but nice.

But she needed to get to the church. At the same time, she didn't want to leave Oz alone.

So she made a phone call. First to Martha and then a second one to ask a favor.

Ten minutes later, a blue Honda pulled into Oz's drive. Nola stood up from the porch as Clyde McNally stepped from the driver's seat. He gave Nola a little wave before turning to the back door of the car.

Oz came to stand next to her, his arms crossed. "Who's that?"

"That's Mr. McNally. I asked him if he could come stay with you until your mom comes home."

"I don't know him. I'm not—" Oz let out a little gasp.

Nola smiled as Snuffles lumbered out of the car with Clyde's help.

Oz moved forward as if on automatic pilot. He reached out a hand. Snuffles gave it a lick. Oz giggled, and Nola knew it was going to be all right.

Now, she shifted in her seat in the church parking lot. There was only a handful of other cars. Two of them she knew belonged to the reverend and his son. Those two also happened to be the most expensive cars in the lot. The reverend's was a white Mercedes E-Class sedan. Junior's was a bright-red Ford Mustang.

The lights from the church spilled out of the windows, which, when added to the sound of the choir, gave the small church an incredibly welcoming feel.

But the knowledge of what the reverend had been up to behind those doors chased away all of that pretense. Nola knew when it was made public, the church would be devastated. It might not recover.

Or it might take a page from other scandals that had plagued other religious institutions and simply sweep the whole problem under the rug. The girls would be cast as Lolitas, luring the poor innocent reverend into sin. Everyone would focus on all of his good works, not the lives that he had destroyed.

The side doors swung open, spilling light and laughing conversation out into the night air. Three people stepped outside, all women in their twenties, talking and laughing as they made their way to one of the cars. Another group followed, this one a mix of men and women, all older. Their conversation was slightly less animated but no less vocal.

A blue Taurus pulled into the parking lot, its engine idling. The driver honked the horn. A group of four young girls between the ages of twelve and fifteen hurried from the church. Smiling and laughing, they clutched their binders to their chest as they piled into the car.

Another three people stepped from the church and started to walk back toward Baker Street. Nola waited until all the cars had pulled out of the parking lot. None of them glanced toward her. Perhaps they felt safe being so close to the church.

She eased out of the car, closing her door quietly as the lights in the church began to dim one by one. Only one light was left on in the church, but the lights in the house attached to the church flared to life.

Nola had counted the people coming out the doors. She'd gotten there early enough to watch the choir arrive, so she knew there was one missing.

A young girl, maybe eleven or twelve years old. Nola crossed the parking lot quickly and silently slipped through the doors that the choir had exited from. She was in a small side hallway next to the main room of the church. A bright-red commercial carpet covered the floor, and wood paneling adorned the walls. A billboard to her left displayed a listing of community events. They included a potluck lunch, clothes drive, weekly AA and NA meetings, and notices for jobs.

The rest of the hall was decorated with religious pictures. Besides a few of Jesus, Nola didn't recognize the others.

Straight ahead, double doors led to the main room of the church. She could see row after row of wooden benches. The same red carpet blanketed the floor, leading to a large dais. Hallways spanned to the right and left. The right led to the larger foyer at the front of the church. The left headed in the direction of the reverend's home. Light and a low hum of music came from a crack in the door down that way.

Quietly, Nola made her way toward it. She paused just outside, peeking through the crack. It was an office. The reverend's son, Cornelius Junior, sat at the desk, taking notes on a yellow legal pad.

Nola quickly slipped past the door. Ahead was the door leading to the reverend's living area. She stepped into a small mudroom of sorts. There was a door to the outside on her left and another door to the actual home. It looked like the mudroom had been an afterthought, a way to connect the reverend's home to the church and protect him from any inclement weather.

As she tried the door to the residence, she was unsurprised to find it locked. She slipped her tools from her back pocket, and in only a few seconds, had the door open. She left it open a crack, scanning the small hall beyond the door. She slipped through, closing the door behind her.

Unlike the wood paneling in the church, the reverend's home had wallpaper adorning every wall: a combination of red, white, and gold in an Italian-inspired design. An eight-foot-tall grandfather clock stood to Nola's right. Even with a quick glance, she could tell it was expensive. She'd seen similar clocks before, and they cost upwards of $3,000.

A large circular table sat in the middle of the hall, a giant arrangement of flowers on top of it. The dark cherry wood of the tabletop gleamed. The floors were all wood and wide planked. Not a speck of dirt marred them. The scent of lemon was in the air, indicating a recent cleaning.

A chandelier above the table had four tiers and dozens of lights, each capped with a tasseled shade. All the lights were on, although they seemed to be set to the lowest setting, giving the room a dim glow. A staircase at the back of the foyer wrapped around and led to the second floor.

A quick glance into the living room off the foyer showed a room no less sumptuous. The red-and-gold wallpaper continued in there, along with another large chandelier. A deep, thick Persian rug covered the floor. An ornate fireplace with baroque tile dominated the far end. Two couches flanked the fireplace, velvet with dark wooden frames. A massive portrait of the reverend and his son hung above the fireplace. It reminded Nola of the pictures she had seen of monarchs in Europe.

Nola shook her head at all the opulence. Apparently this man of God didn't believe in struggling.

Pausing, she listened for any sound, but nothing came from the darkened upstairs. Light came from down the hall, straight ahead of her, beyond the staircase.

She moved forward, her footfalls easily hidden by the thick rugs. The low murmur of voices followed by a small timid cry flowed down the hall toward her. Nola picked up her pace. She passed a bathroom on her right and a closed door on her left. She paused again at the door on the right. The light emanated from there.

The door was open halfway. A quick glance confirmed that it was a bedroom, although being it was on the first floor, she knew it wasn't the master. *I guess the reverend doesn't want to dirty up his own room.*

Nola toed the door open further. The reverend stood with his back to her. A girl no older than twelve stood on the other side of the bed, clutching the sides of her shirt together.

"Now, Lynette, don't be like that. You know what we do here is sacred." Cornelius stood across the bed from

Lynette, his arms outstretched. He'd already removed his shirt. His white wifebeater stretched tight over his paunch. The buckle on his belt jingled, Cornelius already having unhooked it.

You bastard. Nola kicked open the door. "Get away from her."

Cornelius wheeled around, his large brown eyes widening in fear and surprise. "You, you can't be in here. This is my private residence."

Not removing her gaze from the reverend, Nola rolled her hands into fists. "That's what you're going to go with? That this is your private residence? You don't want to try 'it's not what it seems'?"

Cornelius's mouth gaped open like a fish. "It's not what it seems."

"Yeah, it's a little too late for that one," she scoffed before she looked over at Lynette. "Lynette, why don't you come over here by me?"

Lynette shook her head, her gaze flicking toward the reverend.

He straightened his shoulders. "See? She doesn't want to go with you. There was a little mishap in chorus, and her shirt got ripped. I was merely helping her by—"

Nola rolled her eyes. "Yeah, you might want to work on that excuse a little bit more before the cops arrive."

"Cops? There's no reason for cops. This is a simple misunderstanding."

Stepping further into the room she jutted her chin toward the door. "Out."

His mouth fell open. "Out? This is my home. You don't get to tell me what to—"

Nola reached out and grabbed his arm before he could say another word. She inverted the wrist until his palm was facing the ceiling before she bent it ninety degrees and then pressed down on his elbow, steering him out the door as she ignored his cries of pain. With one last shove, she pushed him out into the hallway, where he sprawled on his expensive rug. Then she kicked the door shut behind him.

Taking a breath to calm herself down, she turned to Lynette. "Lynette? Are you all right?"

Lynette nodded before seeming to think better of it and shook her head. Nola put her hands up and took a small step forward. "I'm here to help. I won't let the reverend hurt you."

Tears sprang to Lynette's eyes, and her chin trembled. "He said, he said God wanted it to happen." Her voice lowered and shook as tears rolled down her cheeks. "But I don't think God wanted that."

Nola didn't answer right away, trying to get a hold of the anger roaring through her. She knew pedophiles groomed their victims. She knew pedophiles needed victims to feel as if they were the ones responsible for the acts. And apparently the reverend was no different from any other disgusting monster that preyed on young children.

It was an effort for Nola to hold back all of the rage burning inside of her. She kept her voice calm as she spoke to the terrified child in front of her. "No. None of this is your fault. What the reverend said is not true. You are a good person. And he is not."

Nola's words seemed to cut the strings holding Lynette up. She swayed for a moment, and with a small cry, dropped to the ground. A wail burst out of her, coming from somewhere deep.

Hurrying over to the child, Nola crouched down next to her. It was the second time in a few short hours that a child had been overcome in front of her. Once again, Nola hesitated, not sure if Lynette would welcome her touch.

But then Lynette threw her arms around Nola, nearly knocking her over. Nola clasped the child tightly to her while she pulled her phone out of her back pocket. "It's going to be okay. It's going to be okay."

Chapter Thirty-Two

The cops took twenty minutes to get to the reverend's home. They kept the sirens off, so it was only the sound of voices down the hall that let Nola know they had arrived. With one arm around Lynette's frail shoulders, she led her toward the doorway. But Lynette shrank back, shaking her head. "I don't want to go out there."

Nola understood her fear all too well. "I know. The police are here, and I think it's time we left this room."

Lynette shook her head, taking another step back. "They won't believe me. No one will believe me."

Nola wanted to tell her that wasn't true. She wanted to tell her that of course the people in her life would believe her. That of course the cops would believe her. But she knew all too well that victims of sexual assault were often not believed. There was no guarantee that anyone would take Lynette's word over the reverend's. In fact, in all likelihood they wouldn't believe her, and her words would be ignored in favor of the respected male in her life.

Leaning down, Nola leaned looked into Lynette's eyes.

"They might not believe you, and I hate that for you. But I know you don't want this to happen again. And I know you don't want this to happen to anyone else. The only way there's a chance of preventing that is if you speak up."

Lynette's eyes were wild. Her gaze darted around the room. Her chin trembled. Her hands opened and closed. "But why? Why do I have to do it?"

"It's not fair. And you shouldn't have to do it. But this is where we are. And there is no one else who can take this next step."

Tears crested Lynette's eyelashes, and she sounded so incredibly young as she spoke. "Do I have to?"

Hating what she was about to say, Nola shook her head. It was too big a burden for this little girl. She should only be focused on being a kid. But the reverend had ripped that childhood from her. "No. You don't have to. If you want, you can go home and try to pretend this never happened. But it won't work. You will remember what happened to you. And it's going to take you a long time to understand everything that's happened here. The truth of the matter is that people like the reverend don't stop unless someone stops them. He might stop for a little while. But then there will be another young girl who will catch his eye."

Nola took a breath. "I can't guarantee that even if you say something, you will be able to prevent another young girl from being victimized. But I can guarantee that if you don't say something, a young girl will definitely be right back where you are right now."

Lynette looked around the room as if searching for an answer. Nola didn't say anything. There was nothing more she could say. Like Charlene, Lynette had had all of her choices taken away from her. This one needed to be her choice, hers and hers alone. And Nola would be damned if she would let anyone take that away from her.

The young girl's voice was shaky as she spoke. "I have a little cousin. Everybody says we look so much alike, even though she's four years younger than me. Will he go after her?"

"I don't know if it will be her or some other girl," Nola said truthfully.

"But he will go after someone?" Lynette asked.

Nola nodded. "Without a doubt, I know he will go after someone else. Predators like him, they can't and won't just stop."

Lynette took a deep breath. "I want my nana."

"I called her. She should be here soon," Nola assured her.

As if summoned by the words, the sound of raised voices reached them from the end of the hall. One of those voices was distinctly female. "Where is she? Where is my Lynette?" Olivia Granger demanded.

"Stay here." Nola moved to the door and then stepped into the hallway. Olivia, all four foot eight of her, had the reverend and Detective Rascal backed up against the wall. "Where is my—" Lynette's grandmother's head whirled around, catching Nola's eye.

Nola nodded her head. Without another word to the men, Olivia strode down the hall. Nola stepped forward so she was out of view of the door. Her grandmother stopped and looked up at her. "How is she?"

"Scared, confused. I called the police," Nola said.

Still eyeing her, Oliva demanded. "You're not the cops?"

"No. I told Lynette that she doesn't have to speak with them if she doesn't want to. I figure she's had enough of her decisions taken away tonight."

Closing her eyes, Lynette's grandmother's hand flew to her chest. "I heard rumors. But I thought that's all they were. I never imagined . . ." Her words drifted, pain etched across her face.

Speaking softly, Nola said, "She's right in there. She's been asking for you."

The words spurred Olivia into action. She bustled around Nola and into the room.

"Granny!" Lynette sobbed.

Giving them a moment and herself, Nola rolled her hands into fists. That girl was going to go through hell for the next couple of weeks, probably years, even if people believed her. But she knew that more likely than not, people wouldn't. Regardless, this event, when it became known, would define her.

Strangers, and some who knew her, might even say that somehow she had led the reverend on.

Because that was how it went with sexual assault victims.

For some reason, the idea that someone would sexually assault someone was completely inconceivable to some, even though it happened to one out of four women. And yet the idea that a man in a position of power would take advantage of that power was completely beyond the scope of believability for some people.

Nola looked down the hallway where the reverend was speaking with Detective Rascal. Gritting her teeth, she headed toward them.

Cornelius's voice was raised, anger and indignation in his tone. "And then she just burst in. She terrified poor Lynette. Lord knows what she's making that girl say. Why, I wouldn't be surprised if—"

"If *what*, Reverend?" Nola's rage, which she thought

she'd gotten under control, boiled just under the surface. It took everything in her not to slam the man up against the wall.

The reverend jumped as if she'd struck him. "How dare you! You have no right to be here. I was just telling the detective how you burst in and upset poor Lynette."

Nola narrowed her eyes. "Is that right?"

The reverend's hand had a noticeable tremor working its way through it as he took a white handkerchief out of his pants pocket and wiped his brow.

Cornelius Junior stormed into the room, sliding his cell phone back into his dress pants pocket. "Pops, don't say anything. I just spoke with a lawyer, and he's on his way." He glared at Nola. "Why isn't she in cuffs? Get her out of our home!" He took a step toward Nola.

She smiled and leaned back against the wall. "Make me."

The son's nostrils flared.

Nola prayed that he took a swing at her. She needed to hit someone. And father or son, either would do.

Detective Rascal put up a hand. "Okay. Tensions are running a little high here. Cornelius, why don't you and your son go into the kitchen, and I will speak with Ms. James?"

"I want her out of my home," Cornelius barked, not looking at Nola as he stormed toward the kitchen. Junior, however, made sure to give Nola a full eye of hatred as he passed. Nola gave it right back. Although in her mind, she was doing a lot more than just watching him.

The detective watched the two men disappear down the hall before his shoulders drooped. He turned back toward Nola. "I seem to be running into you in all of the worst possible places."

Nola shrugged.

The detective nodded down the hall. "How is she?"

"Terrified." Nola met the detective's gaze, not letting him look away. "Will she be treated fairly?"

Not answering right away, the detective glanced down the hall toward the kitchen. "The reverend has a lot of friends in town, and a lot on the city council."

Disgust laced Nola's words. "So he's going to walk. He's destroyed a young girl's life, and he's going to walk."

"I don't want him to."

She studied the detective, who stood with a clenched jaw. "This is not your first case involving the reverend, is it?"

"I can't say anything about that," he said his tone stiff.

Glancing back down the hall to make sure that Lynette and her grandmother were nowhere to be seen, Nola took a step closer to the detective, lowering her voice. "Lynette's grandmother said that she heard rumors. Other girls have come forward, haven't they?"

Rascal nodded his head. "I don't know what you're talking about."

"How many? How many have you heard about?" She asked.

The detective held up five fingers. "I told you, I don't know what you're talking about."

Nola would like to say she was surprised, but there was nothing surprising about that number. If anything, she was surprised it was so low. Only ten percent of sexual assault victims reported the crimes. In all likelihood, the number could be as high as fifty.

Rascal pulled out a notepad. "I'll need to take your statement."

Quickly, Nola ran down what she'd heard about the reverend, although she left Charlene out as the source. She said she had stopped by to have a conversation with the reverend when she found his door unlocked after choir practice. She stepped in after hearing a cry. That was when she found Lynette with the reverend in the room.

Rascal's jaw tightened when he heard the description of Lynette's state. But he said nothing, just took notes.

When she was done, he looked up at her. "So you were coming by to ask about Bible study and happened to overhear Lynette cry out?"

Nola didn't look away. "Yep."

"I guess it's a good thing for her that you had such good hearing," he gave her a small smile.

"Guess so," she agreed.

Then he studied her, his head tilted to the side. "That's two times in as many days that your good hearing has helped people. You're like some kind of superhero."

"Nope. Just an average citizen."

"Uh-huh."

Down the hall, Olivia stepped out with her arm wrapped around Lynette. "I would like to take Lynette home."

Walking quickly toward them, the detective kept his voice soft. "All right. I'll come by there in a little bit and see if Lynette wants to speak?"

Olivia nodded, tightening her arm around the young girl, who looked so incredibly tiny, even next to her small grandmother.

"Do you need a lift?" Rascal asked.

"It's just a short walk," Olivia said.

"I'll see them home," Nola said.

The detective gave a nod of thanks. "I'll be there in about forty minutes, maybe a little longer, depending upon whether or not the lawyer arrives before I leave."

"I'll stay with them until you arrive," Nola said.

Lynette kept her gaze on the ground during the whole conversation, and Nola noted that she cringed away from the detective. The detective seemed to understand. He stepped back to allow her more space. Nola took Lynette's other side as she and her grandmother escorted Lynette from the room. As they reached the front door, Nola glanced back and looked at the detective. Naked emotion was on his face, pain and sadness as he watched them leave.

Nora turned back and stepped through the door, wondering if perhaps Lynette had just found yet another champion.

Chapter Thirty-Three

Nola had escorted Lynette and her grandmother home last night. She'd waited until Rascal arrived before trying to take her leave.

Olivia grabbed her hands as she stepped to the door. "Thank you, thank you for helping Lynette."

"You're welcome."

"Will you come back and check on her tomorrow? I'm sure she would want to see you."

Nola squirmed, not wanting to. But Olivia, who Nola could tell was a strong woman, looked so lost that she found herself speaking before she could pull the words back in. "I'll be back tomorrow."

It was a restless night for Nola. She imagined what she'd do to someone if they tried that with Molly. And she knew the answer: there would be very little left of the body.

She got up early and went for a long run. The humidity sapped her energy after only a mile, but she pushed through, feeling like she was running in soup. But she needed the release. She finished seven miles before she got back home. The sun was still barely up. She grabbed a shower, then stopped by Ma Bell's Diner, which thankfully was already open. After picking up breakfast, she was at Lynette's grandmother's house by seven.

Lynette was still asleep, but her grandmother had the door open before Nola was even out of the car. She looked like she'd been up all night. Olivia took the breakfast Nola brought with a grateful nod and then set it up on the table. The table was set right next to the open living room.

Nola wandered the space, looking at family pictures. There were shots of Olivia and her husband from when they were younger, their three kids as they grew and got married themselves. And then the grandkids. From Nola's count, it looked like Olivia had six so far.

Nola turned as Olivia set the coffee on the table. "You have a large family."

Olivia nodded. "Lynette's parents are overseas. They're both in the army. They prayed that they'd never be deployed at the same time, but . . ." She shrugged. "Come eat while it's warm."

Nola took a seat at the table, placing a roll and some strips of bacon on her plate.

Olivia had eggs on hers but just played with them as Nola ate. "My poor baby," Olivia whispered, looking toward the bedroom. "I want to kill that man."

"I know."

Olivia met Nola's gaze and read the anger in Nola's eyes. "I don't know what to do now. Detective Rascal called this morning. He wants to know if he can come by."

Last night, Rascal had been running late after the lawyer showed up. And Olivia had pushed off his visit. "He wants her to file a report," Nola said.

"But I don't know. If she does, who's going to believe

her? I mean, you see what they do to victims. My god, she's only eleven. What reason would she have to make anything up? And yet, some people will accuse her of just that." Olivia took a shaky breath. "I don't know what to do."

"You just need to be there for her. She needs to be able to make choices now. She needs to have some control over what comes next."

"She told me that you told her it was up to her."

"I did," Nola said.

"Thank you for not pushing her. I won't let anyone push her. Like you said, it's her choice," Olivia said stabbing her eyes.

"I think Rascal will respect that."

Placing the fork on the plate, Olivia nodded. "He's a good one. He was deployed with my son a few years back."

"Rascal was military?" Nola asked, surprised.

Olivia smiled. "I know. He doesn't give off that military vibe, but he was. Good soldier, according to my son. Got a few recommendations for acts of bravery. You were military too, weren't you?"

"No, not military. I worked for the government. But I've seen some things, been in a few war zones," Nola said with a shrug/

"You've got that look about you."

"What look?"

"The look that says you've seen the dark side of human nature and that you stared it down."

"Or maybe I gave in to the dark," Nola said, surprised when the words came out of her mouth.

"It's hard not to sometimes," Olivia said softly. "Sometimes the world pushes you so much that you just need to push back."

"Yeah," Nola said juts as softly. Then she sat with Olivia

for another hour, just letting Olivia talk. She seemed to need someone to let her vent. And sometimes it was easier to vent to strangers.

When Nola left, she was at loose ends. She headed home and started to run a search for missing girls but then changed her mind and looked up Rascal. He'd graduated from the police academy top of his class, but he also had an exemplary military record. He'd gotten both a Purple Heart and a silver star. He'd done two tours.

You are more than you appear, Detective Rascal.

She shook her head, turning her thoughts from the detective. She needed to find another avenue of investigation.

Her phone beeped. Bishop. She glanced at the message:

I got a signal. It just came up. Someone must have charged it.

It took a moment for Nola to realize what she was referring to: Anna Mae's cell phone. Her heartbeat quickened.

Where?

Only about ten miles from where you are. Just inside the Delford city line.

Send me the address.

Chapter Thirty-Four

Bishop did better than just sending Nola the address. She also sent along satellite imagery of the site.

Nola brought the images up on her laptop. On screen was a warehouse. Four cars were out front: two SUVs, one old sports car, and one sedan. There were two men posted at the front door. They sat around a small table underneath the overhang, playing cards. She shifted the image to get a view of the back door. There was only one man back there, leaning up against the building, sipping from a container. There was no other noticeable activity.

The warehouse was situated in a rundown part of the business district. A broken chain-link fence surrounded the building, with large swaths of the fence missing. The parking lot was a decent size, meaning that anyone who approached would have to cover at least fifty feet of open ground before they reached the door. And with men posted at both entrances, it would be next to impossible for people to sneak up on them.

So it looks like I won't be sneaking. She pulled up the blueprints for the warehouse from the city comptroller's office. The warehouse wasn't huge. Nola had definitely infiltrated larger. But there was a lot of open space. There was a small foyer at the front and then a small office at the back of the building by the loading docks. But everything else was open space. It was possible some alterations had been made to the space over the intervening years. The blueprint was, after all, twenty years old, but she couldn't count on it. She had to go in with the expectation that she would be in view as soon as she stepped through the doors.

Nola leaned back, staring at the screen, her gaze shifting back and forth between the blueprints and the satellite feed. An idea slowly began to take form. At the same time, she knew her approach was foolhardy, if not downright dangerous. But Anna Mae's phone was at that warehouse. It was the first solid lead she had. For a moment, she thought about contacting Rascal, but she almost immediately discounted it. He seemed like a good cop. And a good cop wouldn't support what she was about to do.

Making her way to the bedroom, she pulled open the closet and dragged out the old air-conditioning unit that she'd placed in there when she'd first arrived. She shoved it underneath the window. She stopped by the kitchen and grabbed the crowbar by the back door. Then she made her way back into the bedroom.

Using the crowbar, she pried open the floorboards in the middle of the closet. The first night she'd been here, she'd pulled them up and then nailed them down again. It took a few minutes, and when she was done, she was sweating pretty hard. Placing the crowbar back against the floor, she reached in. Bracing her legs, she hauled out the case. She dragged it over to the bed and placed it on top. Inserting the correct combination, she flicked open the locks and then opened it.

A display of destruction greeted her. Two Glocks, along with seventeen-round magazines. Throwing knives, grenades, flashbangs, even a P90 assault rifle with two barrels. She stared at the supply, debating casting aside options before finally leaning in and grabbing the Glocks, the P90, and the flashbangs. She hesitated for just a moment and then grabbed a suppressor. Quiet was definitely going to increase the chances of success.

Nola loaded everything into the black duffel bag that she pulled from underneath the bed. The P90 was probably overkill. But she'd found over the years that it was best to take just a little bit more than you thought you might need. Because if there was one thing she'd found to be absolute true, it was that Helmuth von Moltke was right: No plan ever survived contact with the enemy.

Nola grabbed the bag and headed to the kitchen. Dropping the bag on the table with a thud, she took a long drink of water from the sink. She filled up her water bottle and added it to the duffel bag. Then with one last look around the kitchen, she headed for the car. It was time to make a little noise.

Chapter Thirty-Five

Dusk was on the horizon, casting shadows along the street as Nola drove slowly by the warehouse. But even with the dimming light, the warehouse looked the same as it had in the satellite photos. There were still only two men by the front door, who barely glanced up as she drove by. And now there was one less car in the parking lot. She drove around the block and noticed that the guy by the back door had disappeared. Maybe he was taking a bathroom break.

She drove another three blocks in each direction, getting a lay of the land. Most of the area was completely desolate. On one side of the warehouse was an abandoned paper mill. On the other side was a former shoe company. Both looked like they hadn't seen a customer or an employee in decades.

The whole neighborhood screamed abandonment. Sidewalks were uneven, with weeds sprouting up between the cracks. Most storefronts were either boarded over or had smashed glass. There were only about six cars on the road. All of them had obviously not been used in a long time.

Most were missing their tires. A few were missing the hoods and no doubt a few parts from inside.

In fact, in the entire neighborhood, she saw only two working businesses. One was a small pawn shop right at the edge of the three-block boundary. The other was a night-club about two blocks away. There were two cars in the parking lot, although a quick internet search indicated that the club didn't open until nine at night.

So it looked like Nola had the whole neighborhood pretty much to herself, at least for a few blocks. She headed back to the warehouse and drove around to the back. The guard had returned to his duty and now stood smoking a cigarette. She pulled over to the side of the road at the edge of the warehouse's perimeter, but out of sight of the guard at the back door.

Stepping out of the car, she opened the back door, and unzipped the duffel. She pulled out her bulletproof vest and slid it on, locking it carefully in place. She rummaged in the duffel bag and pulled out the flashbangs, clipping them to the edge of her vest. She slid extra magazines into the pockets in the front, and then after checking both Glocks, placed them into the holsters on either hip.

She slid a few throwing knives into the other empty slots on her vest and then attached her wristband, where she slid a few more for easy access. She looped the P90 around her shoulders and then closed the back door. She pulled her ski mask from the pocket of her jacket and pulled it on.

And she let herself have one little smile. *Time to play.*

Chapter Thirty-Six

Nola crept along the chain-link fence. The darkness had set in fast, but there was an almost full moon, which provided enough light to see by. The phones of the two guys by the entrance were lit up, telling Nola exactly where they were. A second guy joined the other at the back of the building. It was a toss-up which entrance to aim for.

There were three stories of windows, and only the first floor had lights on, but it was possible that someone might still look out one of those darkened windows. According to the plans, there were catwalks on the second and third levels, although no actual floor. If they were smart, they'd have guards walking along them.

Pausing braced by a hole in the gate for only a moment, she slipped through. Crouched low, she studied the lot. She needed to take out the two guards by the front silently. Not an easy task. Luckily, she was small, so there was a good chance they'd underestimate her until it was too late.

Situations like this were the only time that Nola was thankful for the male ego.

She cast another glance at the windows. Nothing moved beyond them. She was walking along the side of the building, out of view of both the front and back entrances. She waited until a loud car drove by on the road and bolted for the side of the building.

She reached it just as the car's muffler huffed out of hearing. Nola paused, but everything was still quiet. There were no sounds of alarm. She sidled up to a window and peered in. Across the warehouse floor, there were pallets strewn with different goods. She could make out a stack of TVs, PlayStations, cell phones. Apparently, these guys didn't just grab Anna Mae.

She couldn't see Anna Mae anywhere, but she did see two other girls that could use her help.

Both were handcuffed to a stairwell at the edge of the room.

The three men sitting at the table playing cards didn't pay them any attention. Nola scanned the rest of the warehouse, but from her angle, she couldn't see all of it. So she had to plan on at least double the number she could see. Plus the two in front and out back, that made ten.

Damn it. Ten was a lot, even for her. She could take out the ones in the front and back, but if someone raised the alarm, it would not be good.

Well, then, I guess I'll just have to be quiet.

She inched toward the front of the warehouse, careful to stay out of view from the windows. She'd just reached the front when the door opened. Music blared out into the night. Nola flattened herself against the side of the building.

"Hey, any problems?" The man who stepped outside asked.

"Nah, it's dead quiet."

"Good. You guys get a break. Head on in,"

"Thanks, man."

Nola waited until she heard the door close. She cursed her timing. Guys just coming on a shift were more aware than guys at the end of a shift.

The man who stepped outside, hit the other guy on the arm. "What the hell's wrong with you?"

"What? Nothing," the second man said not looking at him,

"Derek, I brought you on. You can't be acting like you don't want to be here. So knock it off. If you weren't my cousin, I'd kick your ass for how you're acting."

"It's just . . ." Derek shook his head.

"Just what?"

Anger laced the man's words. "It's girls. You're running girls."

"So?" The other man asked with shrug.

"So? It's wrong, Devante."

Devante laughed. "What'd you think you were signing up for? Sunday school? You know what the Compton boys do."

"I didn't know it was that. I thought it was drugs or something," Derek muttered.

"So what, you want out? You don't get out," Devante said the threat clear.

"I don't know, man. This is seriously messed up. And I mean—" Derek let out a small yell as Devante slapped him hard against the back of his skull.

Devante's voice got mean. "You listen to me. I brought you in. You do anything that makes me look bad, and it will be the last thing you do. You understand?"

"Yeah, yeah, I understand," Derek said.

Nola peeked around the side of the building. Devante

had his cousin pushed up against the wall. The kid looked young, probably about Anna Mae's age.

Nola tossed a rock at the other side of the building. Both men looked toward it. Devante reached for his gun. "What was that?"

Nola bolted from her position. She slammed the grip of her Glock into the back of Devante's head. He dropped like a stone. She turned her gun on the other guy. "Don't say a word."

The kid's eyes grew wide. His hands lifted in the air. "O-okay."

"The girls. Do you know where they are?" Nola demanded.

He nudged his head back toward the warehouse. "They're inside."

"No, the other girls."

The kid's voice shook. "I know about two others. They moved them. They were at a farm, in some hole in the ground. I was there when they pulled them out, but I don't know where they ended up taking them."

"What's your name?" Nola asked.

"Derek."

Points for him: he didn't lie. "All right, Derek, turn around."

He did, his trembling noticeably increasing. "You should know, there's more girls. I mean, not just the two we had. They were bringing more girls. They're shipping them somewhere."

"When?" Nola asked.

"Next few days."

"Well, they won't be shipping anybody anywhere if I take all you guys down."

Derek shook his head. "No, these guys aren't a part of it

anymore. They did their part. The only one still connected is my cousin, but they'll just replace him. He talks big, but he's just another guy, easily replaced."

Sadly, she didn't think he was lying. His cousin seemed like muscle but not a leader. "Do you know who the boss is?"

"No. But I think he works out of Savannah. Devante has been going there a lot." He paused. "There's two girls inside. The guys will use them as shields as soon as they hear you coming."

"How many guys?" Nola asked.

"Six, four inside, two out back," he said quickly.

Nola paused. "Why are you offering up so much information?"

"I never should have gotten involved in this, any of this. I knew what Devante was doing was wrong." The boy's shoulders shook, and he sniffed. "I deserve whatever you do to me. But those girls don't. Especially not Anna Mae."

Grabbing him by the shoulder, Nola turned him around, shoving him against the building, her gun at his throat. "Anna Mae?"

He nodded, his eyes shiny with tears. "Anna Mae Hayes. She was one of the girls we took from the hole. She's a good person. She doesn't deserve this."

She stared at the boy, a war going on inside of her. She wanted to pull the trigger. A month ago, she would have. But something about his face, his tears, pulled at her. She stepped back. She pulled her phone out and took his picture. Then she lowered her gun. "Run."

His chin jerked up. "What?"

"Run. Now," she ordered.

He stared at her and then flicked a glance at his cousin. He swallowed. "Will you help Anna Mae?"

"If I can," she said.

He met her gaze, and then with one last look at his unconscious cousin, sprinted into the night. Nola watched him go, wondering if she'd made a horrible mistake. He could have been lying. He could have been feeding her a line.

But her lie detector had always been good. And he seemed like a kid who'd gotten caught in something much bigger than himself. She shook her head at the choice she'd made. It wasn't like her.

Laughter came from inside, followed by a girl's cry. She rolled her shoulders. She'd made the decision. There was no changing it now.

And there was still some work to do.

She grabbed the handle and had started to open it when it was pulled open from the other side. She didn't waste any time. She shot the man in the thigh, kicking his gun out of the way before slamming him in the face with her knee, knocking him out.

Between the music and the suppressor, no one inside noticed. She stepped quietly over the man.

Two of the men had the girls in their laps. They didn't even notice as Nola stepped into the room. Only the guy without a girl glanced over. He tilted his head, a frown on his face as if trying to figure out why his buddy was on the ground. It took him precious seconds to look up.

Nola caught him in the shoulder, and he fell back out of his chair with a cry. The other two finally realized something was up. The two girls, one African American and the other Hispanic, neither older than fifteen, screamed. Both men tried to stand and reach for their guns. But between the girls on their laps and the table, it was a struggle.

Nola crossed the distance before they'd freed their

weapons. She yanked one of the girls from the man's lap and shot him point blank in the chest.

The other got to his feet, holding the girl in front of him as a shield, just as Derek had warned. He held his gun to her head. "Drop your gun!" he yelled as he backed away, dragging the girl with him.

Nola followed, her gun hand steady. "No."

He shifted his gun from pointing it at his hostage to pointing it at Nola. "You think I'm kidding, bitch? I'll—"

Nola caught him in the ribs with the first shot. He stumbled back. The next shot caught him in the right shoulder. She hurried forward, kicking the gun out of the way as the back door opened.

"Hey, Kyle, everything o— Oh shit! Max, get in here."

Nola stepped behind a pallet of TVs. The guard hurried forward. Nola waited until both had passed, then she slipped up behind Max. She slammed her heel into the back of his knees and then yanked him back by the hair. His head crashed onto the concrete floor with a thud. She stomped her boot into his face.

His buddy turned. Nola caught him in the ribs with a sidekick followed by a round kick to the thigh that buckled his knees. He screamed. She grabbed him by the back of the head and shoved his face into the edge of the TV tower.

Blood exploded across his face. She stomped on the back of his knee and shoved him to the floor, then slammed his face into the concrete. She quickly yanked his arm behind his back and then the other. Using a zip tie, she secured him and then quickly did the same to the other men in the room. She grabbed one of the cell phones still on the table, wondering which one of the guys had taken Anna Mae's phone. "Siri, call 9-1-1."

"9-1-1, what is your emergency?" The dispatcher asked.

"I'm at the old warehouse on Sweet Oak. Two girls are being held hostage, and there's a bunch of stolen equipment. Come fast." She ended the call, tossing the phone on the table.

Then she turned to the two girls who cowered in the corner. Mascara tears ran down their cheeks. Nola approached them slowly, her hands in the air. They scrambled back against the wall as she approached. "It's okay. I'm not going to hurt you. The cops will be here in a little bit. Are you okay?"

One of the girls looked up at her and nodded.

Nola pulled out her phone and showed them the picture of Anna Mae. "Have you seen this girl?"

The girls looked at the picture, and then both shook their heads. "Okay. Just hold tight, the police will be here in a little bit."

She headed for the front door. Derek's cousin knew where Anna Mae was. She'd grab him and get him to talk. Glock in hand, she opened the door and scanned the small covered area.

But Devante was gone.

Chapter Thirty-Seven

Nola closed her eyes as the hot water cascaded over her. She replayed last night's events. She'd been kicking herself ever since. She should have secured Devante before she went inside. It was a stupid mistake.

She'd driven around looking for him but had to stop when the cops arrived. It took ten minutes for the first car to get there. She watched from down the block as two more arrived, and then a few minutes later, a detective she didn't know arrived along with Rascal.

Nola put the car into gear. If Rascal was there, the girls would be all right. She drove slowly away from the ware-house, taking the long way home. And with each street she passed, she wondered why she had let Derek go.

Something inside had told her he wasn't like the others. That he didn't deserve their fate. But she'd be damned if she understood what made her think that.

She'd done a search on him this morning. Derek Rivers hadn't been hard to find. He'd actually lived in Delford until a few years ago. He had no priors and had been a decent student. It looked like his family had fallen on hard times lately from the financials she'd pulled up.

Derek's cousin, however, was a different story. He'd been in and out of juvie since he was a kid and had even gone away for a two-year stint for armed robbery, getting out just six months ago. Nola had the feeling Derek might have turned to his cousin in desperation. A quick run of his mom's financials showed a mountain of debt.

She stepped out of the shower and quickly toweled off. She dressed and headed to the kitchen as her phone beeped. She glanced at a text from Teddy.

Any luck?

Nola sighed. The kid texted her twice a day. She normally sent him a short no, but she figured she could throw him a bone.

Some. It looks like Anna Mae's disappearance is linked with the Compton boys. Any idea who that is?

She opened the fridge, and her phone beeped again.

I may have something. I'll send it now.

Nola frowned, not sure what that was all about, but if he had something on the Compton boys, she'd be shocked.

But ten minutes later, she was. Teddy sent video footage, but she wasn't sure what to make of it. It showed a couple of guys at the Retreat, and they definitely did not look like members. They were decidedly rough around the edges, with tattoos, beat-up cars, and a general sense of menace. From what Teddy had sent, they had been at the Retreat at least a dozen times over the last two years. Who the hell were these guys? And what did they have to do with anything?

She pushed away from the desk and headed for the kitchen. God, she felt like she was drowning in puzzle pieces, but none of them fit the puzzle she was trying to solve. She opened the refrigerator, just staring at its contents.

Derek had said the main guy was based out of Savannah. Nola debated whether or not to head out there. If Derek was telling the truth, and she thought he was, then Anna Mae was no longer around here.

Nola slammed the fridge shut with more force than necessary. Damn it. The haystack had just quadrupled in size.

Her phone beeped again. This time it was a text from Bishop.

Had a forensic accountant go through the church's books like you asked. He found some interesting stuff. Sent you the file.

Nola quickly switched over to her email and brought up the summary of the report. She smiled. *Well, well, well, what a shock.*

A knock sounded at the front door. Nola frowned. She hadn't heard a car, and Oz would probably come to the back door. She grabbed her Beretta and stood to the side of the front door. She peeked out, shocked at the sight on her porch. She unlocked the door, careful to keep her gun aimed at her visitor but out of his view.

Derek stood, shifting from foot to foot. "Um, hi. I, uh, was hoping I could talk to you."

Chapter Thirty-Eight

Nola did not get surprised often, but Derek Rivers standing on her front porch was definitely surprising. She scanned the street beyond him, but there was no unusual activity. He seemed to be alone.

She stepped back. "Come on in."

Derek ducked past her and stood, shifting nervously in her small living room. The kid—and he was still a kid— looked more stressed than any teenager should be. There were dark circles under his eyes, his clothes had been slept in, and his left cheek was swollen with the beginnings of a nice bruise.

She waved him toward the couch. "Take a seat. How can I help you?"

Sitting, he perched on the edge of the chair. "Um, I, uh, um. I, uh, thought maybe I could help you, um, find Anna Mae."

"What makes you think I'm looking for Anna Mae?"

"Ma Bell. She talks a lot," he said with a shrug.

Nola cursed the friendly diner owner.

"And, um, I think maybe we met last night?" he hurried on. "I didn't tell anyone. I— After I left, I just walked around, trying to figure things out. Ever since I saw Anna Mae and the little girl with her, I've been trying to figure out a way to help them. But on my own, I didn't know how."

"Why didn't you go to the cops?"

Derek scoffed. "I didn't know which ones to trust. I know some are on the payroll. Devante said as much, but I don't know who. And I don't know where the girls are now, so I didn't know what to even tell them."

Noting the fresh new bruise on his cheek., Nola asked, "How'd you get that?"

Derek's hand flew to the bruise. "My, uh, cousin. He was mad I left him at the warehouse."

"Did you tell your cousin you think I'm the one who was at the warehouse?"

"What? No! He'd kill you. I don't want that. I want to . . . to help."

Leaning back against the wall, Nola crossed her arms over her chest. "So how can you help me?"

Derek ran a hand over his head. "I don't know. I thought maybe if I found Anna Mae again, I could contact you and let you know where they are. Then you could figure out a way to get them, keep them safe."

"You're still working with your cousin?"

"Yeah, but only to find the girls. Look, I screwed up. I never should have started working with Devante. But my mom . . ." He shook his head. "It doesn't matter. But I need to make it right, so I'm staying with Devante. He said the shipment's going to happen soon, and he's going to be a part of it. I'll get him to bring me. And then when I find them, I can call you."

"What if you don't find them?"

Derek swallowed. "I don't know. I guess I'll just go to the cops and tell them my story. Maybe they can do something to the Compton boys. Maybe the cop I tell won't be linked with them and I won't end up dead. All I know is, I can't do this. This isn't who I am. I can't live like this."

The signs of stress were splashed all over the boy: darting gaze, sweaty brown, nervous energy. He did seem like someone in way over his head. She pulled out her phone and carefully started the cloning program. She pushed off the wall. "Well, I don't know about any warehouse, but I am looking for Anna Mae. So give me your phone. I'll plug in my number so you can contact me if you find her."

Derek's shoulders dropped, relief covering him like a blanket. He scrounged in his pocket, pulled out his phone, and handed it over. "Thank you, thank you."

Nola took the phone and turned to the side while she fiddled with it, taking her time while she cloned his phone. Finally, she handed it back. "Okay. Let me know if you find anything."

"I will. I promise."

Nola escorted him out the door, then she walked to the kitchen table and took a seat. She pulled out her phone and carefully scrolled through all of Derek's texts. He had a lot from Devante. Devante issuing orders, and Derek following them. Most were orders for Derek to run errands: pick up food, pick up Devante. The other texts were to his mom, checking in, asking how she was feeling. A few were from what seemed like friends, but Derek kept those exchanges brief. Otherwise, there was not much on there.

She twirled the phone on its edge, picturing the young man. He had no criminal history. He'd been a good kid until he'd gotten mixed up with his cousin. His mother was really struggling. She had three jobs, none of which paid more than minimum wage. It looked like he might actually be a kid with a guilty conscience. Nola wasn't going to count on him coming through, but she couldn't help but hope that he did.

Chapter Thirty-Nine

After Derek left, Nola headed over to the Hayeses. As much as she didn't want to hurt Anna Mae's mom, she knew she'd want to know what was happening.

Oz had been sent out to play as the two of them sat down.

"It's bad, isn't it?" Martha asked.

"Not exactly. I haven't found her, but I did find her phone." She explained about Teddy, the phone, and tracing it to the warehouse.

"That was the big hubbub over on Sweet Oak?"

Nola nodded.

Martha cleared her throat. "And the two girls you found, they didn't know Anna Mae?"

"No. Why didn't you mention Teddy when I asked about Anna Mae's friends?"

"Honestly? I forgot. I was thinking about friends around here. I knew they were friends." Martha took a deep breath. "Anna Mae didn't talk about him a lot. I asked her why. She said it was because he was hers, and hers alone. Like this piece of her life that no one else had a part of. She didn't want to share him.

"Not in a bad way," Martha said quickly. "I understood what she meant. Anna Mae . . . she was always helping other people. She didn't do anything just for herself. Her friendship with Teddy, that was for her. I got that. I wish I'd known about the phone, though."

"He's been calling it every day, multiple times, trying to find her. He really cares about your daughter."

"I know. He's a good boy. It took me a while to see past his last name. But he's a good boy." Martha took a shuddering breath, her eyes haunted.

Nola found herself in the unusual position of wanting to provide comfort.

But she really didn't know how. She was completely out of practice. The only thing she could offer her was a little time to clear her head. She cleared her throat. "I was thinking of walking down to Ma Bell's Diner and getting some ice cream. Would it be okay if Oz came with me?"

Martha wiped at her eyes. "Yeah, that would be great, thank you."

Rascal's car was conspicuous from down the block as she and Oscar returned with ice cream cones in hand. Oz's had been reduced by just a few inches because he was obviously making his last. His eyes, though, zoomed in on Rascal leaning against the hood of his car in Nola's driveway.

"Who's that?" Oz squinted as he licked the side of his cone as ice cream worked its way down onto his fingers. Nola had the feeling he needed glasses.

"It's a detective."

Oz looked up at her, betrayal in his eyes. "He a friend of yours?"

She shook her head. "No. But I ran into him the other night."

Oz nodded, seemingly affirmed by her lack of friend-ship with the officer. "He came when Anna Mae went missing, along with another one. They never came back."

"What do you mean they never came back?"

"They never told us anything after that one time. Mama was so mad and so sad."

Rascal stepped away from his car and smiled as they approached. "Hey there, Oz. That ice cream looks good."

Oz rolled his eyes. He turned his back on Rascal and nodded at Nola. "Later."

He walked past the detective without a word, heading for his own yard. Nola admired his spunk. There was a lot of attitude in a little body.

The detective frowned, watching him go. "He mad at me?"

"Well, he's got this crazy idea that when police officers come over and say they'll find your sister that they'll actually find your sister. Or at least call you and let you know what the hell is going on."

Rascal turned to Nola. "What are you talking about?"

"You and another detective came and took the information down about Anna Mae. Then you never followed up."

Rascal's mouth fell open. "No, that's not true. Chanel said that she . . ." His voice drifted off as realization crossed his face. "She said she'd take the lead. She never got in touch with them?"

"No. And apparently Oz's mom called quite a few times. No one would give her any information about the

status of the investigation into her daughter's disappearance."

Rascal closed his eyes, leaning against his car. "God
dammit."

Nola was very aware that the curse was not meant for
her ears. It seemed Rascal was finally becoming aware of
the less-than-savory aspects of the Haverford-Delford Police
Department.

But Nola wasn't here to be the guy's shrink or to help
him get through his work issues. She crossed her arms over
her chest. "Can I help you, Detective?"

"Did you hear about the incident over on Sweet Oak?"

She nodded. "Yeah. Why?"

"The person who took the Compton boys down asked
the two girls there about Anna Mae."

"Interesting. What did they say?" She asked.

"They didn't know her. But here's where it gets really
interesting: Apparently Anna Mae had a cell phone. And
one of the guys at the warehouse had it. Strange, huh?"

"Sure is," she drawled.

"So I showed the girls another picture again this
morning of Anna Mae, and they still said they didn't know
her."

"Do you think they're lying?" She asked.

He kept his gaze on her as he spoke. "I think they are
traumatized and in shock, but no, I don't think they were
lying."

"What do you know about them?" Nola asked.

"They were grabbed three weeks ago on Atlanta's east
side. They couldn't describe their kidnappers, said they were
kept in the dark until five days ago when they were brought
to that warehouse."

"How old are they?"

"Fourteen."

Nola's hand rolled into a fist, her nails cutting into her palms. "Bastards."

Rascal grunted his agreement. "It's funny. We got five Compton boys dead to rights with the goods, the girls. None of them would say anything about any of that, but all of them were real talkative about the person who tied them up. And they all agreed on one thing: there was only one assailant, some sort of cross between a ninja and a soldier of fortune."

The silence stretched between them. Nola simply counted, wondering how long it would take Rascal to speak, knowing he was hoping his silence would force her to fill the awkward quiet. She counted to fifty-two before he spoke. She tried not to smirk.

"Have you ever heard of someone like that?"

"Like what?"

"Ninja, soldier of fortune."

"Maybe in the movies." She took a step toward the house. "If there's nothing else, Detective."

He raised an eyebrow. "Actually, there is, I heard you went by Lynette's yesterday morning."

"Is that a crime?"

Rascal put his hands up. "No, no. God, no. I'm glad you did. She swore out a report."

"That's good." She studied him. "Isn't it?"

"I hope so," he said softly before continuing. "The reverend got a high-priced attorney out of Atlanta. He's already making a lot of noise about false arrest and defamation of character."

Nola snorted. "Figures."

"Anyway, he won't be out on bail until at least tomorrow.

The judge set a high bail amount, which shocked just about everyone."

"Good. Well, thanks for the update." She took another step toward the house.

"Actually, that's not why I stopped by. I was coming to ask you for a favor of sorts."

Nola raised an eyebrow. "I don't believe we're at the 'asking for favors' level of friendship, do you?"

Rascal winced. "No, I don't think we are either. But I'm hoping that maybe you might be willing to help me out with something."

"And why is that?"

"Because you helped out Charlene." Rascal met her gaze.

Nola didn't look away. "I don't know what you're talking about, Detective."

"Well, it seems that someone walked into the Crenshaw Street house and rescued Charlene Hudson from one of the bedrooms upstairs. She then took her out to lunch and then took her to her grandmother's house over in Clarkson. And from the description I got, I'm guessing that person was you."

Nola stared at him, because once again he had not asked a question.

Rascal became uncomfortable under her gaze. He ran a hand through his hair. "Look, I get it. Cops in this town aren't exactly known for being the good guys. And I'm guessing from what little there is on your background, that you don't have the best experience with them either. But I *am* really trying to help here. And in order to help, *I need* some help."

"What kind of help?"

"I got a tip." He put up his hands at the roll of her eyes.

"It's a reliable one. This guy's come through for me a lot. And I could tell he was scared to give me this one."

"So what's the tip?"

"It seems Reverend Cornelius's son has been asking some questions. Questions about girls going missing." He gave her a pointed look.

"And I'm guessing he's not investigating their disappearances?"

"No, he is definitely not. Anyway, I'm worried about Lynette. She filed a report. It's now official. And if she testifies, she's credible. I mean, there's always a chance that the jury could ignore her testimony and believe the reverend, but there's a lot of smoke right now. But if Charlene steps forward as well—"

Nola cut him off. "What do you know about Charlene?"

"After I heard about her appearing at her grandmother's, I looked into her a little bit. She tried to file a report about a year ago. I didn't know anything about it. It was buried pretty deep. But I found it. And if she can testify along with Lynette . . ."

Nola hoped that Rascal was right. But she also knew that the criminal justice system didn't always work like that. There were good victims and there were bad victims. Lynette was a good victim. She was a young girl. She'd never been in trouble before and looked as innocent as a child could.

But even then, a skilled defense attorney could twist her background and make it sound like she was the one seeking out a father figure to make up for the absence of her own parents. And for Charlene, well, her last year was definitely not going to add to her credibility. It was true that being that there were two of them there was a better chance of the reverend being found guilty. Or at least brought to trial.

The sad truth was one victim telling the truth was very rarely, if ever, enough to get the case to trial.

"So what's your tip?"

"I think the reverend's son is arranging for someone to go after one of the girls. I just don't know which one. I can watch Lynette, but I need someone to keep an eye on Charlene. And I was really hoping that maybe you would be willing to do it."

"Why me? Why not someone else from the police department?"

He closed his mouth and looked away. "Because as much as I hate to admit it, I can't trust anyone in the police department with this. No one's looking out for the girls, and everyone's looking out for themselves. But I know you have no dog in this fight, and I have a strong feeling that your work at the 'Department of Agriculture' means that you can handle yourself pretty well."

Nola studied the detective in front of her. He seemed earnest. And after getting Charlene out of that mess, she didn't want anything coming near her that might possibly send the girl back in again. "Okay. I'll keep an eye on Charlene. I'm going to grab a few things and then I'll head out."

Rascal's whole body seemed to sag with relief. "Thank you. Thank you so much. Let me give you my cell phone so you can call me if anything happens." He rattled off the number.

Nola put it into her phone and then quickly called him so that he would have her number as well. "I'll be on the road in five minutes."

She turned to the house when his phone rang, but Nola ignored it and him. She headed up the stairs and let herself in. She made her way to the bathroom, did her business, and then quickly went to the kitchen, throwing together a few snacks that she could use for dinner and then filling up two water bottles.

And the whole time she thought about what Rascal had said. If one or more of the girls disappeared, the case against the reverend fell apart. They wouldn't need to grab both of them. Just the disappearance of one might be enough of a threat to the other girl to keep her from testifying. Nola picked up her phone and quickly dialed Charlene's grandmother. Chantilly answered after only one ring. "Hello?"

"Hi, Chantilly, it's Nola James."

Happiness surged through Chantilly's voice. "Oh! It's so good to hear from you. Charlene and I were just talking about you. And I prayed for you this morning at church."

Nola wasn't sure what to say to that. She couldn't remember anybody ever saying they had prayed for her, at least not in a positive way. "Thanks. Charlene okay?"

"Great. She helped me around the house and in the garden this morning. I know there's stuff she doesn't want to talk about yet, but she's good."

"I'm glad to hear that." She paused. "But I just found out there's a chance that someone might be coming for Charlene. I need you to keep an eye on her. I'm heading over to you now. Is there somewhere safe you can take her?"

Chantilly was quiet for a minute before she spoke. "No one will get near my baby."

"The people that are coming will be armed. It won't just be a matter of you telling them to stay away."

"Miss Nola, I am a god-fearing woman. And as far as I'm concerned, God created everything on this planet, including the guns created to defend ourselves. I got a Smith & Wesson from my daddy sitting in my bedroom, and

I know how to use it. Don't you worry about Charlene. I will keep her safe no matter what."

Nola smiled at the image. She had no doubt that Chantilly would make sure her grandbaby was safe. "That's good. I'll be there in about an hour. You just hold down the fort."

"Nola!"

Nola glanced at the door at Rascal's yell. "I've got to go now. Trust your instincts."

She disconnected the call and crossed to the living room. Rascal was already opening the front door. "Nol—" He cut off in mid-name when he caught sight go her.

"What?"

"We're too late. Someone just grabbed Lynette."

Chapter Forty

A squad car sat in the driveway of Lynette's grandmother's house. Nola pulled up in front of the house just behind Rascal. Rascal got out and strode toward the front door. Olivia and a uniform stood on the front stoop. From Olivia's agitated hand movements, she was not happy with whatever the officer was saying.

Nola followed behind Rascal. He didn't tell her to stay behind, and she wouldn't have anyway. But as he reached the path to the front door, he glanced behind him. Surprise flashed across his face. He must have figured she'd stay in the car.

He figured wrong.

As soon as Olivia caught sight of Rascal, she turned her back on the other police officer in order to march over to him. She grabbed onto Rascal's hands as if completely unaware of the black eye spreading across her face. "They took her. They took my baby."

Speaking quietly, Rascal said, "Now what hap—"

She cut him off with a glare. "Exactly what I just told

you. They took my baby. I was in the kitchen, and they broke in the front door."

Nola glanced toward the front door. The screen door was wide open. The wooden door behind it hung crookedly on its hinges.

"Do you know who it was?" Rascal asked.

Lynette's grandmother looked like she wanted to spit. "They wore masks, but you know damn well who it was. We all know it was the Compton boys. Three of them stormed into the living room. I rushed out of the kitchen and one backhanded me. I flew across the room. Got my stars shook, that's for sure. Then they went into Lynette's room and grabbed her. I tried to get to them. She was screaming the whole time. Oh my God, the screams."

This time, it was Rascal who grabbed Olivia as her knees buckled. She straightened, taking a shaky breath. "I'd only gotten to my hands and knees when one of them kicked me in the ribs."

Nola took a long look at her. She had one hand over her ribs, and the side of her face was starting to swell painfully. Someone had definitely roughed her up.

Olivia caught sight of Nola behind Rascal. Her eyes lit up. "You'll get her back. You'll get her back, won't you?"

Nola gave her a nod and then strode back toward her car.

Rascal spoke with Olivia for only another minute before he hustled after Nola. "Nola! Nola! Wait up! Nola!"

She ignored him. He had to sprint to catch her before she reached her car. He put a hand on the door to keep her from opening it. "What are you doing?"

"I'm going to get Lynette back. What are *you* doing, Detective?"

Rascal looked back at the house before he spoke. "We don't know where she is. She could be anywhere."

She nodded toward Lynette's grandmother. "Well, she seems to have a good idea. So I'll start with the Compton boys and work my way from there."

"You can't just walk in on the Compton boys. They're an Atlanta gang. They started making inroads into Delford the last couple years. There're too many of them. They have a way of making people disappear."

Nola smiled. "Don't worry. I'm good with unpleasant people."

Rascal muttered something under his breath.

"Look," Nola said, "I'm not going straight at them. I'm going to stop and speak with another source first."

The detective paused, looking at her. "Who's the other source?"

"I think perhaps it's best if you don't know."

The detective hesitated for a moment and then removed his arm from Nola's door. "I'll start with the Compton boys. I have some sources I can tap too. Look, I don't know what you're about to do, and I'm pretty sure I don't want to know, but if you find out anything about Lynette, call me."

Nola looked into the man's eyes. She knew that he felt responsible for Lynette going missing. It wasn't his fault. But that wasn't going to help him sleep at night, so she nodded. "If I find out something, you'll be my first call."

He held her car door open for her with a nod. "Then happy hunting."

Chapter Forty-One

The Delford First Baptist Church was quiet as Nola pulled into the parking lot. There wasn't a soul in sight. In fact, the only car in the lot was the red convertible Mustang that belonged to the reverend's son. After the reverend's arrest, church activities had been cancelled. Apparently Junior didn't want to take up the sacred mantle.

Nola pulled into a spot two spaces down from the Mustang. She stepped out, pausing to listen. The church was far enough back from the road that the sound of any cars that passed was muted. And the church had bought the lots on either side, meaning that even the neighbors were too far away to hear much.

Making her way to the back of the Mustang, she uncurled her keys, clasping the ignition key between her fingers. She walked along the side of the Mustang, digging the key into its side. The sound of metal on metal would make most people cringe. But right now, it made Nola smile.

She walked up to the church but found the front door was locked, so she made her way around the side. She had no luck there either.

The front door to the reverend's home was locked as well. Nola looked around, but no one was watching. She slipped her lockpick case out of her pocket and made quick work of the door. Stepping inside, she closed the door quietly behind her. Loud music played somewhere toward the back of the house. She walked past the opulent front hall and headed toward the kitchen area. She hadn't been in this part of the home during her last visit.

The kitchen was modern in design, with sleek white cabinets and white quartz countertops. The floor was a dark wood, matching the rest of the house. Along the right-hand side was a huge picture window with a table and six chairs set in front of it. A large island dominated the space. The cabinets underneath were black, with the same white countertop. Sleek, modern, expensive. The kitchen was a chef's dream.

But Nola had the distinct impression that it didn't get much use. There were a couple of takeout boxes on the counter that suggested the most important meals were prepared somewhere else. Off the kitchen was a screened-in porch with French doors. The French doors were thrown wide, and music blared from inside.

Junior sat on a lounge chair with his back to the kitchen. His head bopped in time with the beat, as did his bare feet. A glass of scotch was in his hand, a cigar in his other hand. His shirt was unbuttoned.

Apparently Junior's not overly broken up about his dad's incarceration.

A wireless Sony speaker sat on the ground to the left of

the French doors. Nola walked over and pressed the power button. The music cut off immediately.

Junior's head jerked up. He looked over with an annoyed frown, then jolted to his feet when he caught sight of Nola. "What the hell you doing here? Get out!"

Nola shook her head. "Oh, I don't think so, Junior. We've got some business to discuss."

His eyes hard, he glared. "I don't have any business with you. Get the hell out of here before I call the cops."

She smiled. "Oh, you don't want to do that. Because then I'll have to have a long conversation with the cops about your extracurricular activities."

"What the hell you talking about?" he demanded, but the slightest pause in his reply gave away his worry.

Shrugging, she said, "I had a friend look over the books from the church. You'd be amazed at what they found. There seem to be quite a few discrepancies in the finances. That's your area, right, Junior? You keep track of all the money for your daddy's little business, don't you?"

She straightened his shoulders. "A church is not a business. It's a calling."

Nola snorted. "Yeah, sure. Now I can guarantee that this conversation isn't going to go very well if you keep up with that line. I think it's time we laid all our cards on the table."

"I don't have anything to say to you. You can talk to my lawyer." He went to grab for his cell phone, which lay on the table next to the lounge chair.

She snatched it from the table before he could reach it.

"What are you—"

With a dead expression, she tossed it to the tile floor. The unmistakable sound of crunching glass cut through the air.

Junior's nostrils flared. "You Northern bitch. I heard they don't teach their women lessons up there." He cracked his knuckles. "Well, you're about to learn one down here."

The memory of Deacon Baker saying almost exactly the same thing wafted through her mind. She shook her head. "You boys all need some new lines."

Junior didn't respond, at least not verbally. Instead he tucked his shoulders and dove toward Nola, trying to tackle her at the waist.

The move was so obvious, she was almost embarrassed for him. She backed up only a step and then grabbed the back of his head, twisting his neck to the left while shifting her body to the right to redirect his energy.

Junior let out a screech as his feet came up off the floor. He slammed to the ground on his back. Nola picked up her left foot and slammed it into his face.

He let out another scream. His nose was now a fountain of blood. As he wailed, he revealed a new chip in his tooth.

She felt zero sympathy for him. She crouched down next to him. "Where's Lynette?"

"My nose! You broke my nose!" He wailed.

"And I'll break more than that if you don't start talking. Where. Is. Lynette?"

"You bitch." Junior rolled onto his side, flailing wildly with his left fist for Nola's face. Nola slapped the punch away before grabbing onto his wrist and then slamming her own fist into his already-broken nose.

Another scream this one extremely high-pitched. She'd never actually heard another man make that particularly noise before She leaned down again. "This is not going to get easier for you. I suggest you start talking before I lose my temper."

Big ugly sobs shook Junior's shoulders. But instead of pity, all she felt was disgust.

"Where. Is. Lynette?" She grabbed onto his hand, pulling on his little pinky and starting to extend it back toward his wrist. "I'm getting annoyed at having to ask the same question over and over again."

"I don't know!" He cried.

"Wrong answer."

Nola yanked the pinky back to his wrist, which resulted in a satisfying pop. Junior screeched.

Nola kept hold of his hand even as he tried to pull it away. She grabbed his index finger. "You have nine more fingers. And then we'll start on some body parts that you might really care about."

"I don't know!" he wailed.

She started to apply pressure to the finger. "Then what *do* you know?"

Junior's chest heaved. Sobs wracked his frame.

Nola added more pressure to his index finger.

"The Compton boys! All I know for sure is that the Compton boys said they'd take care of her."

An image of Lynette looking terrified when Nola had first met her swam through her mind. It took everything in her not to snap the man's arm in two. She spoke through gritted teeth. "And at *whose* suggestion did they decide to take care of her?"

"I don't—"

Nola yanked his index finger all the way back.

Junior screeched again as the finger broke. He tried to curl into the fetal position, but Nola's hold wouldn't let him, so he simply writhed on the floor.

Sweat poured down his face along with the blood

staining his shirt and painting his chest. His eyes were bloodshot from tears and pain. "Okay, okay. I did it. I called them. But she was going to testify. If she did that, everything my dad and I built would've gone away. The church, the cars, the money, all of it."

Her rage barely contained, Nola spoke softly. "So you had them make the problem disappear."

Junior nodded his head.

Nola punched him in the ribs. "Out loud."

"Yes, yes! I had them make the problem disappear."

"Use her name." She latched onto another finger.

His whole body trembled. "Lynette! I had them make Lynette disappear."

She took a breath, trying to calm herself down. She wanted to paint the room with this guy's blood. First his father tried to take the child's innocence, and now the son was trying to finish the job. "*What* exactly did you tell them to do with her?"

Junior tried to shrug, but it came out as more of a painful contortion. He refused to meet her gaze as he spoke, staring at the opposite wall. "I didn't tell them anything to do with her. I just told them that she was causing problems."

"Why? Why would you tell *them* that she was causing problems?"

He was quiet for a few moments.

Nola squeezed his pointer finger.

He shook harder, trying to pull his hand back, but once again Nola refused to let go. Tears streamed down his face. He moaned. "No, no. They have a reputation. For being able to get rid of girls that are causing trouble."

"Where did you hear that?"

"I don't know."

"Think harder." Nola pulled on his finger.

The words burst from in, his face pinched with pain. "S-somewhere over at Haverford, the Retreat!"

"The Retreat?"

Junior nodded, saliva flying from his mouth as he spoke. "There were rumors. They could get rid of problems. You just had to know who to ask."

"And who did you ask?"

"A friend. At the club. He got in touch with the Compton boys. I don't know how. You'd have to ask him."

"What's his name?" She demanded.

"Craig. Craig Bradford."

Nola had no idea who that was. But she pictured the hoity-toity Honoria Haverford.

Damn it. I should have looked for more connections to the Retreat. She knew Anna Mae and Tasha had connections, but the Compton boys had thrown her off. Then she thought of the video Teddy had sent her. God dammit, it had been in front of her the whole time. She stood up, shoving Junior back against the floor as she did so.

He cringed, closing his eyes. When no strike came, he opened them slowly. "What are you going to do with me?"

She glared at him, rolling her hands into fists to try and keep herself from reaching for him again. She even took a step back to keep him out of kicking distance. "Not what you deserve. But I'm sure the cops will be very interested in the story you just told me."

His eyes grew wide, his head shaking from side to side. "I'm not . . . I'm not telling them that. I'll go to prison."

Nola shook her head as she stared down at the man. "You're really not very bright, are you? You *will* tell them everything you just told me. In fact, you already have." She held up her phone. The red light shone brightly, indicating that it was still recording. She turned the recording off.

His eyes grew large as he stared at the phone and then Nola. "You won't use that. If you do, you'll get in trouble too."

She leaned forward. "You don't understand, Junior. I'm a ghost, and the law doesn't touch us ghosts."

Chapter Forty-Two

Nola snagged the zip ties tight around Junior's wrists. She grabbed one of the kitchen chairs and pulled it into the entrance of the porch room. Then she hauled him up and deposited him in the chair. She used more zip ties to attach him to the chair.

He offered no resistance, as compliant as a doll. Nola wasn't surprised. Guys like Junior lived in a world where their toughness was never tested. They just assumed they were tough because, hey, why not? But like all faux tough guys, a little pain took all the bravado away.

"You can't leave me here like this. You can't—" He grunted as she tightened the zip ties behind him.

She grabbed the dishtowel from the counter. "Sorry, what was that?"

He glared at her. "I said—"

As soon as he opened his mouth, she shoved the dishrag inside. His eyes went wide. He rocked from side to side, his cheeks flaming pink.

"Sorry, can't hear you," she said with a shrug.

He screamed behind the rag.

She walked back into the porch room and picked up the speaker. After turning up the volume, she headed back to the kitchen and placed it on the counter right next to Junior.

Taking his phone, she grabbed his thumb and pressed it to the screen, unlocking it.

Junior's face was now bright red. She raised an eyebrow. "You're going to give yourself a heart attack if you keep screaming like that."

She scrolled through the station options on Amazon Music before settling on a big-band station. Then she placed the phone in a drawer on the other side of the island before returning to Junior. She patted him on the head. "Now, don't you go anywhere. I'll be back in a little bit after I've spoken with Bradford. And you better pray that he has something to tell me."

Junior struggled against the ties, shooting daggers at her. Nola turned her back on him and headed for the front door. Once in the foyer, she pulled her cell phone from her pocket and dialed Rascal. He answered quickly. "What do you know?"

"Craig Bradford. What do you know about him?"

Rascal answered after only a short pause. "Former gangbanger. Works in the kitchen over at the Retreat. Did a stint for a few aggravated assaults, got out about five years ago. He's been relatively clean ever since."

"What does 'relatively clean' mean?" She asked.

"He never did anything that would get his parole revoked. So as of a year ago, he's officially off state supervision. He's caught up in this?"

"According to my source, he is. You got an address?" Nola asked.

"Yeah. He lives over on Magnolia Lane. Number 16. I'll meet you there," Rascal said.

"Okay." Nola disconnected the call and immediately pulled up a map of Delford. Magnolia was only a few blocks away. As she let herself out of the reverend's home, Nola called Bishop. glancing around the parking lot, she hustled out to her car. No one was around.

It took Bishop a few rings before she answered. Her voice was breathless when she did. "Nola. Hey. What's going on?"

Nola frowned. There was something odd in Bishop's tone, but she didn't have time to suss it out. "I need some surveillance."

"Uh, sure, sure. How's the case going?" Bishop asked.

"Another girl was taken."

"Oh, man. Okay, go ahead, give me the address."

"16 Magnolia Lane, Delford," Nola said.

"Hold on." Bishop went silent, but Nola could picture her hunched over the keyboard, the glow of the monitor reflecting off her cheeks. Her hair was probably pulled back in one of those messy buns, a pencil stuck in it.

The sense of homesickness came out of nowhere. Nola started at its unfamiliar appearance as she slipped behind the wheel of the Bronco. No time for that now. Lynette was the girl she needed to focus on. She quickly put the car in gear and tore out of the parking lot.

Pushing down heavily on the accelerator, she pictured Lynette's face the last time she had seen her. *God dammit.* There were predators everywhere she looked. They'd just gotten the reverend behind bars, and now she had this Bradford guy. It was like an unending game of whack-a-mole.

"I've got it," Bishop's voice came through the speakerphone, pulling her from her thoughts. "It's a residential home. Couple of cars on the street. It looks like about maybe a quarter-of-an-acre plot. Not a lot of movement on the street, and the house looks quiet. But there's lights on, a car in the drive."

Nola frowned. "How'd you get that? That seems a little too accurate for satellite imagery."

"Um, I tapped into some security cameras in the area. The house across the street and the one behind has one, as well as a few street cams."

"Can you keep an eye on it for me and let me know if you see any movement at the house?" Nola asked.

"Will do. Is that where the girl is?"

Picturing Lynette, Nola's jaw tightened. "I sure hope so."

Chapter Forty-Three

Magnolia Lane was a step up from Crenshaw, but it still had a feeling of neglect to it. There wasn't anybody out walking around at this hour, but there were more than a few cars. In a glance, Nola recognized that at least half a dozen of them were permanently in their spots until the town towed them away.

She drove slowly past 16 Magnolia. It was an old two-story colonial with a chain-link fence around it that had come undone in eight- to ten-foot swaths. An old pink flamingo stood straight up in the yard, as if guarding the front lawn. Nola pulled into the side of the street across from number 16 and one house down. "Any movement?"

"Quiet. There's been no movement since I started watching." Bishop paused. "You sure this is the right address?"

Nola shook her head. "No."

She grabbed an earpiece and mic from the bag on the passenger seat of the car. Placing the bud in her ear, she clipped the mic to her collar and activated them. "Can you hear me?"

"Loud and clear."

"I'm going in."

"Hold up. A car's coming down the street."

Nola glanced in the rearview mirror and recognized Rascal's car. "It's okay. That's my backup."

Shock reverberated through Bishop's voice. "You brought backup?"

Nola ignored the question and got out of the car. She pulled the duffel bag over to the driver's seat and stood in the driver's door while she slipped on her bulletproof vest. She grabbed her Glock and slid it into the holster at her waist, then she grabbed a couple of magazines.

By the time Rascal joined her on the sidewalk, she was fully loaded.

Rascal eyed her from head to toe and just gave a nod, not making a comment on her accessories. He'd removed his jacket and his hat, and he'd put on his own bulletproof vest. He nodded to the two cars in front of 16. "Those two belong to Big Boi and Shane. They're members of the Compton gang."

There was a look of disgust on his face as Rascal stared at one of the cars.

"What is it?" Nola asked.

"Big Boi. He was suspected of abusing his neighbor when he was a kid. The girl was six years younger than him. He was accused again in high school and once again a few years back. But the victims disappeared." The detective met Nola's gaze.

She just gave him a nod while inside she cursed the system that let these monsters walk the street, preying on young victims. "How do you want to play this?"

"We've got probable cause to believe Lynette's inside. We're going in." Rascal said.

"Got a warrant, Detective?" She asked.

Shaking his head, he continued his surveillance of the house. "I'll take the heat for it."

"Okay, I'll take the front, you take the back," Nola said.

Rascal shook his head. "No, I'll take the front. You take the back."

She rolled her eyes. "Seriously?"

"If anyone's watching, it's better if they see a cop busting in the front door than you," he reminded her.

"Fine, whatever." She tapped mic by her throat. "You got anything?"

"Still quiet," Bishop said.

Rascal frowned. "Who are you talking to?"

"My inner demons."

Bishop snorted into the earpiece.

Nola smiled. "Let's go."

Chapter Forty-Four

Nola crept along the driveway. She'd told Rascal to give her to a count of twenty to get into position. She moved quickly, staying in the shadows. She wasn't sure how many people were inside or what to expect. But if Lynette was in there, she was getting her out. She knew that much.

Shadows moved along the windows at the back of the house as she rounded it. She glanced inside and noted two men sitting around the kitchen table, a box of pizza in between them. A shotgun sat on the counter behind them. She caught sight of a handgun at the waist of one of the guys. She assumed the other was equally armed, although she couldn't see from her vantage point.

"Police!" A crash sounded at the front door.

Dammit, he's early.

Nola sprinted up the three steps at the back of the house and kicked in the door. One of the men had already run toward the front of the house. The other one turned to the back door, gun in hand.

Nola didn't give him a chance to raise it. She caught him center mass. He fell backward, crashing into the kitchen table and dropping to the ground. She kicked his gun away from him as she checked the corners of the room before stepping into the hall. Gunfire rang out from the front of the house.

Bishop's voice called out through the earpiece. "Car's coming up the street."

Dammit. Nola made her way down the hall. Through a bedroom, she caught movement in the house next door. A large man had someone over their shoulder. She caught the flash of a pink shirt and dark hair. Lynette.

Two men stood on either side of the hallway, facing the front door. Somehow, with the gunfire, they hadn't heard Nola coming in the back. She aimed for one and then the other. Both dropped.

"Clear! Coming out!" she yelled as she hustled through the living room and out the front door.

Rascal was flattened against the side of the front of the house. She blew past him as the car in the driveway next door flared to life. She sprinted across the lawn, jumping the fence and continuing across the other lawn. The car had already reached the edge of the street.

Nola pulled out her gun, aiming at the back of the old Cadillac. The tail was low, making it difficult to get to the wheels. And she wasn't sure if Lynette had been put in the trunk.

As if she heard her name, Lynette popped up in the backseat of the car. Duct tape was over her mouth. Her eyes were large, and Nola could tell she was screaming. Nola sighted the car. But it was bouncing too much to get a clear shot. The car put on a burst of speed and charged down the road.

Nola changed direction and sprinted for her car. "Lynette's in the car!"

She leaped into the driver's seat, putting the key in the ignition and slamming on the gas. She initiated a U-turn, going up on the curb on the other side of the road and slamming down hard before taking off after the old Caddy.

Even with the speed with which she managed to get to her car and get it turned in the right direction, the Cadillac was out of sight by the time she was able to follow it.

She tapped the mic at her throat. "Bishop."

The reply came back immediately. "I've got them. Take the first right."

Nola took a right hard. The back left wheel came up as she turned. But she didn't slow. Ahead, she saw the taillights of the sedan. She pressed down on the accelerator.

Come on, come on, she urged the engine.

The car took a left, swinging wide to make the turn.

Nola was only a few feet behind as she did the same. They were now in the old business district, not too far from the warehouse at Sweet Oak. There weren't any houses around. She'd only seen one person walking. There were very few cars on the street as well. She pressed down on the accelerator and slammed into the back of the Cadillac.

It bucked, the back of the car fishtailing and slowing slightly.

Nola slipped along beside it. As soon as the hood of her car was level with the back wheels of the Cadillac, she turned into it.

The Cadillac fishtailed again. The driver lost control. Nola slammed on her brakes as the sedan did a 360 and ended up facing the wrong way on the road.

Nola was out of the car in a second, the Glock in her

hand. The driver's door of the other car kicked open. A man stumbled out, firing wildly.

Nola ducked down behind her own door. The man stepped into view, and she took a shot, catching him in the shoulder. He collapsed to the ground.

The passenger-side door of the car flung open. A man sprinted out as the back door of the car opened as well. Another man lumbered out, carrying Lynette as a shield in front of him.

Rascal screeched to a stop behind her. His driver's door opened quickly, and he stepped from behind it. "Release the girl! Lie face down on the road!"

Nola moved forward and quickly kicked the gun away from the man she'd taken down. She looked up as another shot rang out. The man holding Lynette shot at Rascal as he stood exposed in the open space between his car and the Cadillac.

Rascal returned gunfire, and the man went down. Lynette hit the ground hard, rolling away from the man and lying still.

Nola put three of her own bullets into the man. He stumbled back with each hit and then collapsed on the ground, not moving. She shot a quick glance at Rascal. "Rascal, are you—" Her stomach dropped.

He was on the ground, a large pool of blood soaking his shirt just below his bulletproof vest.

Chapter Forty-Five

Nola stared at the retreating back of the one remaining man. He was out of range. She wanted more than anything to go after him. But Lynette lay unconscious on the side of the road, and Rascal was bleeding pretty badly. She could go after the man, but she'd seen wounds like Rascal's before, and even with medical intervention it was fifty-fifty.

Damn it.

She ran over to Lynette and threw her over her shoulder before sprinting for her car. Carefully, she placed her on the passenger seat and strapped her in, noting the rise and fall of her chest as she did so. She then raced for the driver's side. Throwing herself behind the wheel, she threw the car into reverse, coming to a screeching halt right next to Rascal.

She leaped out and then yanked open the back door. She grabbed Rascal under his arms and dragged him to the door. Crawling in, she hefted him onto the seat, banging his tailbone and then his legs in her attempt to get him in the car.

She grabbed the first-aid kit from the duffel bag and rifled through it, praying Avad had packed it. She found a towel and yanked it out, then let out a shout when she found the XSTAT. "Yes!"

She grabbed the applicator. It looked like a giant syringe. It was filled with small sponges that rapidly expanded. It had been designed for treating gunshot wounds on the battlefield. She lifted his vest to reach the wound, and blood immediately poured out. She pushed past it, blood coating her hands as she found the entry wound. She injected the sponges, feeling as they filled up the space. Then she placed the towel on top.

"Rascal, wake up. Wake up, Rascal!"

He didn't stir.

Nola reared back and slapped him hard, leaving a bloody handprint on the side of his face.

Rascal's head stirred. His eyes flickered open. "Wh—"

She grabbed his hands and placed them on the towel. "You need to hold this down. Do you hear me?"

He blinked.

"Damn it, Rascal, you are going to bleed out. You need to keep the pressure on."

Rascal blinked a few more times before he nodded. "'kay."

Nola knew that was as good as she was going to get. Backing out of the door, she sprinted back to the driver's seat and floored it as soon as she was inside. A quick glance at Lynette showed that she was still out, a large goose egg beginning to grow on the side of her forehead. But she was still breathing.

She glanced in the rearview mirror but couldn't see Rascal from her position. "Rascal, you still with me?"

It took a long time for him to answer. "Here," he mumbled.

"You keep pressure on. We're almost there. Sing me a song."

His eyes flickered open. "Wh—"

"A song, sing me a song, any song," Nola ordered.

He gave the slightest of shakes. "I don't—"

"The Star Spangled Banner. Everyone knows that one."

His voice was weak as he began to sing. "Oh, say can you see . . ."

She pressed down on the accelerator and prayed that they made it to the hospital in time.

Chapter Forty-Six

Rascal sang almost all the way to the hospital before his voice fizzled out.

"Rascal? Rascal, you still with me?" Nola's tires squealed as she turned into the hospital driveway.

No answer.

Honking her horn, she pulled up right in front of the emergency room with an abrupt stop. She vaulted out of the driver's seat as a man in scrubs appeared through the sliding doors.

"Get a stretcher. Gunshot wound."

The man disappeared back inside and reappeared seconds later with a stretcher and two other individuals. Nola had the back door open as they wheeled the stretcher up to the car. She reached in and grabbed Rascal underneath his shoulders. One of the other residents moved to quickly grab him underneath the waist as Nola pulled him out of the car. A third grabbed him at the feet. Together they got him onto the stretcher with a little more jostling than Nola would've liked.

"He took a shot to the stomach," she explained.

The first man that had stepped out of the doors nodded, checking the wound. Two uniformed police officers rushed to the door, a hand on their weapons.

Oh crap. Nola had hoped there wouldn't be police at the hospital. That way she could drop Lynette and Rascal off and then track down Anna Mae. She had the feeling time was of the essence.

"Ma'am, ma'am, you need to step away from Detective Nealon."

Nola closed her eyes, letting out a frustrated breath. She had blood up to her elbows, and she was the one dropping him off. They were going to hold her for hours. Hours she did not have. More importantly, hours Anna Mae did not have.

"No," Rascal croaked out. "She didn't do this."

Rascal's voice was so low that the police officers couldn't hear him. One of the doctors spoke up. "He said she didn't do this."

One of the officers moved so he could keep an eye on Nola while he leaned down to speak with Rascal. Nola took a step back, but the other officer twitched. She stopped moving. She had a feeling that if she took too many steps, he would pull that trigger. "Lynette Granger is in the car. She needs help too."

The officer with Rascal straightened. "She's not the shooter."

The other officer watched Nola and finally nodded, removing his hand from his weapon. Nola quickly turned to the car and yanked open the passenger door. Lynette was still out, her head turned to the side. Nola unstrapped her and carried her into the hospital, shocked at how light she was. "It's okay, Lynette. You're safe now."

With her eyes closed, she looked so young, so peaceful. Nola would've liked to have been shocked that someone could target a young girl who looked so innocent. But those blinders had been ripped off her at a young age. And the evil that people could do to one another no longer shocked her.

At all.

But it did still make her angry. She placed Lynette on an empty stretcher. One of the police officers stopped next to her. "What happened?"

Nola took a moment before responding, wanting to make sure she didn't say anything that would cause her or Rascal more problems down the road. "Rascal and I found her. He was shot by one of the Compton boys. They were holding her."

The officer pulled out a notepad. "I'm going to need you to take me through everything that happened."

"I will. But we need to call Lynette's grandmother first."

Nola stepped from the stretcher, but a small hand reached out and grabbed hers. Nola looked down. Lynette's eyes flickered open. "Nana?"

Nola winced as she noticed the blood transfer from her hand onto Lynette's, but there was no helping that now. "She'll be here soon, sweetheart. You're safe now," Nola said softly.

Lynette's eyes closed, but she didn't let go of Nola's hand. So Nola leaned back against the stretcher and called her grandmother to let her know she'd found Lynette. Then she explained to the officer about the Compton boys holding Lynette. Lynette held on to her the whole time.

A nurse came by and washed her hands for her. He even managed to wash most of the one Lynette held.

A detective arrived, and Nola had to go through the

whole spiel again. She did, staying next to Lynette while from the corner of her eye she watched doctors work on Rascal. They set up a couple of lines and worked furiously around him. Nola's gut clenched.

Please let him be all right.

The doors to the emergency room opened and closed a half dozen times during her recitation. Nola didn't recognize any of the people stepping through. An ambulance pulled up, and the police officers left her to go help bring some drunk individuals into the ER.

Lynette's eyes were closed again, but her hand was firmly clasped around Nola's. Yelling erupted from the ambulance bay. A tall muscular man with a knife sticking out of his skull was being wrestled through the door by the two cops. The guy had to be high as a kite, because the knife in his skull wasn't even slightly bothering him. But from the horrified looks of the people in the emergency waiting room, it was disturbing everyone else.

The police officer had just managed to wrestle the man into one of the rooms when the emergency room doors opened again. Olivia bustled through, her eyes wide. Her head shifted from side to side before she caught sight of Nola and hurried toward her.

Olivia's steps faltered as her eyes locked on the blood across Nola's jeans.

"It's not Lynette's," Nola said as Olivia reached her.

Olivia stopped at the edge of the stretcher, her eyes taking in Lynette's form, searching for any injuries.

"She got hit on the head. It knocked her out. She'll need to get checked out to make sure she doesn't have a concussion. But other than that, I don't think she has any major injuries. A doctor hasn't been over yet, though. The ER's been a little busy."

"Lynette, baby? It's Nana," Olivia said as she leaned down.

Lynette's eyes flickered open. "Nana?"

Olivia smiled down at her, her eyes bright. "It's me, baby girl. You're safe."

The young girl's eyes immediately filled with tears. She released Nola's hand and reached for her grandmother. Olivia gathered her up into her arms and held her tight. "It's okay, baby. You're safe. You're safe. It's going to be okay."

Lynette sobbed, leaning against her grandmother.

Stepping away, Nola let the two of them have their moment. But she knew that Olivia hadn't been entirely honest with her granddaughter. It wasn't going to be okay. Not for Lynette, and not for any of the other girls. Not for a very long time.

Chapter Forty-Seven

The lights were bright in the hospital bathroom. They flickered, reminding Nola of a flytrap. She washed the blood off her hands that the nurse had missed. The water slowly turned from red to pink to clear as it swirled down the drain.

She turned the water off and leaned against the edge of the sink, looking at her reflection. "Dammit."

She ripped two feet of paper towels from the roll sitting on the counter. Crumpling it up, she ran the edge of it under the water and then rubbed at the blood that had somehow gotten on her face. Satisfied that she'd gotten all of it after inspecting her face and tilting her chin in the mirror, she dried off her hands and dumped the used towels in the receptacle. Blood was sprayed across her black tank top and on her jeans. The tank top wasn't a problem. The blood couldn't be seen. But it had dried, leaving the top stiff. Occasionally flecks of dried blood would fall off as she moved.

Her jeans were even worse because there was no hiding the blood splashed across them.

Tearing her eyes from the macabre display, Nola leaned against the counter, her head down. Rascal had been taken into surgery. A doctor had examined Lynette and thought there was a good chance she had a concussion. She'd stay overnight for observation.

The cops had made it clear they wanted Nola here for further questions. But that did not work with Nola's plans. Her mind raced, trying to figure out her next steps. Finally, she straightened, grabbed her phone from her back pocket and her keys from the front one and strode out of the bathroom, heading for the stairwell.

She ducked into a room as a police officer headed toward her. She knew that they were going to want to ask more questions. But she needed to get out of here.

She slipped out and into the stairwell and went up one floor. Stepping out, she turned left, heading toward the main entrance. Five minutes later, she was back in her Bronco and heading for home.

The third Compton guy was long gone by now, and she'd never gotten a good look at him. The only other link she had was the Retreat. But she didn't know who there was the connection. Maybe it was only Bradford.

Damn it. Nothing about this case was going right. It had completely blown up her usual approach. She'd gotten to know the people involved, she'd been interacting with law enforcement, and now she was about to call Bishop.

Again.

She didn't want to take this step. It would make everything so much harder. But right now, she needed help. Anna Mae needed help.

But she didn't know who to ask. Between Delford and

257

Haverford, they had maybe ten cops, including part-timers. Plus she wasn't sure who in the police department she could trust. And there was always a chance they would tip off the guys that she was looking for. So they were out.

So where did that leave her?

Her phone rang. She glanced at the name, and with a grunt, answered it. "Bishop?"

"Hey, Nola. Are you okay?"

Nola's voice was tougher than she had planned, but the emotions clawing their way up her throat were also unplanned. "I'm fine. Do you have something?"

"Yeah, I, uh, followed that guy. He doubled back to his car on Magnolia," Bishop said.

Relief flowed through Nola. "Where'd he go?"

"He stopped at another house, picked up two more guys. Then they went east. But I lost them after that."

Damn it.

Bishop continued quickly. "But I backtracked and actually managed to track them down pretty much up until you showed up. And right before they grabbed Lynette, they went over to Haverford. They stopped at—"

Nola cut in. "The Retreat."

"Yeah. They stayed for about thirty minutes and then headed right for Lynette."

"Were you able to get eyes on them inside the Retreat? See who they met up with?"

"No," Bishop said.

Nola's mind whirled. "Okay. I think I know how to see who they met. Thanks, Bishop."

"You're welcome. I'll see you soon." Bishop disconnected the call.

And Nola frowned at her choice of words. Maybe it was

just a slip of the tongue. A normal ending to a phone conversation. Bishop always said that to her before . . .

Well, just before.

She put Bishop out of her mind. Scrolling through her contact list, she punched the button for Teddy Haverford.

"Hello?"

"Teddy, it's Nola. I need your help again." She quickly explained what she needed, and they hung up. Nola had just turned onto her road when her phone rang again. "Teddy?"

"I'm sending you the data. I'll go through it here on my side too."

"Good. I'll be home in two minutes."

She slowed as she approached her house. A car sat in her spot on the driveway. And sitting on its bumper was Bishop.

Chapter Forty-Eight

Trying to calm the rage of emotions rushing through her, Nola pulled in front of the house. But there wasn't enough time to hold back the wave. Throwing open the door, she stormed up the drive. "What the hell are you——"

Avad stepped out of the shadows on the front porch.

Nola glared at him. "What the hell are the *two* of you doing here?"

"Um, hi, Nola. It's good to see you," Bishop said, stepping away from her car.

Nola growled as she climbed her porch. Avad opened the front door. She strode past him. "What are you two doing here?" she repeated.

"Don't be mad," Bishop said as she followed her in, her messenger bag slung over her shoulder. "We thought you needed some help."

"I don't," Nola said through gritted teeth.

Bishop stared at her. "You have multiple missing girls, they've been taken by a dangerous gang, and your only backup just got shot."

"I don't want you near this." She turned to include Avad, who had stepped into the room and closed the door behind him. "Either of you."

"Well, we're here. And we're helping," Bishop said. "Look, I've been going through the data, and I don't think it's just Anna Mae and Lynette. I think girls are being grabbed all over the state. And I noticed a pattern. It happens every year at this time. I don't think this is a simple disappearance. I think we're talking human trafficking."

Sighing, Nola rubbed her forehead. "Yeah, I've been thinking the same thing." Her phone beeped. "That's Teddy. He's sending me the recordings from the Retreat. I want to see who the Compton boys were meeting with."

"Why don't you go get changed? I'll go through the data," Bishop said.

Nola wanted to argue, but she felt this ticking clock at the back of her head pounding away. "Okay. I'll show you my setup and log you in."

"No need. I already hacked into your system. I can do it from here." Bishop waved her hand toward her laptop.

Nola wanted to be mad, but it was such a Bishop thing to do. "Fine. Tell me when you've found something." She headed to her bedroom and closed the door. She pulled a fresh pair of jeans from her bag, but instead of getting changed, she sank onto the bed.

Bishop and Avad were here. She hadn't seen Bishop in person in two years. She'd changed a lot in that time. When she'd last seen her, Bishop still had traces of baby fat. But now, now she was all angles and sharp edges. She looked good. She looked grown up.

A pang rattled through Nola's heart. *And I missed it.*

She stood up. *No. It's better for Bishop this way. She had a chance to grow up. I can't be selfish.*

Nola locked down the rest of her thoughts, shoving her feelings aside. Right now, she only had time to focus on Anna Mae. She deserved all her attention. Bishop was safe. Anna Mae was the one in danger.

And that's where my focus needs to stay.

By the time Nola got back to the living room, Bishop had the Retreat recordings queued up. Bishop sat, leaning forward, her hair pulled back with a headband as she studied the screen, searching for the Mustang.

Nola slipped into the kitchen. Avad sat at the kitchen table. Walking over to the cabinet, she pulled out a protein bar. "Want one?"

"No, I'm good," Avad said.

"So how long have you two been in Georgia?"

"What do you mean?"

Nola unwrapped the bar and took a bite. She couldn't remember the last time she'd eaten, and she knew she'd need some fuel for what lay ahead. "You got here too fast. It should have taken you hours. Yet here you are on my doorstep, an hour after Rascal was shot. So how long have you been here?"

"We never left. We stayed in Atlanta. Once Bishop learned about the shooting, she insisted you'd need our help." Avad paused. "I think she was right."

Nola sighed. "If it's a human trafficking ring, then yes. But not if we can't find it."

"Guys?" Bishop called from the other room.

Nola met Avad's gaze, and then they headed into the living room. Nola leaned over Bishop's shoulder to stare at the screen. The scent of vanilla wafted off Bishop's skin.

She always smelled like vanilla. Nola had first gotten her a vanilla-scented moisturizer when she was fourteen. She had fallen in love with the scent and never went without it.

Nola cleared her throat, chasing away the memory. "What have you got?"

"I found the car." She pointed at the screen.

"When was this?" Nola asked.

"About three hours ago."

Before Lynette was grabbed.

The Mustang entered the estate through the servants' entrance and headed down the long drive. She frowned as the car turned away from the main house.

"Do you know where that road leads?" Avad asked.

"Yeah, there's an old boathouse. But no one really uses it. Or at least, that's what I was told."

The car disappeared from view. Bishop frowned, searching for more images on the feed, but apparently there weren't many cameras along the road leading to the boathouse. And they weren't getting any good angles on the car. Every once in a while, they'd catch a flash of a bumper or the edge of the hood but no complete shots of the car.

"Huh," Bishop grunted.

"What?" Nola asked.

"There aren't a lot of cameras along this way, but it's almost like the driver knows where they are and is keeping out of sight." Bishop fast-forwarded until the car reappeared on the road.

It didn't go back to the main house this time either. Just headed for the main entrance and out the gate. It took a right, heading toward Delford.

You just got your marching orders, didn't you? Nola thought. Out loud she asked, "How long was the car out of sight?"

Bishop glanced at the time stamp. "Only fifteen minutes."

"Can you see who they met with?"

"Hold on." Bishop switched to look at the other cameras to see if anyone else had headed toward the boathouse. Just before the car arrived at the boathouse lane, a single golf cart cut across the lawns and headed in that direction. Bishop followed it, and sure enough, it headed down a separate path that also led to the boathouse. Then it disappeared from view. Nola glanced at the time stamp. Just about the same time the Mustang had headed to the boathouse.

Bishop fast-forwarded again to the time the Mustang left. Sure enough, the golf cart reappeared, heading toward the main house. The angle was wrong, so she couldn't get a good look at the driver. Bishop followed the cart all the way back to the main house. Finally, it pulled up around the back. The driver stepped out and turned toward the camera.

Freezing the shot, Bishop zoomed in on the man's face. "Do you know who that is?"

Recognition jolted through Nola. She'd never met him. But she knew. "That's Beau Haverford, Teddy's brother."

Chapter Forty-Nine

Nola stared at the image of Beau Haverford frozen on the screen. She'd never met Teddy's brother and Honoria's stepson. But she'd done her research on him. He was the same age as Honoria, and as far as she could tell, lived a life of luxury. He'd never had a job and lived off of his investments, which a hedge fund managed for him.

"Where is he now?" Nola asked.

"Um . . ." Bishop traced Beau's movements. He stopped at the main house for only a few minutes before reappearing with a basket. He put it in the back of the golf cart and then drove off, heading farther into the Retreat. Nola had never been to that part.

Bishop fast-forwarded as Beau followed a paved path. Finally, he parked next to a Porsche at a small house. All the lights were on inside. Beau grabbed the basket and hurried to the door. He opened the door and closed it quickly behind him.

"Okay, good. It looks like he's going to be there for a

little while." Nola turned from the screen, heading to her bedroom. She'd reload on weapons and then head out.

"Wait, good? What does that mean?" Bishop asked as she followed her.

"It means I'm going to have a chat with Teddy's big brother," Nola said as she flipped open the lid of her trunk and then frowned. She should take all of it. If Beau was connected, she would get the address out of him where Anna Mae was being held. And she didn't want to waste time by having to come back for any of her gear.

Locking the trunk, she started to drag it out to the living room. "Hey, Avad, can you throw this in the back of my car?"

"Yes." He walked over and with enviable ease, lifted the heavy trunk and headed for the front of the house. Bishop hustled over and opened the front door for him.

Nola headed into the kitchen and grabbed a couple of power bars and refilled the water containers.

"So you think Beau's going to just tell you what you need to know?"

"After some persuading, he will."

Bishop bit her lip.

"Look, I didn't ask you to join me. You're not a part of this. But I need answers from him, and . . ." Nola took a breath. "You know what? I'm not doing this. I'm not explaining my methods or asking for permission. He has info. I'm getting it from him. End of story."

She walked past Bishop, grabbing her car keys and heading for the door.

"What about us? We want to help," Bishop said following once again.

"Not with this part." Nola stepped outside.

Bishop was right behind her. "Okay, but we're coming."

Nola turned to tell her no, but Bishop spoke before she could say anything. "Look, I know you don't want us there. But if you get the location, you're going to need our help. We'll stay outside the Retreat. And once you have a location on the girls, we'll take off. The girls will need us."

Nola looked at Bishop. Her face was set, her eyes determined. This was not the young girl she'd last seen two years ago. "Fine."

Bishop pulled a flash drive from her pocket. "But before you go, there's something I need to show you."

"What is it?"

Bishop smiled. "A way to get Beau to talk."

Avad and Bishop followed Nola over to Haverford. They pulled off at the main street, in front of a cafe that was still open.

Nola watched them through the rearview mirror. Bishop stepped out of the car, highlighted by the streetlights, and watched Nola drive away. It felt like a fist was clutching Nola's heart, memories of the last time she'd driven away from Bishop tormenting her.

She pulled her gaze away and focused on the road. She took a few deep breaths, concentrating on her breathing. In, out. In, out. Her heart calmed, and she turned her attention to the mission.

She needed to know where the girls had been sent. If Beau was the conduit, then he would know. If not, Nola would have to track down Derek and see what she could get from him.

But she hoped Beau would be able to tell her.

Nola turned into the servants' drive. It was unmanned.

She passed the turn for the clubhouse and continued on. Once she was about half a mile from the clubhouse, she made another left. She followed the curving road to a small but beautifully landscaped cottage. Beau's golf cart still sat outside along with the white convertible Porsche.

Pulling in, Nola blocked the Porsche's exit. She stepped out of the car, rolling her shoulders while she tried to come up with a game plan. She needed to get information from him. But she didn't have time to quietly needle the information out. And Anna Mae had already been gone for days. It might be too late to save her. This guy was up to his eyeballs in Lynette's disappearance. And she needed to get the information.

But she couldn't go in guns blazing.

This was much easier to do when you were in a foreign country and could just grab someone and drag them over to a CIA safe house. Then you could take your time getting the information. Or use whatever method was necessary to get intel quickly.

Sometimes just the abduction alone was enough to convince the person that they needed to spill. Here, though, Beau was in his regular surroundings. He was going to feel powerful. After all, this was his family's land. It had been for generations. This was his family's town. Which meant that Nola needed to come up with something that would scare Beauregard.

And what scared an entitled rich boy?

Losing that money.

The main path was lined with lush hydrangea bushes. They were in full bloom. Someone had to water them regularly to make them grow that large and that colorful. There was a covered arbor entrance over the front door. Flower baskets filled with a riot of colorful blooms spilled out of window boxes. The whole place really had a fairytale look to it.

And a feminine touch.

Beauregard certainly hadn't designed this place. And Nola had a sneaking suspicion she knew who did.

She rapped on the door. No one answered for a few moments, so she knocked again before trying the door. It was unlocked. She opened it. A cold blast of air-conditioning hit her.

The room was a well-appointed living room with deep white couches framed around a brick fireplace. More flowers dotted the mantel, and a colorful print was above the fireplace. Along the right-hand side was a dining area, and beyond that a well-appointed kitchen. There was another shaded porch toward the back that she could see off the kitchen.

"Beauregard Haverford?" Nola called as she stepped in.

The man himself stepped out of a door at the back of the room, buttoning up his shirt. His face was red. Whether that was from catching sight of Nola or for whatever exertions he was engaging in in the other room, she wasn't sure.

"Who the hell are you?" He demanded.

She smiled. "A woman who wants to talk to you about Lynette Granger."

He frowned. "Who?"

"The girl you had Craig Bradford kidnap in Delford."

Beau stormed toward her. "I have no idea what you are talking about. Now you need to get out."

She stepped toward him rather than backing away. From the surprise on his face, Beau apparently wasn't used to that reaction.

"I have you on tape meeting with Bradford," she said.

"It will go to the cops unless you tell me where the Compton boys are taking the girls."

"I don't know what you're talking about." He crossed his arms over her chest.

Nola pulled her phone from her back pocket. "Okay. Have it your way."

Beau hurried forward. "No need for that. Why don't we just—" He lunged toward her.

She sidestepped him, and he nearly fell face first into the floor.

He whirled toward her. "You are giving me those tapes."

"Yeah, that's not happening," Nola said.

He glared, his chest heaving. "I've heard about you. You're causing a lot of trouble. Well, looks like your trouble-making days are over." He seethed before he lunged again.

Nola rolled her eyes as she took a small step back. What was with the corny 1980s bad guy movie lines? She slammed her foot into his groin. He let out a cry, his face turning redder as his knees buckled. But he still managed to stumble forward and grab Nola by the arms.

She reached her hands up in between his and clinched him by the back of the head as she brought her knee up three times. Then she brought her left elbow up and caught him in the chin, followed by a right elbow to the cheek. A left straight sent him flying back and slamming into the side of the couch.

"Well, that didn't go as planned." Pulling her white silk robe closed, Honoria stepped into the living room.

Chapter Fifty

The matriarch of the Haverford dynasty grabbed the belt of her robe and tied it around her waist as she strolled over to the kitchen. She glanced at the ground where her lover and stepson lay sprawled. "For god's sake, Beau, get up."

Beau stumbled to his feet, his face still pinched in pain as he pulled himself onto the couch. Honoria poured herself a tall glass of water from the pitcher on the counter.

Nola noted the lack of fear and the lack of concern for the man who'd just gotten his ass handed to him on the living room floor of their love nest.

"So you two have been together since you were teenagers?" Nola asked.

Honoria tilted her water glass toward Nola in salute. "True love."

Nola narrowed her eyes. She took a long look at Beauregard. He and Teddy shared the same eyes, although Teddy's build was more like his mother's. It was possible they both looked like Honoria's husband, but Nola had a sneaking suspicion she was looking at Teddy's actual father.

But that wasn't what really struck Nola. What surprised her was how unsurprised Honoria was at finding Nola there. And she must have overheard their conversation. "You know about the girls."

With a shrug, Honoria said, "One hears things, as you can imagine."

Nola shook her head, stepping forward. "No, it's more than that."

She narrowed her eyes, studying the woman in front of her. Honoria had gone from poor girl on the wrong side of the tracks to the most powerful woman in Haverford by getting knocked up by the Haverford scion. She remembered what Ma Bell had said about there being other girls along the way, but none of them had ever managed to wrestle the senior Haverford from Honoria's clutches.

"You know about the girls because you helped some of them disappear as well," Nola said.

Honoria smiled. "I have no idea what you're talking about."

Nola looked up at Beau, who was leaning his head back, a pillow pressed to his face to staunch the bleeding. The guy wasn't very bright. He simply didn't have the mental capability of keeping this quiet and keeping it running.

"You sent him out. You gave him instructions. He does what you say. You're the one behind all of this."

The woman said nothing. She simply took a sip of her water.

The lack of response infuriated Nola. This woman had everything money could buy, and yet she was destroying the lives of young girls. "Why? Why Anna Mae? What did she do?"

"Anna Mae." Honoria nearly spit out the name. "She was

making moves on my *son*. I saw how she looked at him. I found his little phone. Texting every day, talking every day. She saw her way to get out of Delford, and she was holding on to it with both hands. She was going to trap him and make sure that she never had to worry about money ever again. I couldn't let that happen. Teddy deserves better than that."

Nola stared at Honoria in shock. She thought Anna Mae was going to try and get herself impregnated by Teddy? Obviously the woman didn't understand friendship, and she sure as hell didn't understand her son if she thought that was even a possibility.

"So you did it, you got rid of her?" Nola asked.

Honoria shrugged. "Of course. Her mother should be thanking me. The woman apparently is struggling to make ends meet. One less mouth to feed will make that so much easier. What did the girl have going for her, anyway? Just another girl who's going to put her feet up in the air for untold men throughout her life. Teddy deserves better. The world deserves better. Her disappearing, it's a blessing for everyone."

It was an effort to hold onto her rage. Nola rolled her hands into fists. "Except for Anna Mae. Did you have her killed?"

Honoria had the gall to look shocked. "Of course not. I'm not a monster. I merely facilitate people who have certain needs, and I provide a product that helps meet those needs."

Nola quickly interpreted the doublespeak. "You *sold* her?"

"I don't sell them. At least, not exactly to their final destination. I merely provide them to a broker who will facilitate the transfer of them to their new location."

"How could you?" Nola demanded. "You were once a poor girl from Delford."

Honoria narrowed her eyes. "Which is why I know *exactly* how they think. I got out by whatever means necessary. I know what that desperation is like. And girls there haven't changed. Do you know how many times over the years some little tramp has gotten herself knocked up and then stood waiting for a handout? As if they deserve it. For what? Lying on their back for five minutes? Please."

"How many girls have you disappeared?"

The question only elicited another shrug from Honoria. "I've never really kept count. People come to me with their problems, and I help solve them. And as a result, they are thankful, and they are also now mine. I solve their problem, and whenever I need them to, they solve mine. Tit for tat." She smiled. "It's been a very lucrative endeavor."

"Lynette Granger. Did you give her away too?" Nola asked, trying to keep her tone even.

"Why would I tell you? You're nothing. I have all the power here," Honoria proclaimed.

The sound of feet heading toward the path was audible. Nola stepped toward Honoria.

Honoria smiled again, tilting her glass slightly toward Nola in a second salute. "That will be my security team. Time for you to go."

A loud banging erupted at the door. "Mrs. Haverford? Security."

"Come in!" She called.

The door opened, and two burly guards stepped in.

Honoria nodded toward Nola. "She's trespassing. Get rid of her. And make sure she learns a lesson to never return."

This time it was Nola's chance to smile. "Stupid move."

One of the men walked over to Nola and grabbed her arm. "Let's go."

Nola slammed the edge of her hand into his throat before grabbing his wrist and contorting it to ninety degrees, his elbow now facing the ceiling. She brought her other forearm down and slammed it into the elbow, breaking it. The man screamed and crumpled to the floor.

The other guard took his baton out as he hurried forward. He took a swing at Nola's head.

Shifting quickly to the side, the baton sailed harmlessly past her. She grabbed onto his arm with the weapon and slammed it back into his knee. Then she continued the momentum forward past him, and then on the reverse swing, slammed it again into the back of his knee.

She wrenched the baton from his hand and then slammed it across his face. Blood burst from his cheek before he joined his partner on the ground.

Her anger not even slightly sated, she turned to Honoria. The baton still in her hand, Nola watched the woman who had carelessly destroyed young girls' lives finally show an inkling of fear.

Nola stalked toward the kitchen. Honoria darted around the other side of the kitchen island, her eyes large, her façade of control gone. "You . . . you can't do this. This is my place. You can't do this."

Glancing back at the bodies sprawled behind her, Nola said loftily, "Oh, I think I can."

Honoria darted to one side of the island. Nola swung out with the baton, and the pitcher went crashing across the island. With a cry, Honoria leaped back out of the way. Nola sprinted around the island and grabbed her by the arm.

Whirling around, the entitled woman tried to scratch

her in the face. Nola punched her in the jaw. All the fight went out of her. She crumpled.

Gripping her, Nola pushed her up against the refrigerator, her forearm at the woman's throat. "Where is Anna Mae?"

"I don't know."

Nola shook her head. "Not possible. Women like you wouldn't leave anything to chance. You know every angle. You *know* where Anna Mae is. You know where they take those girls."

Honoria glared back at her. Nola raised her other fist. Honoria cringed. "There's a farm. It's out at the edge of Haverford and Delford. On Lake Ridge Road. They keep the girls there until they need to transfer them."

"And where do they transfer them to?" Nola demanded.

Honoria pursed her lips as if mulling over the answer.

Nola put extra pressure on her neck. "Where?" She said through gritted teeth.

"Savannah."

Slamming her head against the wall, she demanded, "Where in Savannah?"

"The Port. Ocean Terminal. The girls are sent out on containers."

Disgust rolled through Nola, along with frustration. The Ports Authority was the second-busiest container exporter. It would be like looking for a needle in a haystack.

"What berth?"

"I have no idea."

Nola pressed against her throat. Honoria gagged, tears cascaded down her cheeks, her skin blotchy. "I don't know!" She screamed.

"Then give me something more. What's the company name?"

She pursed her lips.

"The name!" Nola demanded, putting more pressure on the other woman's throat.

Honoria grabbed at Nola's hand, her face turning red. "Oceania Limited!"

Releasing only some of the pressure on her neck, Nola asked, "When's the next shipment?"

"I don't—"

"When?" Nola slammed her back against the refrigerator.

"Tomorrow night," Honoria choked out. :The next one is tomorrow night."

Nola stared at the woman, wanting so desperately to do more than bruise her pretty little face. But she knew if she started, she would never stop.

And she wasn't ready to cross that line just yet.

She flung Honoria to the ground and headed for the door. Both guards looked at her with big eyes and cringed away from her as she strode by. But as she passed, one of the guards tried to reach out and grab her. She kicked him in the face. His hand dropped as his eyes rolled back in his head.

Behind her, Honoria struggled back to her feet. "You're nothing. You're a brute who thinks violence solves things."

Nola didn't look back as she spoke. "No, violence doesn't always solve things. But sometimes it damn well helps."

Chapter Fifty-One

Nola called Bishop as she stepped out of the cottage. Bishop answered immediately. "Nola? You okay?"

"I'm good," she said rolling her neck and trying to rein in her anger. "The girls are at the Ports Authority in Savannah. We need to get there now."

"We're in the car and heading out."

"Good. I'll be right behind you. Is Avad driving?"

"Of course," Bishop grumbled.

"Good. I need you to send those files about the Retreat to the appropriate authorities. Whoever you think will move on them quickly."

"Okay."

"And write something up for the newspaper, anonymous, showing Honoria's connection to the girls going missing."

"It was Honoria?"

"Yeah. She's the ringleader. Beau's just one of her minions."

"Man. That's a messed-up family."

She pictured Teddy. "Not all of them. Now get going. Find a spot not too far from the Ocean Terminal and send me your location."

Nola glanced up at the sky. It was already starting to lighten. It would be early morning when they arrived. But she didn't want to wait until nightfall. If the girls were being shipped out tomorrow, they could be loaded onto a ship at any point now.

"Is Anna Mae still alive?" Bishop asked quietly.

"She should be. Call me when you get there." Nola disconnected the call.

She stepped into her car when her phone beeped again. With surprise, she realized it was from Derek. With everything going on, she'd almost forgotten about him.

Anna Mae and the other girls are being held in a container at Ocean terminal.

Nola texted back quickly. *What container?*

I don't know. But they're somewhere around berth 17.

Smiling, Nola replied: *Good. Now find out which container.*

Chapter Fifty-Two

DEREK

"What are you doing?" Devante demanded.

Shoving his phone into his back pocket, Derek shrugged even as his heart raced. "What? Nothing."

Devante whacked him on the shoulder. "No looking at your phone. Boss man doesn't like when his people are distracted."

"Okay, sorry."

Devante shook his head. "You better not mess this up for me. This is the big leagues, not just hanging out in some warehouse with stolen TVs."

Yeah, just hanging out on the water with stolen girls, he thought, but he kept his mouth shut. He glanced around. He and Devante had arrived two hours ago. Devante had woken him up and told him to get moving. He hadn't put up a fight and had gotten in the car quickly. He hoped that wherever Devante was taking him might have something to do with

Anna Mae. When they'd pulled into the Ocean Terminal, though, his hopes had dimmed.

Until he'd heard some of the other guys talking about the delivery and getting a chance to "sample some of the goods" before they were shipped out. From the description, he knew they were talking about the girls. He felt nauseous at the thought. How the hell had he gotten caught up in this? These guys had no spark of conscience in them.

He studied his cousin from the corner of his eye. Devante had taken part in their wishful planning right along with them. God, he felt sick.

Taking a breath, he watched a large ship float past on the Savannah River. It would be okay. Nola was on her way. He didn't know what she planned on doing, but he hoped it involved lots of cops. He knew he'd get arrested too, but he figured he deserved at least that much.

He looked around at the dozens of guys, all armed, ostensibly on guard duty. None of them seemed to be taking it too seriously. He got the feeling they'd been through this a few times. And from their ease, he figured it had always gone off without a hitch.

He tried to keep his disgust off his face. *If I deserve prison, then these guys all deserve something much, much worse.*

Chapter Fifty-Three

NOLA

Her knuckles swollen, Nola gripped the steering wheel of the Bronco. Her back was sore from driving for two hours. Or maybe from any of the fights she'd had in the last day . . . days.

She hadn't even realized her knuckles were in such bad shape. She'd grabbed an ice pack from her first-aid kit as she was driving, but it had long since gone warm. And she wasn't about to pull over for a few bruises. So she downed some ibuprofen and stayed on the highway.

In her mind, she reviewed the Google Earth views of the dock that she'd pulled up earlier. The area surrounding the port was relatively quiet. Ocean Terminal had five deep-water berths. Large cranes lined the edge of the Savannah River to aid in the loading and unloading of the immense containers. Containers were neatly lined in rows along the 200 acres of the terminal. The Google Earth view almost made it look like some sort of kids' game: all bright and colorful, everything in their spot. But it wasn't a game. It was a busy seaport. But being it was Sunday morning, she hoped the terminal was going to be quieter than normal.

The terminal's size wasn't the only problem. Containers were piled two or three high. There were also a few warehouses and offices. Plus, there was a lot of open space, which was necessary to move the containers. It wouldn't offer much cover, which would definitely be a problem.

In fact, all she could see were problems. She glanced at her phone again, but there was no new text from Derek. She didn't want to take the chance of contacting him unless she had to. They needed to know which container the girls were in. They couldn't search the entire terminal. It would take too long.

Avad and Bishop had contacted her a few minutes ago to let her know they'd reached Savannah. They would send her their coordinates once they found a good spot to hole up. Nola still wasn't sure about bringing them. On the one hand, she knew they were right. It was too big an area to cover on her own. If she wasn't going to call in the cops or the Feds, she needed someone backing her up.

But on the other hand, she didn't like how seeing them made her feel. For the last two years, she'd seen Avad maybe a half a dozen times, generally at an airport. And Avad being Avad, he didn't speak much. He just took stock of how she was and reported back.

Nola was okay with that. She knew Ileana and Bishop were worried about her. But she couldn't step back into that life. It wasn't one she wanted anymore. Or rather, she didn't want it as it was.

But seeing Bishop . . . it was painful. It brought up all sorts of memories and emotions that were better left buried. At the same time, she'd missed her.

She just didn't know how to keep Bishop in her life and stay sane. She didn't think it was possible. These last two years had been her way of working things out.

And she wasn't done yet.

She passed a sign announcing that there were only ten more miles to Savannah. She pressed down on the accelerator. *One case. One case, and then everything goes back the way it was.*

The highways had been clear, and she kept her foot on the accelerator the whole way. The Bronco had been surprisingly responsive. She'd worried that when she'd side-swiped the car with Lynette in it that she had done some damage. But it appeared to be just body work.

Now it was approaching ten. The traffic had picked up a little bit but still wasn't too bad. She kept an eye on her rearview mirror and noticed at least two cars had followed her most of the way here. Being she was still on the main highway, that wasn't necessarily indicative of anything.

She put on her indicator for the next exit, one that wouldn't be as well traveled to Savannah. She switched lanes, flicking yet another glance at the rearview mirror. The Chevy stayed where it was, continuing on toward Savannah. But the SUV farther back switched lanes as well.

She cursed silently. *I should have dealt with this sooner.* Now they knew she was on her way to Savannah. That was why Avad and Bishop showing up was dangerous. It put her off her game. Instead of keeping an eye on her surroundings, she was getting lost in feelings and memories.

And that's when people I care about get hurt.

She took the exit and then made a quick left. Her tail followed her a minute later. She was in an older commercial area of Savannah. Small derelict storefronts lined the road. There was a pawnshop, a bar, a dollar store, and a dentist. A quarter mile down the road was an old restaurant with two cars in the parking lot. An abandoned real estate agency was next door. More abandoned storefronts were on the other side. In between the strips of commercial businesses were older smaller homes with overgrown yards and long-abandoned cars.

None of them suited her purpose. Soon the derelict storefronts gave way to more modern creations. A few recognizable big-box stores appeared. She passed a supermarket with a large parking lot out front. Next to it was a storage facility.

Perfect.

Nola drove into the parking lot. The facility was set up in long rows of garages, each used for storage. In the back, four smaller units ran perpendicular to the ones in the front. She headed for the back, taking note of the cameras.

She turned at the end of the row, nodding her head as she saw the office. It was a separate building, really more of an old trailer than an actual permanent structure. A closed sign hung on the door.

Nola parked in front of the office. There were no noticeable cameras aimed at it. Hopping out, she quickly made her way around the back of the trailer.

Only a few seconds later, she heard the quiet creep of the other car. Using the railing for the ramp at the back of the trailer, she hoisted herself onto the roof, staying low. She made her way toward the front. Inching toward the edge of the roof, she caught sight of a brand-new dark-blue Chevy Tahoe pulling in only a short distance away from her.

The driver sat behind the steering wheel, the engine idling. He sat for a few moments before he turned off the car. She couldn't see his face, but from the movement of his hand, she got the feeling he was scanning from side to side, looking for her. He opened the door and got out, a hood over his head.

The driver glanced around and then walked toward Nola's car. He peered in the windows and tried one of the doors. He looked around, but his back was to Nola, so she still couldn't get a look at his face. He started toward the edge of the trailer.

Nola crept along the top of the roof, staying parallel to him. She waited until he moved only a few feet from the building's edge.

Then she jumped.

Chapter Fifty-Four

Nola landed on the man's back. He let out a scream as he fell forward. He managed to get his hands in front of him so his face didn't slam into the concrete. But that was as far as his luck went.

Nola slipped her arm around his neck, trapping it with her other arm and locking it in place. She wrenched the man to her side as she got to her feet.

He scrambled, trying to get his feet underneath him.

She increased the pressure. "Who the hell are you?"

The man hit at Nola's arms. "Nola, Nola, it's me. It's Teddy."

Swallowing a curse, Nola loosened her grip and swung the man around. She pushed him up against the side of the trailer, her forearm at his throat. Teddy Haverford's blue eyes were wide with fear, his mouth hanging open as he stared at her.

Nola released him and stepped back. "Teddy, what the hell are you doing?"

Leaning heavily against the trailer, Teddy rubbed at his throat. "Helping you?"

"You're doing a bang-up job. I could've killed you."

He nodded his head, dropping his chin. "I know. It's just, I saw you on the cameras down at my brother's place. When you left, I figured you were going after Anna Mae, and I wanted to be there to help you help her."

Nola stared at him. "How much did you see?"

"Not much. I, uh, know about him and my mom. Beau, he's not bad, exactly, he's just selfish."

"Yes, he is." She studied the young man in front of her. His whole life was about to get unraveled. She felt a twinge of guilt at that. Honoria and Beau deserved what they got. Teddy didn't deserve any of the blowback, though.

His tone plaintive, Teddy wrung his hands. "Look, I don't know what they did. I'm not sure I want to know. But I do want to help Anna Mae."

Nola was shaking her head before he finished speaking. "Teddy, this is dangerous. You're not ready for something like this. You need to go home."

This time it was Teddy who shook his head. "No, you need my help. Look, I get that you're a badass. I know I'm not. But I *can* help. When you find Anna Mae she . . . she might need help walking or something. You wouldn't be able to carry her and then fight off whoever the hell has her. I can help with that."

He had a point. And more importantly, he had a big car. If there were multiple girls, and they needed to get them out in a hurry, that could come in handy. But protecting him while getting Anna Mae out was going to add a whole other level of complexity that she did not need. "I know you're worried about her. But you can't help me, not like this."

Teddy yanked his hood off in frustration. "I'll . . . I'll

stay in the car. I'll stay in the back. And then if you need me, you can just call, and I'll come. I can't go home, Nola. I need to help her. Please."

Everything inside of Nola was screaming at her to send the kid home. But she knew that look on his face. He wanted his best friend back. Anna Mae was more than a friend. She was the only family he truly had. She sighed, knowing she was probably going to regret this. "Okay. But you do exactly what I say. You don't move unless I tell you to move, you understand?"

"Yes, yes, yes," he said quickly.

Spearing him with a glare, she said, "You're staying in the car until I signal you. I will only signal you if I need help getting Anna Mae out and if it's safe for you to come in. If you come in before then, I will shoot you myself."

Teddy laughed, and then his laughter died away. "You're kidding, right?"

"No, I'm not," she said. "This isn't a game, Teddy. These people are serious. And if you don't follow my instructions, you will get hurt. Anna Mae will get hurt."

"I'll do whatever you say. I promise," he said.

Nola looked into his earnest face. He was a good kid by some miracle. She just hoped she wasn't making a mistake by not sending him home.

Chapter Fifty-Five

Savannah was a city steeped in history and ghosts. From the Revolutionary War to the siege of Savannah, the nation's first planned city had seen its share of violence. Ghost and haunting tours were executed daily to take people through the historic streets, pointing out where the ghosts were said to still arise.

Savannah's waterway was similarly steeped in history. Gunships had patrolled its banks during the Civil War. And now it looked like its banks might be used for something even more morally bankrupt: the sale of young girls.

Thanks to Bishop, they knew that the security was light on Sundays. Only two men at the front gate and another four wandering the yard. But the ones wandering the yard kept on a pretty strict routine. Nola didn't want any record of their coming and going through the front gate. Plus, she wasn't sure that the guys at the front gate wouldn't raise the alarm. If she was right, and this was a regular operation, the Compton boys had to have at least a few members of the boatyard on their payroll.

So they needed to make their own entrance. Nola chose a spot on the southeast side of the boatyard. It couldn't be seen from the road or the water. Plus, there was a tangle of deserted containers blocking the view of the fence. Obviously this was not a high-traffic area.

Nola put down the wire cutters, and Avad ripped away the portion of chain-link fence that they had cut through. There was now a gap four feet by five feet leading into the boatyard. Nola turned and looked at Teddy. He gulped nervously, his Adam's apple moving rapidly. "You get back to your car. You stay out of sight. We will call you in when we have Anna Mae and we need you to get her out. You come through the southeast entrance. Okay?"

Teddy nodded nervously.

"If things don't feel right, you get yourself out of here, okay?"

"But—"

Nola shook her head, cutting off his argument. "No. Like I said, this isn't a game. This isn't a movie. Things could go very wrong. You need to trust your gut. If it tells you to run, you run. Do you understand?"

Teddy nodded his head.

Nola shifted her gaze to Bishop. "That goes for you too."

Bishop balked. "Nola, I know how to—"

She cut Bishop off too. "I'm not doubting that you can handle yourself. But Avad will tell you that even the most experienced operator will listen to their gut even when their gut is telling them something that goes against the plan. So, if something doesn't feel right, you trust that. Ego will only get you killed."

Bishop nodded, her mouth a tight line. Nola sighed, knowing that it was in fact Bishop's pride that was talking and not her head. She wanted to prove that she was good enough. Nola didn't actually doubt that. But with experience came the understanding that being good enough wasn't always all you needed. Experience had taught her that luck and instinct played an important role too. And Bishop hadn't been in the game long enough to know that.

Avad, on the other hand, was a creature of instinct. Ileana had found him during the Bosnian wars. At that point, he'd already been an operative for five years when she had saved his life. And the lives of the rest of his family. So now he worked for Ileana, and occasionally he worked with Nola as well. She respected his skill and his judgment.

"Okay, Teddy, take off. Stay hidden," Nola said nudging back toward his car.

"I . . . I will. Thanks." He looked at each of them and then hurried away. Nola hoped once again it wasn't a mistake bringing him along. But she had a feeling if she hadn't, he would've followed anyway, and then he would've been in even more danger.

"Bishop, you ready?" Nola asked.

Nodding, Bishop stepped back from the case she'd carried in. It lay on the ground, open. A small drone with tiny cameras whirled into motion. It hovered for a second and then flew off over the containers. Watching the screen, Bishop said, "Immediate area is clear."

"Okay, I'm first. Bishop, you're next. Avad, you bring up the rear. From this point on, no talking. I know there's only a small skeleton crew of security, but there could easily be other people in the boatyard. We need to keep quiet. Understood?"

Avad and Bishop both gave her a nod.

Turning Nola took a breath. She patted her Glock at

her waist for good luck, a habit she'd gotten into years ago, then she stepped through the opening. "Let's go find Anna Mae."

Chapter Fifty-Six

ANNA MAE

The container was so hot that most of the girls had taken to lying flat on the floor in an attempt to get some cool air. There were now seventeen girls inside, but Anna Mae had heard the man who dropped off the last two girls talking about another container. Which meant that there was probably at least a total of thirty of them that were being shipped God knew where. She swallowed thinking about what was to come.

How am I going to get through this?

She had no answer for that. But she knew she had to. She had to find her way back home. She had to make sure that Oz didn't grow up thinking that the world was a cold dark place.

But even as she thought that, she wasn't sure that she would be the one to teach him that lesson anymore. Because she was no longer certain that the world wasn't in fact a cold dark place. These men had grabbed all of them. They didn't care about the lives that they were ruining. They didn't care about the torture and horror that they were going to inflict upon any of the girls. All they cared about was making a few bucks. And destroying dozens of lives in the process was just the cost of doing business, and for them, there didn't appear to be any cost at all.

So even if she got out of this, how was she going to be herself again? Was it even realistic to think that that was possible?

Natalie sniffed next to her and wiped a tear from her face. Anna Mae had no words of comfort to offer her. So she just reached down and gently squeezed her hand. Natalie held on to her hand like it was a lifeline. She held on so tightly that it hurt.

But Anna Mae didn't ask her to loosen her grip. She knew the young girl needed that contact, and in truth, so did Anna Mae. The rest of the girls in the container didn't talk much. Anna Mae had the feeling that they had been here a lot longer than she had. The container smelled so awful. They had a bucket in the corner that they were supposed to use to relieve themselves, but it was only replaced every two days. And usually whoever was carrying it spilled some over the side as they made their way out of the container with it. Anna Mae knew she herself had never smelled so bad in her life. Vaguely, she hoped that the fact that she was so disgusting right now would protect her a little bit. But she had a feeling it wouldn't.

This was a horrible situation, but it was also an organized one. These people had done this before. They knew what they were doing.

A sob wended its way up through Anna Mae's chest. She clamped her mouth shut, not allowing it to escape. She couldn't do that to Natalie. She couldn't break down. She had cried quietly at night when Natalie was fast asleep. But she had been careful to make sure that she didn't cry when Natalie could see her.

But she couldn't stop the shudder of the sob working its way through her body. Natalie clung to her hand even tighter, as if to give her strength.

Anna Mae clung back just as tightly, wondering not for the first time who was comforting whom.

Chapter Fifty-Seven

NOLA

Nola put up a hand after they'd been walking in the boatyard for five minutes toward berth 17. They had slipped in through the containers. The drones had warned them that two trucks were heading their way. It had given them enough time to slip around the side of a container and hide.

Now Nola crouched at the edge of a long container. Her phone buzzed in her pocket. She quickly pulled it out. It was a text from Derek.

I know which container. But it doesn't have a number. I hope you're here because I'm going to try to signal you.

Nola slipped the phone back in her pocket without responding. She didn't want to let Derek know they were here in case he was playing them or in case someone else had gotten his phone. She ushered Avad and Bishop closer.

"Watch for Derek. He's going to point out the container," she whispered.

Both nodded back at her. Nola noted Avad was as cool as usual, not a sign of nerves. But Bishop was a little jumpy, her head constantly swerving from side to side.

In front of them was a large crane. From the state of it, it was obviously in disrepair. She nudged her chin toward it. "Okay, Bishop, you're up on that stack of containers there. It'll give you a good view of the boatyard and give you multiple egress avenues."

Without a word, Bishop slipped around the side of the container. Nola stayed where she was, keeping an eye on the boatyard as Bishop reached the crane and started to climb. She leaped from the top of the crane to the edge of the container and swung herself over.

Nola waited until Bishop had flattened herself against the roof of the container before she looked up at Avad, who stood silently next to her. She nodded to another stack of containers, these only two high.

Avad nodded and took off at a brisk walk. Nola followed behind him, her head scanning from side to side and behind her. In another few minutes, they were on top of the containers, lying flat as well. Nola pulled her binoculars out from her bag and scanned the boatyard.

The ship that the container was supposed to be loaded onto hadn't docked yet. Bishop had gotten into the boatyard's manifest and knew it was supposed to arrive within the hour.

From her perch, Bishop was going to send the drone out to scan the boatyard to look for Derek. But Nola knew they couldn't count on him being able to ID the container. He was a low man on the totem pole. He wouldn't have much say in where he was assigned. Which meant they needed to keep looking on their own.

It was a needle-in-a-haystack approach. But Nola was

hoping they would catch sight of one of the Compton boys, which would lead them to the correct container.

Barring that, they would have to wait until the ship docked and they started to move the container. Then they would have to move on the container while it was in motion. Or climb aboard the ship and release them there. Nola hoped it didn't come to that. Those two options were definitely more dangerous for everyone involved.

So what they needed right now was just a little bit of luck. But that had never really been something that had worked out for Nola in the past. She hoped that maybe she could borrow a little from Avad or Bishop. Surely their luck was better than hers.

Chapter Fifty-Eight

ANNA MAE

Voices grew closer. Anna Mae tensed, as did all the other girls in the container. Anna Mae sat up, moving herself so that she was slightly in front of Natalie. All the other girls who had been lying down sat up as well. None of them wanted to be caught in such a vulnerable position. It was bad enough they were in this situation; they needed to do something to make themselves feel slightly more powerful.

The door to the container started to open. All the girls scurried back, as if somehow they could hide.

Five men stood framed in the doorway. Anna Mae recognized one guy. He was the one from the farm, the one who had seemed nice. Or at least as nice as any of them could be. He met her gaze and then looked away. She could swear it was guilt that flashed across his face. And there was still something familiar about him.

But she only spared him a quick look, because he wasn't the one that she needed to worry about. No, the one she needed to worry about was in the front. He wrinkled his nose. "It stinks in here. You girls are disgusting."

No one said a word.

The man chuckled. "Well, you ladies are certainly looking worse for wear. And smelling worse. But don't worry. When you get to where you're going, you'll get cleaned up. But first, a few lucky ladies are going to get a chance to get cleaned up sooner." His eyes scanned the group, a predator looking for prey. Anna Mae dropped her gaze to the ground, not wanting to meet his eyes. Not wanting to draw his attention.

"That one, that one, that one, and that one." The other men with him moved into the container. The one who looked familiar made a beeline for Anna Mae. He grabbed her arm, speaking quietly. "You have to come with me."

Natalie let out a little squeal of fright next to her. Anna Mae patted her hand, even as tremors ran through her. "It's okay. It will be all right. Just stay with the other girls, okay?"

Natalie didn't say anything, just stared at her with big eyes. Anna Mae leaned forward and kissed her on the forehead, the same way she kissed Oz every morning before he went to school. "I'll be back in a little bit," she said before standing.

The guy took her by the arm and pulled her toward the entryway. Three other girls were already being pulled out of the container. None of them put up a fight. Anna Mae didn't either. What was the point? They couldn't overpower these guys. All of them were weak from hunger. Anna Mae's legs shook just from walking. She certainly couldn't run.

She blinked hard, her eyes tearing as she was led out into the sunlight. It wasn't even that bright. It looked like late afternoon. But the light was shocking compared to the darkness of the container.

Ahead, the man who'd chosen them stepped into a warehouse. Anna Mae swallowed, her eyes following him. She waited until the door closed, and after a quick glance to make sure there was no one close enough to hear them, whispered, "Where they taking us?"

The man next to her didn't look at her as he spoke quietly. "To get cleaned up."

Anna Mae didn't ask why they were being cleaned up. She unfortunately knew the answer to that. Her stomach rolled.

"Please don't let them do this. You're a good person. Don't let them do this."

The man said nothing. He just pulled her forward, and then it was too late. They were stepping into the warehouse, and there were seven men inside. The girls were led to a room at the back. The other three girls were there already, and two guards stood.

"There's a sink at the back of the room. Get washed up. You have fifteen minutes," one of the other men ordered.

The man who'd led her here gave her a long look that Anna Mae couldn't read before he stepped outside. The door closed shut behind him.

Anna Mae jumped at the sound. Fifteen minutes. Fifteen minutes, and then she knew the horror of the last couple of days would feel like a vacation compared to what was about to come.

Chapter Fifty-Nine

DEREK

Derek closed the door, trying to block out the image of Anna Mae's face. She didn't deserve this. None of them deserved this. He'd already given up any hope that he might somehow be a good person. But maybe if that woman came through, maybe she could at least keep Anna Mae from being hurt.

But he didn't know what to do right now. He'd told Nola the girls were in the container. And they were. But Anna Mae was no longer there. Should he lead her here or back to the container?

Derek walked through the room, not making eye contact with any of them inside. They were all looking forward to the "treat" to come. Derek was afraid if he looked at any of them, they'd see the disgust in his eyes.

He stepped outside. The boss's guards were outside the door. They were much better armed than any of the Compton boys, and they were also much more security conscious. He nodded at them and headed back toward the container. He'd figured out a way to signal where the container was. And then, once those girls were secure, he'd show Nola where Anna Mae was.

But all of this relied on that woman being here. Because if she wasn't, Derek wasn't sure what he was going to do.

Chapter Sixty

BISHOP

Bishop's nerves were on edge. She hadn't lied to Nola about being field certified. But she definitely did not feel comfortable in the field.

Not like Nola.

Nola seemed to walk through danger like most people walked through a park. Her and Avad both seemed completely unbothered by the potential damage that could be brought down on them in the coming hours.

But that wasn't what really got to Bishop.

What really got to Bishop was thinking about those girls and what they were going through. If they were right, and there was a container full of girls, then only horror was ahead of them. They'd already been through so much, and if Nola, Bishop, and Avad were unable to find them, then they were going to go through so much more.

And Bishop knew that from personal experience.

A tremor worked its way through her hand as she

gripped the edge of the controller, scanning the images that the drone had relayed. She let out a slow breath, trying to calm her racing heart. Her fear would do nothing but hurt the girls she was here to help. She needed to keep it under wraps.

But that was proving difficult.

The girls' predicament, seeing Nola again, the nature of this particular case, it was all blending together to result in an overload of emotions that Bishop was struggling to keep locked away.

At the same time, she knew she was right in insisting that Avad and she come along. This was too much for anyone, even Nola. And if Nola had faced this alone . . .

Bishop cut off the thought, not willing to go down that road. She had been down that road so many times in the last two years. Each time Nola had started a new case, fear had taken root in Bishop's chest as she wondered if this would be the time that Nola finally found a case that would be the death of her. And at the end of each case, she'd hoped that maybe that would be the last one and that Nola would finally come home.

But she never did.

For Nola, there was always one more case, and then one more after that. Bishop knew that without some sort of interference, it was always going to continue like that until Nola's luck completely ran out. Nola would never return to them, not unless they did something drastic. Not unless they gave her a case that got her thinking about home again.

What Bishop hadn't counted on was how difficult this kind of case would be on her.

Giving herself a shake, Bishop pushed away the thoughts. There'd be time for all of that later. She frowned as she caught movement close to where the berth was for the ship. She redirected the drone so she could get a closer look at the car that had just pulled in.

It wasn't the blue Mustang they were looking for. But the individual just slipping into the warehouse along with three other men, he might be the boss man. She did a freeze-frame on his face and quickly blew it up.

Bingo.

It was Chris Dylan. He was one of the leaders of the Compton boys. His pockmarked face and the scar through his left eyebrow gave him a distinctive look not easily hidden.

Bishop scrolled back to the image, checking out where it was that he had disappeared into. It was one of the warehouses. Warehouse 17. She tapped the mic at her throat and spoke quietly. "I have confirmation on Chris Dylan, one of the heads of the Compton boys. He headed into warehouse 17."

Nola's voice came back whisper soft. "*The Louisiana* just pulled into the waterway."

Bishop scanned the river, and sure enough, she saw the ship heading for the boatyard. "Any sign of the girls?"

Bishop scanned the images, flitting from screen to screen before she stopped. "I've got a blue Mustang."

She quickly rerouted the drone near the Mustang and caught sight of six men standing near a series of containers. She zoomed in and got another hit. "I can't confirm the container yet, but I've got eyes on the Compton boys. They're two rows over from where you are now."

"Roger, we're moving."

Bishop wanted to move the drone to keep an eye on Nola and Avad, but if it was discovered, she didn't want it leading to them, so she kept it parked on top of the container, keeping an eye on the Compton boys.

The men joked and laughed as they stood around waiting. Bishop rolled her hand into a fist. These guys were not even slightly concerned about the lives they were destroying. They looked like they were out having a good time. Bastards.

Three minutes later, Bishop's phone beeped. *In position.*

Bishop quickly typed back. *Plan?*

We're going in.

Chapter Sixty-One

BISHOP

Bishop was a bundle of nerves. They were going in? What did that mean? Going in where?

She sat staring at the screens, looking for some indication of which container the girls might be in. But there was nothing about any of the people to indicate it.

Then a tall young black man walked over to join the group. He looked different than the others, a little less happy to be there. She zoomed in on his face. It was Derek Rivers.

"Nola, hold. I've got eyes on Derek."

"What's he doing?"

"Give me a minute."

One of the men called out to Derek. He gave him a smile. As soon as the man looked away, the smile dropped from Derek's face. He looked around, scanning the top of the containers. Bishop's breath hitched. He knew they were there. He walked over and tied his sneaker in front of one of the containers.

But something was off with the movement, and Bishop couldn't figure out what it was. She rewound the tape and studied him before realizing what was wrong.

His shoe hadn't been untied. And while he'd been tying his shoes, he stared at the container the whole time.

"Did you catch that, Bishop?"

"Yeah," she said, realizing that Nola had somehow seen Derek drop in front of the container. Now he stood in front of it, shifting from side to side. He was signaling them.

"That's our container."

"Are we sure he's on our side?"

"Most likely. He stays safe. All the others are targets. When I give you the signal, you take out the three on the left. Avad and I will handle the others. Going in two minutes."

"Roger."

Bishop looked through the sniper rifle, sighting each of the individuals. She saw the two that were her targets. Both were big guys. Both were armed, and both were laughing and having a great time while waiting to ship off a group of girls.

She tightened her finger on the trigger. She itched to pull it, a little scared at how eager she was to do so. She'd shot people before, but never like this. Never without them being a direct threat to her. Of course, all of these guys were a direct threat to each of the girls in that container.

She looked through the scope. Right now, in her mind, that was the same as holding a gun to their heads.

Chapter Sixty-Two

NOLA

Nola and Avad climbed down the side of the container, heading for the one that Derek had identified. Nola hoped he wasn't leading them into a trap. She hoped that her faith in him wasn't misplaced.

She and Avad inched closer and then separated. They would each come in from a different side of the container, trying to split the focus of the men.

But she actually wasn't too worried about the men. All of them were chatting, laughing, having a good time. None of them were looking for any problems. They'd probably done this so many times that it was old hat by now. Right now they were just looking forward to their payday.

Nola crept up to the side of the container. She held her breath. Around the side, the men were exactly where they'd been two minutes before, still laughing. One guy was doing some sort of impression, drawing everyone else's attention. The only one not part of the frivolity was Derek. He stood with his hands in his pockets, looking around. The kid looked like he was about to be sick. Nola couldn't blame him.

The targets she'd given Bishop were still in the same position. She and Avad had divvied up the rest. Nola clicked on her mic so that it went through to both Avad and Bishop. She spoke softly. "Here we go. Three, two, one."

Three gunshots cut through the air, one right on top of the next. Three men dropped. The other three men stood gaping at them for a moment before, in another rush of bullets, four more dropped.

Derek was the only one still standing. He stood with his hands up, his eyes wide. Avad stayed behind the container, covering Nola as she stepped forward.

Derek's shoulders relaxed as he caught sight of her.

"Thank God." He started to lower his arms.

"Keep them up."

Derek's arms shot back to the sky. Nola moved toward him, scanning the area for any movement. The men on the ground groaned and cried out. Nola quickly kicked their guns out of reach. Then she patted down Derek, who was unarmed. Finally, Nola nodded. "You can put your arms down now."

Derek's chest heaved. But Nola knew it was from fright, not exertion. "This is the container. But there's a problem."

Her gaze constantly scanning the area, Nola asked, "What's the problem?"

"They took four of the girls inside. Anna Mae's one of them."

"Dammit." She tapped her mic. "There're four more girls inside. Contact Teddy. Get him in here and get the girls in this container out. Bishop, you cover them from your perch. Once they're in Teddy's truck, Bishop, you join them and get them out of here. Avad, you stay with them until they're clear, and then you come after me."

"Nola—" There was a warning in Bishop's voice.

"Follow orders, Bishop." She turned to Derek. "Show me."

Chapter Sixty-Three

BISHOP

From her bird's-eye perch, Bishop typed quickly. *Need you at berth 17.*

It was only a minute later that he pulled to an abrupt stop in front of the container. He must have been already inside the boatyard.

Avad had gotten the door to the container open. He stepped back and looked up at Bishop's position, his usual mask of neutrality one of anger and despair. Bishop felt her throat catch at the sight of his face.

But when the first girl stepped out into the light, her stomach felt like it dropped to the floor. She was just a girl. She was tiny.

Avad towered above her. Teddy bolted around the side of the Tahoe and came to an abrupt halt, his mouth dropping as he caught sight of the girl. For a minute, Bishop worried about how he'd react. She could imagine the smell that accompanied the open door, not to mention the human suffering he was seeing.

But Teddy hurried forward, stopping when he was only a foot away. Bishop couldn't hear what he said as he stretched out his arm.

The girl looked at his hand for what felt like an extremely long time. Bishop knew they needed to get moving. There was no guarantee that other people hadn't heard those shots. But looking at the traumatized girl in front of her, she couldn't imagine hurrying her along.

After what felt like minutes but was only seconds, the girl reached forward and grasped Teddy's hand. He pulled her toward him, wrapping an arm around her shoulders and speaking quietly to her as he led her to the Tahoe. More girls appeared from the door. Some of them glanced at the bodies and then looked away with a shudder. But most just quickly moved to the Tahoe, seeming to understand that help had arrived.

Bishop removed her gaze from the scene to take in the surroundings. Cars were heading toward their location. She tapped on the mic and warned Avad.

He nodded. "Get down here and go with Teddy. I'll take the high ground."

"But what about Nola?"

"Our job is to get these girls to safety. Then I'll go after Nola."

Bishop wanted to argue with him. She wanted to tell him that Nola was the priority. But she knew Nola wouldn't agree with that. So she said a quick prayer as she climbed down the stairs and packed up her gear. "Okay, I'm on my way."

Chapter Sixty-Four

NOLA

Nola ran next to Derek, heading farther into the boatyard. "How many men?"

"I think about eight."

"Armed?"

"Yeah. Mainly automatics. But the guys on the door have ARs."

Nola's mind whirled, taking in the info and quickly devising a plan. "Okay. I need you to distract the guys on the door."

"Distract them how?"

Nola glared at him. "I don't care. Point out a bird in the sky, tell them a joke. But get them to look away from the direction I'm coming from. I need to get in close or else it will warn everybody inside. It'll turn into a gunfight. Quiet is key."

Derek swallowed noticeably. "Okay."

"Now, where exactly are the girls in the building?"

"They should still be in the back room. They were getting cleaned up for—" He broke off, his mouth a tight line.

Nola's anger simmered, and this time she didn't put a lid on it. Not only were these men going to sell these girls, but they were going to try out their product beforehand. They deserved all of her anger.

They reached the edge of the container closest to the office. Nola grabbed onto Derek's arm. "Get them to look the other way for twenty seconds. That's the time it will take me to get across there and get the first one down."

His whole body shaking, Derek nodded his gaze darting around.

Gripping him by the shoulders, Nola looked into his eyes. "You only have to be brave for a short while longer. You're doing the right thing. Don't stop now."

Derek nodded again, this time a little less nervous. "Okay." He stepped out from the container and started toward the guards. He was moving quickly.

"Slow down," Nola whispered.

As if he could hear her, his pace slowed. One of the guards called out to him. "What was all that noise?"

Derek shrugged. "That fool Pete brought some fireworks. Idiot."

One of the guards slapped the other guard on the shoulder and said something that Nola couldn't hear. The two of them laughed.

"He set some up on the other side of the yard. Look that way. You should be able to see them," Derek said.

Both guards turned toward where Derek had pointed. Nola bolted from her spot, crossing the open ground as Derek stepped behind the two men.

"Should be any second now," Derek said.

One of the men glanced back at Derek. "Where did he get the—"

Nola's knife plunged into his neck before he could get out the rest of the statement. She yanked it out and had it in the other guy's back before he could even fully turn around. She yanked it up and twisted. All he had the time to do was let out a puff of air as he dropped to the ground.

Stumbling back, Derek looked between the two men. "Holy cow. You just . . . you just—"

She wiped the blade on one of the men's jackets. "Yes, I did. Now let's get going."

Easing the door open, she peeked inside. One man stood with his back to the front door, looking into a large room beyond it. Nola put up a finger to indicate Derek should wait. "Call him outside," she said quietly.

Popping his head in the door, Derek called out, "Hey, Tito, can you come here for a minute?"

Tito made some kind of remark that Nola couldn't make out, but Derek just waved him toward the door.

The man stepped outside. "What the hell are you—"

Nola slammed the side of her hand into his throat. Tito's eyes bugged out. Before he could do more than gasp, she placed one hand underneath his chin and the other on the back of his head. She twisted and broke his neck. Tito tipped to the side. Derek grabbed him as he fell and then lowered him to the ground.

Mouth open, Derek stared at the three bodies and then at Nola. His face was a few shades paler than it had been seconds ago. "Oh my God."

"I need you to hold it together," Nola said. "Your job is to get Anna Mae and the other girls out. Do you understand?"

His eyes still large, his Adam's apple bobbing away, Derek nodded.

"Stay behind me," Nola said before she eased the door open, her gun in front of her as she scanned the hallway.

No one seemed to have noticed Tito's disappearance.

She hurried down the hall, casting a quick glance into the room to the left, but there was no one there. She stepped to the spot where she'd first seen Tito and glanced into the room. It was an office. Six metal desks stood in the middle of the room, although some were at odd angles now, looking like they'd just been shoved aside. A few chairs had been scattered about. Three men stood. One leaned against the desk at the back while the head honcho sat at the desk, his feet up, a cigar at his mouth.

"Let's get this show on the road," he barked.

One of the men grinned and headed for the door at the back of the room and threw it open. "Time to party, ladies."

Nola took him out first. Her shot caught him just behind the ear. He pitched forward, but due to the silencer and the noise of the other men in the room and his location, no one noticed right away.

But then a cry of alarm went up from the other room. Still in the doorway, Nola took out two more of the men. The others, finally clued in that something was going on, turned around. But they didn't reach for their guns.

Stupid.

Targeting one more, she caught him center mass, which left her with only the boss and one other guy. The boss ducked behind a desk while the other guy dove for the floor. Nola knew she wouldn't be able to get him from this position.

But she also knew if the guys were smart, they would duck into the other room and grab the women to use as shields. She couldn't allow that.

Rolling into the room, she took a spot behind the front desk.

Gunshots peppered the desk, but the old steel beast held so she ignored them. She lay down on the floor and lined up her shot. She could see the gunman's shoes, one desk over.

Smiling, she pulled the trigger. With a cry, he dropped to the ground, His eyes widened when he caught sight of Nola. But there was no time for him to do anything but receive three more bullets to his chest. His screams died as he did.

It meant nothing to Nola. She was already looking for her next target. Movement came from the other side of the room. The boss sprinted for the other door. Lining him up, Nola caught him in the ankles. With a scream he fell face first.

Vaulting to her feet, Nola stormed toward him, kicking guns away from clawing hands as she did so. She reached the boss, who scrambled for his gun which had tumbled from his hand as he fell. His fingers were inches from it when Nola's bullet punched through the middle of his palm. His screams grew louder, mixing in with the groans and cries from two other men. The others were deathly silent.

Keeping her gun trained on him as her gaze scanned the room for other threats, she ordered, "Derek, get the girls out of here."

After tripping over the threshold, Derek hurried into the room, pausing for only a minute to look at all the bodies, before he dashed into the back room.

"Take them out to the boatyard and meet up with the others," Nola called.

The boss cried, cursed, and wailed as Derek moved. Nola kept her gun trained on him the whole time. Derek disappeared into the room and then reappeared a minute later with four girls following him. The first was Anna Mae Hayes. Nola met Anna Mae's gaze. She felt like she knew the young girl, but Anna Mae's gaze glazed over Nola looking for the exit.

Ushering all of the girls across the room, Derek led them around the bodies. Nola waited until they were out of the building before she spoke. Her voice was deceptively calm. "You ran all of this? You were going to sell those girls?"

Sweat and blood drenching his shirt, he shook his head, trying to scamper back. "No, no, of course not. I would never do anything like that."

Without a word, Nola shot off his pinky. He let out a shriek.

"Lying can be painful," Nola said her voice still even. "You're done. You're going away for a good long time. So take your last look at the free world. Because after today, you're never getting out again."

Narrowing his eyes, the man spat at the ground. "Doing time? That's just the cost of doing business. I can do time in a heartbeat."

Leaning down so she was over the man's back, she grabbed the back of his head and pulled. "Yeah, but you see, this time you're going in as a child molester. Because, you see, most of those girls you grabbed, they're not adults. And I'm going to make sure that everybody in that prison yard knows exactly what you were up to. You do know how prisoners view child molesters, don't you?"

"I'm no sicko. I never touched a kid," he stammered.

She smiled. "Well, good luck explaining that inside. I'm sure they'll take your word for it." Then she slammed his head into the hard tile floor once, then twice.

It was an effort for her to step away. Chest heaving, she pulled out her phone and texted Bishop. *Call in the cavalry. We're done here.*

Chapter Sixty-Five

Nola wanted to disappear. Once again, she didn't want to deal with any of the cops. But this time, she didn't want Bishop to look bad.

Bishop's friend from the FBI came through. She knew a couple of people in the Savannah PD that she trusted and had sent them over immediately. Bishop had waved her badge and given them the rundown on the situation. They'd been a little bit miffed at an operation going down near them without being notified.

But once Bishop explained that she was happy for the Savannah PD to take the credit, their demeanor definitely changed. Breaking up a human trafficking ring would lead to a lot of promotions.

Ambulances arrived to look the girls over. There'd been a second container with another twelve in it. All were shocked, dehydrated, malnourished, and traumatized, but none had any pressing medical needs. However, from the vacant look in most of their eyes, Nola knew that their psychological needs were what was going to be the most lasting for this group.

Derek had been arrested, but Bishop had explained to the officers about his cooperation. And as long as he continued to cooperate, he should be all right.

Teddy sat on the edge of an ambulance with Anna Mae, his arm wrapped around her.

Nola walked slowly over to the two of them.

Teddy whispered something in Anna Mae's ear and then hopped off the back of the rig to envelop Nola in a hug. "Thank you. Thank you so much."

He wiped his eyes. "When I first saw you, I hoped you'd get her back. But I don't think I ever really believed you would. Not with everything we found out. But you did it. You got her back."

Nola met Anna Mae's gaze and knew that Teddy was only partially correct. They had gotten Anna Mae back physically, but part of her would always be stuck in this situation. She would never be the same again. And yet, Nola had a feeling that Anna Mae would be one of the ones who came out stronger because of it. Nola gave her a small smile. "You've got an amazing little brother. He's going to be very happy to see you."

Anna Mae just nodded before her gaze shifted to something behind Nola. "That's Derek Rivers, isn't it?"

Nola turned to look. Derek was being led across the space toward a waiting squad car. Nola nodded. "He helped us find you. He was in a bad situation, but he did the right thing in the end."

"I always liked him," Anna Mae said softly as Teddy took a seat next to her, wrapping his arm protectively around her once again.

A yell went up from the other side of the boatyard. Nola whirled around and saw Devante fighting with two cops.

A sick sort of premonition coming over her, Nola strode forward, her pace picking up until she was flat out running.

Devante wrestled one of the cops' guns from their holster. "You bastard!" He aimed the gun at Derek.

Nola dove at the same time Devante pulled the trigger. She tackled Derek to the ground, barely feeling the bullet as it entered her ribs.

Chapter Sixty-Six

BISHOP

The sound of the gunshot cut through the air. Bishop looked up from her computer where she been relaying the drone feed to the Savannah PD. She saw Nola dive and tackle Derek to the ground.

She waited and she waited, but Nola didn't get up.

Bishop sprang to her feet, her computer crashing to the ground. She sprinted across the space, dodging people and shoving others out of her way. "Nola!"

A paramedic beat her to Nola's side. He placed a pressure bandage to the wound. Bishop crashed to her knees next to Nola as the cops dragged Derek away. Derek stared, his eyes giant saucers.

Bishop grabbed Nola's hand. Her face was pale, her eyes closed.

And the blood, the blood was everywhere.

"Nola, no. Don't you do this to me. Don't you do this," Bishop all but yelled.

Bishop wanted to grab her and shake her, but she was so scared she could barely move. She could barely think.

Avad crouched down next to her. "The doctor is on the way."

Bishop looked up to him in confusion and then remembered that they had brought the doc with them. The doc was Dr. Obed Ahmad. He'd been staying at the airfield. They'd contacted him once they headed to Savannah. Darius had flown them to an airfield in Savannah. They hadn't told Nola, but Ileana had had a bad feeling and had insisted the doc be nearby.

The paramedics pulled over the stretcher, but Avad intercepted them, saying they had a medevac on the way. They rolled Nola onto a board as a chopper appeared on the horizon. Bishop shifted her gaze between Nola and the chopper. She prayed the chopper would move faster and prayed that Nola would hold on a little bit longer.

The chopper landed in the boatyard. Everyone scattered to make room.

Dr. Ahmad scurried out. He was a small man, standing only five foot four, with wrinkled, sun-darkened skin. He had been Ileana's personal physician for years after retiring from the military as a trauma surgeon.

He hustled over to the stretcher and immediately got to work with the paramedic, putting in lines. Bishop couldn't seem to do anything. Even breathing seemed difficult at this point. This case was supposed to change everything.

But not like this.

Avad squeezed Bishop's shoulder. "We have to take her now. We'll take her to the hospital."

Bishop knew that Savannah had some good hospitals, but she also knew that there was one other place that Nola belonged even more. "No. Take her home. We're taking her home."

Chapter Sixty-Seven

NOLA

A light breeze mixed with the scent of lavender ruffled Nola's hair. It was the first indication that she was no longer in Georgia. The soft sheets underneath her body were the second one.

Nola opened her eyes, unsurprised to see the familiar room. Tall windows to her left overlooked a large sprawling lawn. The pale-blue sheer curtains swayed gently with the breeze. The ceiling above her had thick wooden beams across it. She was in a wooden poster bed. A thick white down comforter was neatly folded at the end of the bed. The white sheets underneath her were incredibly soft to the touch. She knew for a fact that they were 800-thread count. A small vase of flowers stood on the bedside table. Lavender, calla lilies, and daisies. All her favorites.

A small whine reached her ears. She glanced down at the small white dog with the red collar who, with her head down, had blended right into the white sheets. "Hey there, Lulu. How long have you been here?"

The dog's only response was a quick wag of her tail.

"She's been there all morning. You slept for a long time," a familiar voice called.

Sitting up, Nola caught sight of her daughter sitting on one of the brocade chairs by the fireplace, her feet swinging a foot above the ground.

"How long have I been sleeping?" Nola asked feeling stiff.

"Nearly two days. Bishop, Avad, and Grandma are really worried."

Her ribs aching as she sat up, Nola grimaced. "Well, I seem to be fine."

Molly shook her head. "You're not fine. You haven't been fine for a long time. Not since Daddy and I left."

With a sigh, Nola swung her feet over the edge of the bed and slipped them into the slippers waiting for her. "That's probably true."

She glanced at the picture frame on the other side of the bed. It had been taken two years ago, just before everything. Molly, David, and Nola had gone to Hershey Park for the weekend. They'd had such a wonderful time.

Molly had insisted that nobody was allowed to use their phones or check their email. It was an electronics-free weekend. David and Nola had balked at the idea at first, but after the first day, Nola realized she loved the freedom of not being in touch. Now she wondered if maybe that had set the stage for everything that had happened, including her going off the grid for the last two years. Maybe she had taken Molly's wish for them to be out of touch to an extreme, a subconscious need to fulfill her daughter's wish.

As Nola stood up, Molly stood up as well. Her daughter

nodded to the large wardrobe in the corner. "Grandma left some of your clothes in there."

Walking over with a wince, she grabbed a pair of pants, a shirt, some underwear, and then headed to the bathroom. "Are you going to visit Daddy?" Molly asked.

Nola nodded. "I always do when I'm here."

Fifteen minutes later, Nola had taken a shower and was already outside. Her hair still wet, it hung down her back, dripping onto her shirt. But she didn't care about that. She put it into a messy bun as she walked down the flower-lined path. Molly and Lulu traipsed ahead, running in and out of the flowers and chasing one another.

Following behind, Nola smiled as she watched them. They were always so happy here. The end of the path emptied into a large green field. In the distance was a row of fruit trees. A line of willow trees bordered the field to the right. In front of them stood a tall, stately oak. It was hundreds of years old. A swing hung from its lowest thick limb. A light wind blew, setting the swing in motion.

Molly ran up to her. Her cheeks were full of color, her eyes bright. "I'm going to take Lulu to the swing."

Nodding, Nola watched her and Lulu race across the field. The wind had picked up, and the swing now moved back and forth in a steady rhythm, as if someone were already sitting in it. For a moment, Nola wondered if perhaps there was.

"I thought I'd find you here."

The voice still held its Afghani accent, even though Ileana Hamilton had left Afghanistan more than forty years earlier.

Nola turned. "Thank you for your help."

Ileana scanned her from head to foot. "You were lucky," she said bluntly. "You won't always be so lucky."

331

"I know."

The sun slipped from beyond the clouds for a moment. It shone on Ileana's face, highlighting the scar from the acid attacks when she was twenty years old that reached from the edge of her chin and down her neck.

Taking a step forward, Ileana put a hand gently on Nola's cheek. She stared into her eyes. "Do you know? Or do you hope?" she asked softly.

Nola looked into her mother-in-law's eyes and just shook her head without answering, pulling her chin gently away.

Ileana took a step back. "I knew you'd visit my son as soon as you were able. I thought you'd like to know that Rascal was released from the hospital. He'll be on desk duty for a while, but he should make a full recovery. The doctors don't think there will be any lasting damage."

"That's good. He's a good man," Nola said.

"So it seems," Ileana said. "It's unlike you to work with anyone. I was surprised when Bishop told me that you had incorporated the detective into your activities."

Nola shrugged. "It was the most efficient way to get things done."

Her mother-in-law raised an eyebrow. "Hmm. Anna Mae was taken home. The police in Savannah arrested most of the members of the Compton gang. A few are on the run, but there's an all-out manhunt for them. It won't be long until they're tracked down. But either way, their days of running girls are over. I contacted some of my sources overseas. They shut down the supplier on that end, and I've been assured they will not be starting up some-where else."

Nola nodded. She and her mother-in-law were of the same mind when it came to what should happen to people who abused the vulnerable and innocent of this world. Nola had no doubt that Ileana had made sure that those responsible for the trafficking in young girls were held accountable.

And then buried.

Ileana Hamilton had worked for the U.S. Intelligence complex for nearly forty years, culminating in her seven-year post as the Director of National Intelligence. She'd started as a CIA agent, and when she'd retired two years ago, she'd cultivated sources and contacts all over the globe. Ones she still unofficially maintained.

"What about Lynette?" Nola asked.

Ileana smiled. "She was released from the hospital within twenty-four hours and is home with her family. And an anonymous benefactor set up a fund for the girls who were recovered from the boatyard. It will help them get resettled and cover any treatment that they might need."

Nola looked at the anonymous benefactor. "Thank you."

Waving away her words, Ileana said, "As for the Haverfords, Bishop released the edited tapes to the police department and the press. Honoria and Beau are claiming that it is an example of a deep fake video."

With a scoff, Nola rolled her eyes. "Is anyone buying that?"

A smile slipped across Ileana's face. "Well, they would be if Bishop hadn't also tracked down the money from the sales of the girls. I'm not sure if Honoria will be held legally accountable, but she most definitely will not be the head of the Haverford Retreat any longer. The board has already ousted her and her family."

"What about Teddy?" Nola asked.

The smile only grew wider as Ileana said, "Actually, he apparently already had some plans in motion."

Nola frowned. "What plans?"

"He had begun the process to be declared an emancipated minor. He has enough money from a trust fund from his grandfather. His father actually supported the effort, even though with him being in a home and his mental state being in question, that might not have held up, but even that is being reevaluated. It seems there's some indication that the elder Haverford's dementia was not entirely natural. Either way, young Teddy had himself declared an emancipated minor early this morning. And he is taking over care of his father. He also bought the house that you were renting in Delford."

Picturing the youngest Haverford, Nola smiled. *Good for you kid,* she thought. Out loud, she said, "That's good."

Ileana's sharp eyes stayed focused on Nola, and she had no way to avoid their inspection. "Yes, good, but not easy. This was a more difficult case than your previous ones. It was a bit more personal."

Nola shrugged. "It was just a case. No more, no less."

Studying her for a long moment, Ileana finally said, "Of course." She handed Nola a bouquet of flowers. "I thought you might want these. They're Molly's favorite."

Nola took the daisies. "Yes, they are." She looked back at her mother-in-law. "If you don't mind, I think I'd like to see them alone."

Ileana nodded. "Of course. I'll wait for you here and accompany you back to the house."

"Thank you."

Turning, Nola headed for the small fenced-in area just beyond the last willow tree. It was the Hamilton family cemetery. Two dozen members of the Hamilton family were buried there.

Nola looked out over the grass to where Molly was

holding up a stick for Lulu to grab. She smiled. It was always so nice here, so peaceful.

But Nola didn't deserve this peace. Not yet, maybe not ever.

Opening the wrought-iron gate, she gave only a cursory glance to the Hamilton ancestors. The graves dated back to the mid-1800s. But Nola didn't know any of them. She didn't know any of their stories, any of their histories. There were only two graves in this cemetery that concerned her.

Her feet slowed as she approached them. Once again, she prayed that when she saw the graves that the names would be different. That the last two years had all been a horrible nightmare and that today was the day she would finally wake up.

But it was a fool's wish.

"David Hamilton, beloved husband, beloved father" was engraved on the stone to her left. And the date of his birth and death were listed underneath.

Nola knelt down at the grave, laying her hand on the grass-covered surface before the tombstone, before she whispered, "Hi, sweetheart."

The wind picked up and blew her hair, almost like a caress. She closed her eyes and leaned into it, thinking for a moment that maybe it was David coming to say hello.

A squeal of laughter made her look up. Molly and Lulu now chased one another around the willow tree. Lulu ran around the back and then didn't reappear. Molly stopped, looked over at her mother, and smiled, giving her a big wave before she too faded from view.

Nola turned to the other grave: Molly James Hamilton. Her day of death was identical to her father's.

And in the bottom-right corner of Molly's grave was the

inscription for Lulu. They had loved each other so much in life, it seemed only right that they be buried together in death. The world had taken the three of them from her two years ago this week. The life that Nola had known had ended, and a new one had begun.

She didn't regret leaving her old life behind. Because the greatest parts of her old life were already gone. And now it was her job to make sure that those who couldn't protect themselves were protected.

She placed the daisies at the base of Molly's grave. Then she reached out and traced her daughter's name. "I love you, little girl," she whispered.

Then she stood, wiping the dirt off her hands, her gaze straying to where she had seen Molly last. She was gone for now, but Nola knew she would return. She always did. She thought back to what Ileana had asked her. Did she wish to join David and Molly?

She didn't know. She was sure a psychiatrist would say that all of her actions over the last two years indicated a death wish.

But no, she didn't want to die, and she wasn't actively seeking it. But she supposed it was also safe to say that she wouldn't mind if she did.

Chapter Sixty-Eight

BISHOP

Bishop waited until Nola had walked away before she approached Ileana. The older woman gave her a smile and took her hand. The two of them stood arm in arm, watching as Nola made her way to the graves.

The graves of her daughter and husband.

Keeping her gaze on Nola, Bishop spoke quietly, "You know she sees them, right?"

"Yes. I think she sees Molly more, and Lulu as well." Ileana turned back to Bishop. "How was your trip?"

"Good. I spoke with the young boy, Oz, Anna Mae's brother. Nola took him out for dinner one night and then took him out for ice cream another night."

Ileana's eyebrows rose, surprise flashing across her face. "Really?" She turned to look back at Nola. "That's a good sign."

"That's what I thought too. And Charlene and her grandmother couldn't say enough good things about her.

Plus, Ma Bell, who runs the diner, was singing her praises to everyone around her. She really made an impact—a big one."

"Don't get your hopes up," Ileana said as she squeezed Bishop's arm.

But Bishop wouldn't be deterred. This was progress this was a good thing. "But maybe she's coming back to us. She hasn't been on the estate for two years now."

Shaking her head slowly, Ileana's eyes were full of compassion. "She didn't have a choice. We brought her here. Circumstances were desperate."

"But she would have come back eventually, right?" Bishop asked, hearing the need in her voice.

"Perhaps eventually," Ileana said softly. "But even so, losing those two and the guilt she feels for it, it changed her. She shut off a part of herself. I'm not sure if she'll ever open the door to that part of herself again."

Although part of Bishop knew that was right, another part wanted her desperately to be wrong. Watching Nola kneel by the graves, she asked with a tremor in her voice, "The part that cares?"

Ileana's reply was emphatic. "No, she cares. She cares deeply. That's why their loss was so great. And that's why she keeps looking for other people who are powerless to help them avoid the same loss that she suffered."

"Do you think she'll ever stop? Do you think she'll ever truly come back to us?"

Sighing, Ileana's gaze strayed to her daughter-in-law. "I think this last case, it was the first one that forced her to get to know the people involved in a way that none of the other cases have. And I hope that maybe, just maybe, it might start her on that path."

"I hope so. I miss her," Bishop said.

Her knowing eyes focused on Bishop's face, Ileana said, "She didn't push you away because she doesn't care. She pushed you away, and she pushed me away, because she does. She lost so much that the idea of losing anyone else she cares about is unbearable. And so she pushes those she loves away in the hopes that should something ever happen to you or me, that it won't hurt as much."

"But she's wrong. If something were to happen to either of us, she would wish for the time back." Bishop sighed, her gaze pulled back to Nola, who was still kneeling at the graves. "It's hard. To watch her putting herself out there, risking herself for person after person, knowing that she's doing it alone."

Wrapping an arm around Bishop, she leaned her head closer. "She's not alone. She has us. You did good, Bishop. You did real good."

Bishop felt her cheeks flush with praise. "Thanks, Ileana."

Ileana tutted. "What did I tell you about that?"

Smiling, she leaned her head on Ileana's shoulder. "Thanks, Nona."

Nola glanced over at them. Straightening, Bishop pulled her arm from Ileana. She didn't know why she did it. She supposed she felt like she should stand on her own, that she didn't want to give the impression that somehow Nola had been replaced. Because there was no replacing Nola. Nola had saved her life long ago. Nola had given her her life.

Now Bishop just needed to find a way to give Nola her own life back.

There was a sheen to Nola's eyes from unshed tears as she walked toward them. But by the time Nola reached them, her eyes were clear, and Bishop wondered if maybe she had imagined it. Now she stood in front of them, her face a mask, no expression.

And the hopes Bishop had that maybe this case had changed something in Nola and somehow awoken the old Nola who used to laugh and hug began to crumble.

Nola looked at Bishop and nodded. "Good. You're here. Find me a new case."

Next in The Nola James Series

www.vinci-books.com/escape-fear

They're on the run. She's their only hope.

Former CIA operative Nola James must outwit ruthless enemies to
protect a family on the run, knowing that one wrong move could
cost them everything.

Turn the page for a free preview…

Escape the Fear: Chapter One

NOLA

The town of Cameron, New Jersey, owed its existence to the vision of Hawley Cameron Senior. Hawley Senior started the first Cameron Canned Goods factory back in 1921, after returning from World War I. During World War II, the factory had been converted to manufacture munitions for the war effort.

While Hawley Junior fought in the Pacific for his country, Hawley Senior had kept the town going, hiring war widows and paying them the same rate as their male counterparts. Instead of firing his war staff at the close of the war, he built a second and then third factory, which his son helped him run.

Hawley Junior had fully taken the reins when his father retired at the age of seventy. Both Hawley Senior and Junior, according to all reports, had an incredible work ethic. And they were beloved by their staff.

The apple, however, had fallen very far from the tree when it came to Hawley Junior's son, Tommy.

Nola sat outside the Gentleman's Club at five a.m. as Tommy Cameron pushed himself out the door and stumbled onto the sidewalk. He misjudged the curb, tipping forward, but managed to keep from pitching himself face first into the parking lot.

At age forty-six, Tommy was the picture of an aging athlete. He'd played football in high school but not college. Ignoring the hundred pounds he'd gained since those glory days, he still wore athletic tanks to show off . . . something. Flabby arms? A sagging stomach? Nola wasn't sure why he thought that was a good look. But Tommy was a die hard adherent to his fashion choice. Even tonight when the temperatures had plummeted to freezing tonight, he wore nothing over his tank top.

With the walk of a man trying to act like he hadn't had too much to drink, he made his way to his black souped-up pickup truck. Flames had been painted on the sides, and twenty-six-inch wheels had been added to allow for the six-inch lift.

Obviously Tommy was compensating for something.

Reaching the car, Tommy leaned against the wheel as he rummaged in his pockets for his keys. The brake lights blinked twice, indicating he'd achieved the milestone. It then took him two tries to reach the door handle and pull it open. Another three tries were needed before he was able to heave himself into the driver's seat.

Nola sat across the street shaking her head in disgust. Why was it the people with all the resources in the world proved to be the ones least deserving of them? At last count, Tommy boy was worth approximately five million dollars.

Plus, in a few months, he would come into the lion's share of his trust, which would tack on an additional ten million.

And what did he do with his abundance? Spent it on strippers and toys for himself.

Oh, and terrorizing the illegal immigrants who worked in his factories.

Across the street, Tommy's engine flared to life. He pulled out of the spot and over the sidewalk before bouncing onto the road. He weaved his way across the yellow line so much that it was a miracle he didn't hit anyone. Halfway to his home, Nola was sure he wouldn't make it. Part of her thought it would be a good thing if he didn't. It would solve a lot of problems.

But the lucky bastard pulled into his drive without even an extra scratch on his custom paint job.

Nola pulled in across the street. Parallel lines covered the sprawling lawn of Tommy Cameron's estate. Bushes shaped like diamonds lined the long drive. The lawn maintenance crew was obviously paid a lot of money to make the place look good.

And it did.

The home stood out amongst the other large ornate mansions in the small New Jersey neighborhood. But then again, it should. It had been the first mansion in the area. Originally it had sat on twenty-six acres. Now it sat on a mere twelve. Of course, all the other McMansions were on lots no larger than two.

Nola watched as the truck's lights went out. Tommy didn't get out right away. She had no doubt he was struggling to figure out either how to unbuckle himself or how to remove the key from the ignition.

What a tool.

With a sigh, she flicked a glance at the recording equipment on the passenger seat of her Bronco. It hadn't been hard to record Tommy's activities at the strip club. The club already had a monitoring system set up to record. It took little effort for Nola to tap into the feed.

The monitoring system itself hadn't been set up to protect either the club's employees or clientele. No, the system was created to enable a healthy side business: blackmail. More than one politician, religious leader, or other pillars of the community had paid handsome sums to keep the high-definition images of their activities in the club private.

But the Gentleman's Club owner had never attempted to blackmail Tommy. With Tommy's money and clout, it would cause too many problems for too many people to risk. In fact, the strip bar owner's brother worked as a manager in one of the Hawley factories. So once again, Tommy was insulated from acts where other people would be held to account.

Across the street, Tommy finally managed to extricate himself from the driver's seat, although his foot got caught in the car door. For one happy moment, Nola pictured him plowing face first into the drive.

Alas, that happy image was not fulfilled, as he managed to free himself from his beast of a truck.

Standing on the driveway, Tommy held on to the door, swaying for a moment before he managed to close it and head toward the house. The dim light made it impossible to pick out the frosted tips Tommy had touched up every two weeks.

Nola watched him go while all that she knew about him rolled through her mind. On paper, he was squeaky clean: no tickets, no arrests, he paid his taxes, and even contributed to charity.

But none of those details provided an accurate portrait of Tommy Cameron. He'd been the late-in-life child to Hawley Junior and his deceased wife, Marjorie. And they'd spoiled the child something rotten.

And the rot had stuck.

Tommy had never married. By the grace of God, he'd never procreated either. Although that was probably less by design and more due to the heavy steroid use earlier in his life.

There was also a string of ex-girlfriends who, if they weren't scared out of their minds, would testify to his abusive nature and extravagant lifestyle.

Tommy boy was in charge of six Hawley factories in New Jersey alone, as well as the factory that had just opened up across the border in Pennsylvania. He didn't go to them every day, of course. According to Tommy, only fools had nine-to-five jobs. No, Tommy would show up at each factory once about every two weeks to check and make sure everything was fine.

And to scare the hell out of the people working there.

Because Tommy hired mainly illegals for the factory floor. He liked hiring people without papers because he could put them on the payroll at the regular pay and then take half of their salary. And if anybody dared complain, he threatened to call ICE.

Amazingly, that wasn't the worst of his crimes.

Nola stepped out of her car. She quickly walked across the road. She wore black, including a ski mask and gloves. She'd already taken care of the cameras earlier. In fact, right now, lights were still on in the house, although with the flip of a switch, she would be able to take care of that. She didn't need Tommy identifying her. Not that she was overly concerned about it. He was so drunk, she wasn't sure he'd recognize himself in a mirror. But old habits die hard.

She walked over to the patio and, hopping over the short wall, wended her way around the fire pit to the side door that she'd left open for herself. She'd been in Tommy's home earlier today. It was kept immaculately clean. Apparently old Tommy was a germaphobe.

Growing up, the Cameron family had had a full-time maid who'd worked for the family for forty years. She had quit last year after Tommy's father had moved down to Florida.

Now Tommy had two maids in their early thirties, Ava and Maria, who were both from Guatemala. They lived together in a room at the back of the kitchen. Neither one had papers and both were terrified of Tommy. They scurried around his home like mice.

Nola had spoken with them earlier. They had been terrified, but she had finally gotten them to open up about Tommy.

And then she'd gotten them the hell out of there.

If she hadn't despised him already, the tales they told her would have ensured it. Their accounts of Tommy's behavior had made her skin crawl. He'd subjected both of them to the triumvirate of abuse: physical, sexual, and psychological.

Nola picked up the bat that Tommy had displayed behind the back of his couch in his entertainment room. He was so proud of it. It was a Mickey Mantle bat from a 1953 Yankees game. Retail value: $81,000.

She took a practice swing. Yup, this would do nicely.

Nola took a right outside the entertainment room and made her way down the hall to the front foyer. A large circular stairwell rounded up the walls, highlighting a twenty-tiered crystal chandelier that dated to the creation of the house nearly a hundred years ago.

Tommy had just reached the top of the stairs. He didn't glance back as Nola silently climbed the stairs behind him. He stumbled down the hall and careened off one wall before bumping into another and then finally making it to his bedroom. He disappeared through the double doors.

Instead of rushing in, Nola waited a few moments outside while Tommy stumbled to the bed and landed face down. After a few minutes, the room went silent. He was well and truly out.

She smiled and then walked over to the closet in the hall. Pulling open the door, she looked down at the trunk that she had put together earlier in the day. Holes that she had carefully drilled lined the top. She lugged the trunk out and pulled it toward Tommy boy's bedroom. Once the trunk was clear of the doors, she shut them and got to work.

"Oh, Tommy. Tommy boy. It's time to wake up." Nola slapped him hard across the face.

Tommy blinked, looking around. Then his eyes closed again.

Apparently he needed stronger measures. She reached into the shower, careful to stay to the side, and turned on the jets full blast.

The water was ice cold.

It only took another two seconds for Tommy's eyes to fly open wide with a yell.

Although Tommy screamed, Nola waited another few seconds before she turned off the stream, by which time

Tommy was mumbling a series of curses at her. She grabbed a towel, drying off her arm.

"What the hell are you—" Tommy's words choked off, his eyes growing large as he stared straight ahead.

Nola gave him a moment to take in the scene. Snakes slithered along the floor of the glass container only a few feet away from him. There were only twelve of them, but Nola was sure that in Tommy's terrified mind, there were triple that.

There were three four-foot-long ball pythons in shades of brown, a half dozen king and milk snakes striped in red, white, and black that stretched to six or seven feet, and finally the three small orange corn snakes that topped out at only three feet. Nola had to admit that all mixed up together, it would be easy to mistake them for more than a mere dozen.

So completely focused on the snakes was he that Tommy hadn't even taken in his own position. Nola had strung him up to the nozzles in the shower. Helpfully, Tommy had a shower system with nozzles on both sides. His arms were stretched out above his head, his feet stretched at the same angle to the lower nozzles. It was a terrifying position to be in, even without the snakes.

Tommy pulled on his arms, and then his bloodshot eyes jolted, finally taking in his predicament.

His mouth went slack, his head turning to the side, making him look like a confused dog. He yanked on the ropes while trying to back away from the snakes. "Wh-what's going on?" He asked stammering.

A wave of BO and beer breath wafted toward Nola. She grimaced at the smell. *Ugh. Apparently I should have dumped soap over him before I turned on the water.* She picked up the bat from where she'd leaned it against the wall. "Well, it seems you've been a rather bad boy, Tommy."

Yanking at his restraints, his gaze constantly darted back to the snakes. His words were slurred. "What? I didn't do nothing."

"Anything. You haven't done anything would be the correct way to say that. But either way, it's not true. You've done quite a bit. Do you remember Gina Torres?"

Fear flashed across his face before he attempted to cover it up. "I don't know her."

Nola shook her head. "Oh, you're not a good liar. How exactly have you managed to not get caught for something in all these years?"

Tommy attempted to puff up his chest, which was rather difficult given his current position. "I know the chief of police. You're going to be in so much trouble when I tell him—" A snake hissed, crawling along the side of the glass container.

Tommy's eyes widened, and he once again attempted to back up, which of course he couldn't do.

"Tell him what, Tommy? Are you going to describe me? Tell them I restrained you in your bathroom and then fed you to some snakes? You think they'll believe you?"

Tommy's voice shook. "Of-of course they'll believe me. So you better let me out right now."

"Not until we finish talking about Gina," Nola said, anger lacing her voice. She took a breath, trying to control her rage. "She was only eighteen. Did you know that? Did you know that before you raped her?"

Tommy glared, his eyes hard. "I didn't do anything she didn't want to do."

"Tell me, Tommy, do you know a lot of women who like

to be hit? Who like to have their jaw broken while having sex?"

"She was into it," he mumbled.

Not even sure why she was going down this road, Nola shook her head. Guys like Tommy thought that whatever they wanted, the woman wanted as well. Gina Torres had worked at the factory in New Brunswick. She was from Ecuador. She and her father had made the dangerous trip to America, but only Gina had made it all the way. Her father had been nabbed at the border and sent back. So Gina had been working for the last two years, sending as much money as she could back home. Of course, Tommy had swooped in every few weeks and taken half of her paycheck, which left precious little for her to send.

Nola pictured the crime scene photos of Gina. In life, she had been a beautiful young woman with dark hair and dark eyes. She'd also been incredibly small, not even reaching five feet. But that hadn't stopped Tommy, who was six foot three. Perhaps her small stature was what had drawn Tommy to her.

A month ago Gina had committed suicide. A friend of hers had written an anonymous blog post detailing the abuses that she'd experienced at Tommy's hand as well as Tommy's abuses of everyone in the factory. Bishop had found it and sent Nola along.

Nola gripped the bat clenched in her hand. Without another word, she walked over to the shower and swung. The bat connected with Tommy's ribs with a satisfying thud.

He screamed.

She swung again and again, aiming for the exact same spot. Tommy screamed and cried. After six swings, she stepped back.

Tommy sagged against the ropes, tears rolling down his cheeks. "Stop, just stop."

"Why should I, Tommy? From what I hear, you don't listen when other people tell you to stop, do you?"

"I told you, I haven't done anything."

Nola swung again, this time aiming at one of his knees. His high-pitched cry reverberated against the tiles.

Instead of eliciting sympathy, each sound angered Nola more. Men like this always acted tough, hiding behind their money. But when push came to shove, they were nothing.

She took a step back, needing to give herself some space from the weak man in front of her. "I have informants everywhere. I have a full accounting of what you've done at the factories. I have a full accounting of what you've done at the Gentleman's Club. And I know where you've hidden all your dirty money."

Tommy's head finally jolted up, his mouth fully open as his eyes widened. "What are you talking about?"

Nola would like to have been surprised that the one thing he cared about wasn't the crimes committed against people but the financial ones.

"I know you've been skimming off the top. You've been taking an extra ten grand a month out for the last three years. You take it from a different factory each time. That works out to close to a million dollars a year that you've been taking from your family's company. How do you think your dear old dad's going to view that?"

"He knows all about it," he said quickly.

Nola shook her head. "Oh, no, he doesn't. Or more accurately, no, he didn't. I sent him the files earlier today. He booked a flight for tomorrow morning. I also sent the files over to the feds."

Eyes widening, his mouth dropped. "The feds? Why would they care?"

"You guys opened a factory in Pennsylvania last year. That means your crimes now extend across state borders, making it a federal matter. Know anybody at the federal level you can bribe?"

Tommy licked his lips. "We can work something out."

"No, we can't. It's already done. Now all that's left is the punishment."

Nola walked up to him, looking into his face. "Gina Torres killed herself because of you. You made her life hell. When you go to prison, I'll make sure that everyone inside knows what you did to her. They're not big fans of sex offenders in general pop."

She took a step back and then swung the bat in between his legs.

His face paled ten shades. He couldn't even manage a scream, just a small exhale of breath. She walked over to the other side of the bathroom and placed her hand on the glass container. "My sources say the feds will be by to get you in a few hours. Maria and Ava are already gone, so no one's coming for you until the feds arrive. But I don't want you to be lonely."

Tommy's eyes had been reduced to slits. The ropes were now all that were keeping him upright, but he managed to lift his head as Nola dragged the glass tank closer.

"It's funny how much you can learn about a person online. So many little reveals that they don't even know they're providing." Nola flicked the lid off the container.

The hissing grew louder now as the snakes slithered and undulated across the bottom of the case. All the snakes were harmless, for the most part. The ball python, despite its name, wasn't large enough to ingest or squeeze Tommy. And generally, when scared or stressed, ball pythons looked for places to hide. Nola had looked at a few more dangerous ones, the kind that would wrap around a target and strangle them. It had been tempting, but she wanted a longer punishment for Tommy boy.

After all, she didn't want him dead. She just wanted him scarred.

"In the next few weeks, when you go to trial, remember that I will be watching. Remember that I will come back to visit you if you do anything but plead guilty to everything you have done."

Sobs wracking his body, Tommy dropped his head. "No, no."

"Look at me," Nola demanded, taking a step toward him.

Tommy's eyes were now as big as saucers. He shifted his gaze from the snakes to Nola.

"If you even think about harming anyone else, I will come back. And you don't want me to come back, do you?"

He shook his head quickly, tears rolling down his cheeks.

Nola patted him on the cheek. "There's a good boy."

Turning, she stepped out of the shower, stepping past the container. The image of Gina Torres in the bathtub of her small bathroom, blood staining the water, flashed through her mind. Nola kicked the side of the container.

It toppled over.

Snakes scrambled out, heading straight for the shower. Tommy began to scream in high-pitched wails.

Nola didn't care. She turned and walked out of the bathroom, letting Tommy live in his nightmare. Gina Torres had had to live in her nightmare too. But she'd been so desperate to escape hers, she'd taken her own life.

Tommy couldn't escape his. Nola had made sure of that. He would only physically live in it for a few hours, but she knew the memory would stay with him forever.

It was the least he deserved.

Escape the Fear: Chapter Two

RAFE

Breakfast dishes were still on the table as Rafael Ortiz, aka Ralph Smith, walked into the kitchen. More dishes from last night were along the counter.

He ran his hands over his face. Both kids had woken up late. It had been a mad rush to get them out the door on time.

Last night, he'd let them stay up to watch the third *How to Train Your Dragon* movie that they'd picked up from the library. They all really liked that series of movies.

A quick glance at the clock told him he had about twenty minutes before he needed to head to the school himself. He was a janitor at Hempstead High School. He was only working a half day today because he worked overtime this weekend.

But he wanted to get in there early to see if he could start a little ahead of time and maybe get out earlier. If not, the kids would have to go to Mrs. Lee's house. He liked Mrs.

Lee. She was a nice woman. And he appreciated her taking care of the kids when he got stuck working overtime, but he was really hoping he didn't have to pay for another babysitting stint. It was really beginning to dig into the small savings he'd managed to accumulate.

He needed to get home before the kids today. He needed to not spend money on a sitter if he was ever going to get them out of here.

Blowing out a breath, he looked around the apartment. It was tiny, only about five hundred square feet. The front door opened directly into the living room, which at ten by twelve was the largest room in the place. Off the living room was a short hallway that led to the one bedroom and a small bathroom. Then there was a kitchen that boasted a small table and next to no counterspace. The walls, which had been painted white a few tenants ago, was now more of a dirty gray while the floor was a dirty brown. He didn't let the kids sit on the floor or even walk on it without shoes.

He didn't want much at this point, but a place where the kids could at least not wear their shoes indoors would be a nice change. But until he built up some more savings, that wasn't going to happen.

And he really needed the savings if he was ever going to get them out of this place.

They'd stayed in some of the worst places in Mexico when they'd been on the run from the cartel, but he wanted to be able to leave those days behind. He wanted the kids to be happy when they came home. He wanted the kids to each have their own room.

Although right now all three of them sleeping in the same bed was what they all wanted. No one wanted to let the others out of their sight.

He'd thought once he'd made contact with the US

government, things would be better. And they were when compared to the nightmare of a trip from Mexico to the US. He knew he had it better than some immigrants, who walked for thousands of miles. But like many of them, they'd spent two months in line at the border. And that had been a short wait.

But the whole time, he'd been terrified that the cartel would find them. And there'd been no way to keep that terror from his kids. The day they'd been allowed across the border, a weight the size of a bus had lifted from his shoulders.

Getting the kids to go to school once they made it to America had been difficult though. He'd had to take the day off for the first two days in order to sit with Enzo so he felt comfortable. And then for the first month, he'd had to rush back to make sure he was there when school let out. Buses had been a whole new process for them to accept, but at least then it was the two of them together.

He sighed. He loved his kids. He wanted more than anything for them to be happy. But they still seemed to feel guilty whenever they laughed or smiled. As if somehow they were betraying the memory of their mother by letting some happiness into their lives.

Mariana wouldn't have wanted that. She would have wanted them to be happy. She would have *demanded* that they be happy.

Oh, Mariana, I miss you, he thought as he stared around the apartment. He'd found them a place to live, but it wasn't a home. Mariana had had a way of making any place they stayed feel like a home. Rafe wasn't sure if he had that skill in him. But he'd need to learn it. His kids needed a home, a place that they were happy to come back to. A place where they were comfortable.

At least he knew they were happy when they were with him. They felt safe when they were with him. He was grateful he'd been able to create that much for them. He hoped he could build on it so that they felt safer in this world in general.

As he walked over to the counter, he collected the plates from the table and placed them in the sink before putting the milk back in the refrigerator. The fridge only had left-over pizza and a carton of eggs. He closed the door. It looked like it would be scrambled eggs again for lunch. He'd leave the pizza for the kids tonight.

Rafe turned on the faucet, running a hand through the water, waiting for it to warm up.

A knock sounded at the front door.

Pausing, he glanced over his shoulder with a frown. People never knocked on doors in this neighborhood. As far as he could tell, that was a rarity in America in general.

Turning off the water, he grabbed a towel from the bar on the stove. He walked to the living room as he dried off his hands.

But instead of going to the door, he went to the window next to it and pushed aside the curtain. Two police officers stood on his doorstep. He let the curtain fall back as a shiver ran through him.

This is America, not Mexico, he reminded himself.

Stuffing the towel in his pocket, he took a deep breath and unlocked the door. He pulled it open, "Can I help you?"

One of the officers was about Rafe's height of six foot three, but he had a few more years on him and a few extra pounds around the waist. He had pale skin and nearly white blond hair. His tag read Malcolm. His partner was younger. He couldn't be more than a few years older than twenty. He looked straight out of the academy. The younger officer glanced around, his eyes shifting, taking in everything.

Rafe estimated his age a little younger than he first thought. He was still jumpy from the get-go. He was the one that, if there were problems, he was where it would come from. The young ones always seemed to jump into problems before they were actually problems.

Officer Malcolm gave him a nod. "Mr. Smith?"

"Yes, I'm Ralph Smith," Rafe said with a nod.

Ralph Smith was the name he'd been given by the US authorities. He wasn't officially in the witness protection program yet, but the IDs were a first step. At the time, he thought the name Ralph was a bad choice. He'd never met a single Ralph in all the time he'd lived in Mexico. But he'd been so glad to get the IDs that he hadn't pushed the issue.

"Is it all right if we come inside for a moment? We have a few questions that we need to ask you," Malcolm said. His partner scanned the parking lot, his whole body tense.

Rafe looked beyond the officers to where their squad car had blocked his car in. Apparently they were making sure that he wasn't going anywhere. He knew time was ticking away, and the sooner he answered the police officers' questions, the sooner he could get to work. The dishes were going to have to wait. Mariana would not have been pleased.

He pulled the door open farther, stepping back. "Sure."

The officers stepped into the living room. The younger officer closed the door behind him.

"What's this about?" Rafe asked.

"There was an incident behind Hempstead High School two weeks ago. I'm sure you heard about it. We're talking to all of the staff to see if they saw anything."

Rafe had, of course heard about the incident. A young

boy, only fifteen, had been killed in the soccer field behind the school. Sadly, it was not an uncommon occurrence. Gang activity was rampant at Hempstead. MS-13 and the 18th Street gang had made their presence known.

Turning back toward the officers, Rafe said, "I'm afraid I can't—"

Malcolm pulled his weapon from his holster. "Hands up."

Rafe froze, staring at the man and then his partner, who also had his weapon cleared of his holster. Slowly, Rafe raised his hands. "What's going on?"

"We're going to go for a little ride, Mr. Smith," Malcolm said.

Grab your copy…
www.vinci-books.com/escape-fear

About the Author

Author, Criminologist, Terrorism Expert, Jeet Kune Do Black Sash, Runner, Dog Lover.

Amazon best-selling author R.D. Brady writes supernatural and science fiction thrillers. Her thrillers include ancient mysteries, unusual facts, non-stop action, and fierce women with heart.

Prior to beginning her writing career, R.D. Brady was a criminologist who specialized in life-course criminology and international terrorism. She's lectured and written numerous academic articles on the genetic influence on criminal behavior, factors that influence terrorist ideology, and delinquent behavior formation.

After visiting counter-terrorism units in Israel, R.D. returned home with a sabbatical in front of her and decided to write that book she'd been thinking about. Four years later she left academia with the publication of her first book, *The Belial Stone*, and hasn't looked back.